CAT
GOT YOUR
TONGUE

The 9 Lives Mystery Series
Book Three

Louise Clark

Book design by eBook Prep
www.ebookprep.com

October, 2017
ISBN: 978-1-61417-974-0

ePublishing Works!
www.epublishingworks.com

back and erase when she noticed a mistake, rather than go on and fix it later, so that slowed her down, but hey, she was accurate and that was a good thing.

Experience with the standard office suite of software. Yup, she had that too. She'd taken a night course through the school district after Christmas. She even had a piece of paper to prove she'd passed. So far so good.

The next requirement was good organizational skills. That she had in abundance, so a big check there. Through her charity work and the parents' council at Noelle's schools, she had a lot of experience organizing events. She could even get references, if she tried. She could also use her volunteer experience for the next requirement, the ability to interact successfully with clients and staff.

She thought rather cynically that she could also parlay her years as the wife of the Jamieson heir for this one. Playing well with others was probably the most transportable skill from her old life. Amusement swiftly followed the critical thought. She wasn't sure that dressing in designer gowns and trading air kisses with people you saw far too often and didn't like at any time constituted a transportable skill for the office setting. Still, it was all in how the information was spun, wasn't it? That's what air kisses and false smiles were all about. *Darling, we're such wonderful friends, but the moment we part I'll be putting you down to anyone who will listen.*

The final condition was where she ran aground. It was computer skills again, this time requiring that the successful candidate be expert in the use of a page layout program and a photo manipulation one. Christy frowned. What was that all about? She knew the programs. That is, she'd heard about them. Both were way too complicated for her limited computer skills. She glowered at the screen, her disappointment keen, then she sighed and moved on to another posting. There was no point in applying when she couldn't do the job. Maybe she should be looking for a clerical position, one that wanted someone to file paper, not

CHAPTER 1

The music pounded from the stereo. An electric guitar whined while the drummer laid down a beat that surged through the blood. The lead singer's voice was rough and deep. He sang about life's downside with an earthy charm that had entranced millions. The group wa' called SledgeHammer and they were Christy Jamieson favorite band.

The band was playing in the background as she stare the screen of the laptop she'd placed on the kitchen t She hoped that having the music on while she job sea would give her heart and take her mind off the drea' of discovering how few employment skills she had.

I was down, Sledge sang. *Down and out till y along. You made me whole. You made me strong.*

Not the world's most articulate lines, Christy t' she stared at the job posting for a secretarial pos' of the local universities. Sledge pulled it ' because he sang with such intensity that he sou was singing to her and her alone.

Very sexy, she decided, using the tho herself as she considered the job skill secretary. Keyboarding: check. She c' quickly, though she'd never timed hersel' publish brochures and posters along with all the other duties a secretary fulfilled.

On the stereo one SledgeHammer song ended and the next one on the CD began.

I left my home to travel far. I had my friends. I had my music. I was alone. Then she found me and I knew she was the one. She completed me. She completed me. Yeah, yeah, yeah.

Behind the simple words Hammer's drumbeat drove home the promise in Sledge's rough, masculine voice. The music flowed over Christy and washed away the frustration of her job search.

There was something incredibly erotic about a man focused on a woman, she thought. She pushed the laptop away and put her elbow on the table, then propped her chin on the heel of her palm. This was one of her favorite SledgeHammer songs. Sledge crooned a sensual melody for the first two dozen bars with Hammer laying down a steady drumbeat behind, then Hammer increased the tempo, until the song tightened into a potent dance that mirrored the sexual battle between a man and the woman he desired.

You completed me. You made me strong. The words echoed in Christy's mind as she allowed her thoughts to drift away from depressing ones on job hunting to much more pleasurable ones about Quinn Armstrong. Since she'd met Quinn, she was stronger than she had been before, and, yes, she was beginning to think he completed her.

She envisioned him in her mind's eye. Tall, with a muscular body. Thick black hair that fell over his forehead in an undisciplined way, no matter how hard he tried to tame it. Gray eyes that saw more than most people could— or even wanted to. An angular face and a mouth designed for kissing. She sighed with pleasure, then laughed a little at herself. She was smitten. She wasn't sure if smitten would lead to something deeper, like commitment, but right now it was enough to have his light in her life.

She went back to the job search feeling much less stressed and for another half hour she perused job descriptions. She saved one for a receptionist that stated the successful applicant would dress well, have knowledge of modern telephone systems, and provide clerical computer support when needed. She figured she had the dresses well part down pat and the clerical computer support probably meant knowledge of the standard office suite. The telephone system was another matter. Still, she had to start somewhere.

The job posting closed at the end of the month, which was perfect, since Quinn was taking her and Noelle down to California for a Disneyland vacation during Spring Break. They'd be back by the time the job posting closed, so there would be no problem making an interview, if she got one. She sighed.

Bringing in an income to supplement the money she received from the Jamieson Trust each month was not yet a necessity, but she was very aware that could easily happen. The huge Jamieson fortune had been embezzled at the same time as her late husband Frank Jamieson was murdered. What was left was a fraction of the original. The amount was enough to provide Christy with an income that she used to pay the everyday expenses. Later, it would stretch to paying for her daughter Noelle's university education. There was no contingency for emergency expenses though, which was why she was looking for a job.

There was a possibility—slight at best—that the Jamieson fortune could be recovered. One of the men who embezzled the money was working with a court appointed accountant to try to rescue it and return the funds, but the way was tangled. Now, almost six months after she and Quinn had proved that Frank was dead and not responsible for the embezzlement, the Trust was still a shadow of its former self.

Thinking about the Jamieson Trust had her frowning and checking her e-mail. Recently, she'd started helping Isabelle Pascoe, the Trust's office manager, handle some of the day-to-day details. In the past, the woman always had a trustee to turn to for decisions. Now that three of the former trustees were facing criminal charges, she only had Frank's aunt, Ellen Jamieson, and Christy to use for guidance. And she preferred talking to Christy.

There were two new messages in her box. One was from Quinn. *Are you home?*

She typed *yes* and pressed send, then turned to the other post, which was indeed from Isabelle asking whether she should reinvest a bond coming due or cash it in. Christy read over the details, then told her to designate it as part of Noelle's university fund and reinvest it. She was not going to dribble away her daughter's future by using capital for day-to-day spending now. That was why she needed to get a job. For today's expenses. The Jamieson Trust might be little more than a nest egg now, but if she managed it carefully the money would give Noelle the head start she deserved.

She put the laptop to sleep and turned off the SledgeHammer CD, then she went outside to wait for Quinn on her front porch. She sat on the top step and turned her face up to the sun.

The winter had been one of rain and cold winds blowing off the ocean. The raw weather meant the spring flowers were slow in coming out, and she was still wearing her winter clothes. Today she had put a jacket on over her jeans and the long-sleeved V-necked sweater she was wearing. The sweater was thin, made of silk and wool, and clung to her curves. It was surprisingly warm on this lovely spring afternoon. She smiled as she basked in the weak sun. This was one of the first days that it was warm enough to sit out on her porch and enjoy her world.

When a shadow blocked the light, she opened her eyes and straightened. Quinn was standing in front of her, tenderness in his expression. He bent and kissed her, then sat down beside her on the step. "Hi," he said.

His voice was husky and the word had been spoken with a low sensuality that reminded her of a SledgeHammer song.

"Hi yourself." Her eyes searched his face. "Do you want to go for a walk?" They usually walked along the woodland path that traversed the greenbelt behind the townhouse complex where they lived. At this hour of the day the path was largely deserted and the shadow of the trees provided privacy for passionate kisses.

Quinn's mouth quirked up into a half-smile. "Maybe in a bit. There's something I need to talk to you about first."

"Okay. Shoot." There were any number of things Quinn might have to discuss with her. A journalist of international repute, he'd written a book about Frank's murder and the embezzlement of the Jamieson Trust that had been the cause of it. He'd sold the rights to a multinational publisher and the book had been optioned by a big name movie producer. He was using part of his advances for their upcoming vacation to California. He might need background information for the revisions he was now working on. Or he might want to let her know that he'd included some personal details they hadn't discussed before. She was sure that whatever it was, they'd talk it through.

He pulled a white envelope out of the inner pocket of the leather jacket he wore over his own jeans and sweater. She stared at it, surprised. This wasn't what she'd been expecting.

She flicked one corner lightly. "This looks just like the envelope Gerry Fisher gave me the day he told me I had to attend the IHTF fundraiser as the Jamieson representative." She smiled faintly. The gala dinner had been a trial, but Quinn had come with her that evening and made it easier for her.

You complete me. You make me strong.

He looked down at the envelope. There was satisfaction in his expression. "This is much better than the IHTF event." He handed her the envelope. "Open it."

She laughed. "What is this? Like a present?"

"You could say that."

The envelope wasn't sealed, so she flipped open the flap. Inside were two tickets. She looked up at Quinn, frowning.

"They're for us," Quinn said. "Or you and Noelle, if you think it's appropriate. I can get another."

She shot him a bewildered look as she reached inside and drew out the tickets, then she could only stare in amazement. "Oh," she said at last.

"A good 'oh' or a bad 'oh'?" he asked, sounding worried. And maybe a bit amused.

She turned to him, her eyes wide. "SledgeHammer tickets," she said, awe making her voice breathy. "This show was sold out months ago. How did you get these?"

Quinn grinned. He looked pleased, and also a bit relieved. "Trevor gave them to me."

Christy slipped the tickets into the envelope, careful to make sure they were safely stowed. She looked back at Quinn. "Why would Trevor have SledgeHammer tickets?" She stopped and waved a hand, thinking about Trevor McCullagh, friend of Quinn's free-spirit father, the well-known author, Roy Armstrong. "Why did I say that? Why wouldn't Trevor have tickets?" Just because Trevor was part of the older generation, didn't mean he wouldn't enjoy SledgeHammer's brand of modern rock.

"The tickets are for the SledgeHammer suite," Quinn said. His lips twitched as Christy stared at him, wide-eyed again.

"The SledgeHammer suite? You mean, the band's *personal* suite?" Her voice rose in a squeak she couldn't quite control.

Quinn nodded, amusement dancing in his eyes. "Sledge told Trevor to bring whoever he wanted. Trevor invited us—my dad, you and me, Ellen, and Noelle if you think it's okay—to be his guests. Hammer is inviting his family, and there will be some music people as well."

"But why would Sledge, the lead singer in a rock band, give Trevor McCullagh tickets to his box? Did Trevor defend him at some point?" Though that seemed unlikely. The band had a squeaky-clean reputation and had been known to compare their tours to a salesman's business trip.

There had never been any hint of the kind of charges Trevor tended to defend.

This time Quinn laughed aloud at the confusion on Christy's face and in her voice. "Why? Because Trevor is Sledge's dad."

CHAPTER 2

"I think this is it." Roy Armstrong peered at the tickets, then up at the number posted above the suite.

It was the night of the SledgeHammer concert. The McCullagh party, consisting of Trevor, Ellen, Roy, Quinn and Christy, had entered through the VIP gates on one side of the arena. While this meant they didn't have to fight the huge crowd flooding through the main doors, they did have to walk almost all the way around the second level of the arena to reach their destination.

Roy studied the doorway critically. He was dressed as he almost always was in jeans and a comfortable front button shirt. "The name plate says it's the general manager's suite." Then he shrugged. "May as well try it. We can't go any further."

Christy looked around her curiously. Just beyond the passageway that led to the box, the main hallway had been blocked off with bollards. These were linked together with yellow and black ribbon that proclaimed there was no entry beyond that point. The passage probably gave access to the seats behind the stage, she thought. Roy was right. This must be their suite, because it was located almost directly above the stage.

Trevor put his hand on the doorknob and turned. "The arena isn't going to say it's the SledgeHammer suite. They'd get fans and paparazzi crashing the place." He threw open the door and guided Ellen, who'd been standing beside him, into the room.

The others followed in their wake. Inside they were greeted by a man of average height who smiled toothily and ushered them into the compact luxury of the arena box with an encouraging wave. "Trevor! Wonderful to see you again!" he said. To the rest he added, "Welcome! I'm Vince Nunez. I manage SledgeHammer."

Christy judged Vince to be somewhere between forty-five and fifty. His black hair was combed back from his forehead and held in place with gel. His jeans were designer and the plum-colored shirt he wore under a bespoke jacket was silk.

He and Trevor shared a manly hug, then Trevor said, "We're all looking forward to the concert, Vince. Let me introduce you. Christy and Ellen Jamieson. Roy Armstrong and his son, Quinn."

They all nodded. Vince's eyes brightened and he focused on Roy. "Roy Armstrong, the author?"

Roy nodded, his expression blank. Christy knew that he was here to enjoy the concert, not to promote one of his best-selling books. He hated having his celebrity horning in on his private moments.

Vince shot Trevor a raised eyebrow look and said "You never told me you knew Roy Armstrong, Trevor. This is great." He grinned at Roy. "I love your books, Roy. We'll have to talk."

Roy summoned up a smile. "Sure."

While the men were chatting, Christy took stock of her surroundings. The concert was being held in the building that was used for professional hockey during the winter season. Eighteen thousand seats were arranged in an oval, rising from the rectangular floor space up three tiers. The box they were in was on the two hundred level and close to the stage. She thought with some satisfaction that they would have one of the best views in the house for the concert.

The suite itself was a simple rectangle decorated in blue and green, with natural dark wood tones. At the back of the space was a cupboard for coats and a bathroom, while the entire front wall was open to the arena and the enclosed seats that belonged to the box. Along one wall was a well-stocked wet bar with beer and wine. A big screen TV hung on the opposite wall above a sofa. At one end of this was an armchair with a low table facing it and the sofa. Platters of crudités and chips had been placed on the table. Christy noted that one of the guests was already stationed on the sofa. He was munching on celery sticks and watching the arriving guests with critical interest.

Christy had seen the expression before. This was a man on the make, planning to milk the evening for all the networking benefits he could muster. She wondered what his relationship to SledgeHammer was, then decided she didn't care. Whoever this man was, he wouldn't be interested in Christy Jamieson. Two years ago the situation would have been different. Then she was the wife of the heir to the Jamieson fortune. She would have worn designer clothes, like Ellen's peacock blue jump suit with the wide flowing legs and plunging v-neck bodice. Now she was a single mom raising her daughter on a limited income, wearing jeans and a pretty cowl neck sweater in a dark gold that did good things for her short brown hair, and she was here tonight as a fan planning on enjoying her evening out.

Vince said something polite to Ellen, then he focused on Quinn and Christy. "You're Sledge's friend from high school," he said. "The journalist."

"I am," Quinn said. "Nice to meet you, Vince."

Christy chimed in with a smile, "We're both looking forward to the concert."

Vince waved a hand. "It's going to be a good one. It was Vancouver fans who made SledgeHammer. The band intends to go all out tonight as a thank you, you know?"

Having done his personal greeting, he was ready to turn them over to the rest of the guests in the suite. He drew Trevor into the center of the room, which was open to allow guests to mingle and move around. The Jamiesons and Armstrongs followed. "Now, folks, let me make you known to everyone else who's already here. Over by the table with the hot foods on it are Kyle Gowdy—he's Hammer's brother—and his wife, Kristine." The table was in the back of the room. The couple there turned and smiled, then said hello after Vince finished his introductions. Casually dressed, they both looked comfortable, though not well off. Working class people who unexpectedly had an international star in their family.

Vince shifted position and waved his arm extravagantly. "Curtis and Rose Gowdy, Hammer's parents, have already settled into the seats. The lady sitting beside them is Jahlina Vuong. She's a friend of Hammer's," he added with the kind of smile that had Christy imagining that Jahlina and Hammer were more than friends.

His features smoothed into expressionless mask. "And that's Syd Haynes sitting on the couch." There was a chill to his tone that Christy didn't understand.

Syd Haynes was an attractive man, well groomed, and stylishly dressed in a silk and cashmere sweater and jeans. Judging from the lines around his eyes and mouth, he was around Vince's age. There were no streaks of silver in his dark blond hair, though, or in the scruff of beard covering his cheeks and chin. At Vince's lukewarm introduction Syd raised a brow and his mouth quirked into a rueful smile that appeared to be a self-deprecating acknowledgement of the introduction.

Christy heard Quinn draw in his breath in a quick, shocked way. Then he stepped forward and pushed out his hand. "Quinn Armstrong, Syd. You may not remember me. I'm a friend of Sledge's."

"I know who you are," Syd said. He wiped his hands on a napkin in an ostentatious way before he took Quinn's offered one.

Trevor wandered over. "How have you been, Syd?" He studied the other man. "Your father mentions you often."

"Does he?" Syd shrugged. His expression said he'd believe that when pigs learned to fly. "With the help of the late Reverend Wigle, I've been clean for the three years, so I'd say I'm doing pretty well."

Trevor nodded. "Good to hear."

Clearly there was a history here. Christy wondered what it was, but she figured Quinn would fill her in when he had a chance. In the meantime, she listened and drew her own conclusions. Syd Haynes, she thought, must be younger than the lines on his face said he was. She guessed he was a man much like her late husband, Frank. Indulged, well-off, perhaps more insecure than he would ever be willing to admit. Always looking for something more, the restlessness making him an easy victim to the promised highs of drugs. Like Frank, Syd had been seduced by the party lifestyle. Unlike Frank, Syd had survived and now appeared to have made himself as successful as the other men in the box.

"What are you doing these days?" Quinn asked with that easy curiosity he used to draw people out.

"I run an organization called Homeless Help," Syd said.

"Homeless Help. I think I've heard of that," Trevor said, his face twisting into a thoughtful frown. "You work with the down-and-out on the East Side, don't you?"

Syd nodded. "We provide a way for the homeless to generate an income beyond their Social Security payments. It gives them a sense of worth that they can't get any other way. And it can help them have a few luxuries, make their lives a little easier. We also place alcoholics and drug addicts into rehab programs when they're ready to change. Anyone who needs assistance and has nowhere else to turn can come to us."

Trevor nodded. "The organization was started by Reverend Wigle, wasn't it?"

Once again, Syd nodded. His lips flattened into a thin line. "We set it up together. When he died I took it over."

"Shame about that," Trevor said, referring, Christy thought, to the Reverend's death, not Syd's decision to carry on the man's good works.

Syd nodded again. There was sadness in his eyes now, and his expression said that he still felt the loss of his mentor.

The door to the suite opened and two more people entered. The man was wearing a SledgeHammer T-shirt with jeans and his muscular arms were tattooed down to his wrists. His hair was spiked with gel and streaked with neon blue. As they came through the doorway, the man laughed loudly and bumped against the girl. She bumped back. They both giggled.

Vince did his enthusiastic greeting again. The man was one of the musicians Vince managed, an up and comer Vince talked up enthusiastically. The girl was his current bedmate and they were both flying high under the influence of some substance. Syd's mouth hardened into a straight, disapproving line and he deliberately turned away without speaking to the new arrivals.

A young woman wearing a blue and green uniform that indicated she was arena staff slipped into the box behind the two new arrivals. She circulated through the growing crowd taking drink orders and reminding those she hadn't met before that there was food in the chafing dishes on the table where Kyle and Kristine Gowdy stood and urged them to serve themselves.

Quinn nudged Christy to the food display where they talked to the Gowdys as they loaded their plates. They took them to the far end of the box, where an eating bar set with four stools had been strategically placed between the interior of the suite and the arena seating. Quinn settled in with his back against the wall, and Christy perched on the stool beside him.

"I sense there are old, unresolved issues between Syd and Vince," she said, tucking into an eggroll that was stuffed with crabmeat and shrimp.

Quinn, who was eating dried spareribs, stared over her shoulder at the interior of the box. "Syd's a couple of years older than I am. His father is a partner at Trevor's old law firm," he said in a low voice. "Syd got pretty much anything he wanted as a kid."

Like Frank, Christy thought. She wondered if Syd felt as unconnected with the adults in his young life as Frank had.

"He played the guitar and he had a pretty good voice. Before Rob and Graham became SledgeHammer, they played gigs with Syd."

Christy frowned. "What happened?"

Quinn shrugged, his gaze still on the interior of the suite. "He couldn't handle the lifestyle. While Rob and Graham focused on the music and their career, Syd got into drugs. Hard stuff. He spent more time stoned than he did sober. When Vince discovered them, he gave Syd an ultimatum: get clean or get lost. Syd didn't get clean."

"So Rob McCullagh and Graham Gowdy became Sledge and Hammer of SledgeHammer and went on without him," Christy said softly. "Sad story."

Quinn refocused on her face and nodded. "The split was nasty. Syd was pretty bitter." He looked across the box at the sofa where Syd sat alone. "I wonder what he's doing here?"

Christy smiled. "Making amends?"

"Maybe." Quinn didn't sound convinced, though.

The suite attendant appeared holding a tray. A tag attached to her uniform said her name was Chelsea. She smiled as she lifted a wine glass and handed it to Christy. She was a pretty girl, with honey blond hair pulled away from her face and bound in a French braid. Her smile held genuine warmth that had Christy smiling back as she said, "One chilled chardonnay for you, Mrs. Jamieson. And a beer for Mr. Armstrong. Is there anything else I can get for you right now?" They shook their heads. "I'll be back later then. Enjoy your meal." She flashed that bright smile again, then flitted away to serve someone else.

A rustle of movement had Christy turning so she could see into the suite. A dark-haired man dressed in a navy suit, white shirt, and a blue and silver striped silk tie paused in the doorway, surveying the occupants with raised brows, waiting for an introduction by Vince. Christy's discerning eye identified the suit as being handmade, tailored specifically for the new arrival. She'd bet that his shoes were Italian leather and his socks the finest wool. He looked wealthy and his manner exuded power. Whoever this man was, he expected to be noticed and catered to.

Beside him was a woman about twenty years younger than he was. Her hair was long and artificially blonde. It fell over her shoulders and halfway down her back in cascade of loose curls, framing a face that that was very close to perfection. She was wearing ankle-breaker heels, body hugging pants, and a sheer top over a dark cami. As the man paused at the doorway, she put her hand on her hip and struck an attitude.

"Trophy wife or mistress?" Quinn murmured wickedly.

"She's very decorative," Christy said. She shot Quinn a disapproving look, though she added a chuckle with it.

"He's got to be a businessman of some kind," Quinn said. "Maybe a record company exec. She could be a singer he's grooming, I suppose."

Vince had been down in the stands, talking to Curtis and Rose Gowdy, who were seated in the front row. When he noticed the new arrivals, he bustled to the doorway to greet them. Introductions were then made to the rest of the group. It turned out Quinn was right. The man was Mitchell Crosier, a senior executive with SledgeHammer's label and the woman was his wife, Kim.

The introductions were hardly finished when two more people rushed into the box. The contrast between the two couples couldn't have been more pronounced. Where everything Crosier and his wife did was calculated to create an impression, the two newcomers were refreshingly open and down-to-earth.

"Sorry we're late. Got caught in traffic," the man said breathlessly to the box at large. He was not quite six feet and heavyset. "We live out in the Valley and there was an accident on the Port Mann. I'm Bernie Oshall and this is my wife, Emily. Rob—Sledge!—and I went through school together." He looked around the box and his gaze lit on Quinn. "Quinn Armstrong! What's up, man? Mr. McCullagh, I heard you were ill, but you're better now. I'm so glad." He beamed around the group, good cheer radiating from his round face. "What a great evening this is going to be."

Smiling, Chelsea the suite attendant came over to ask for the couple's drink orders. Vince shook Bernie's hand, and Trevor sauntered over to say hello. Christy raised a brow at Quinn. "A friend of yours?"

Quinn looked amused. "I think I told you I lived with Trevor and Rob for a couple of semesters when my dad was doing time for his part in a tree hugging demonstration and my mom was in jail for contempt of court. I went to school with Rob. He and Bernie were tight, so I became part of their gang."

At that point, Bernie and his wife came over to join them. He and Quinn greeted each other with the easy informality of old friends, even though they hadn't seen each for years, and Quinn kissed Emily's cheek before he introduced them both to Christy.

"I'm happy to meet you," Christy said with a smile. "I'm finding all sorts of things out about Quinn because of this concert."

Bernie grinned. "When you meet Rob, all the dirt will come out. Quinn and Rob used to feed off each other's energy. Quinn came up with the ideas, and no matter how loony they were, Rob took them on."

Beside him, Quinn snorted. "Don't try to whitewash your part."

Bernie contrived to look innocent. "I did the planning. If I hadn't, you'd both have spent more time behind bars than out."

Quinn managed to look innocent and offended at the same time and Bernie laughed.

Christy sipped her wine as she examined the two men. "Sounds ominous. What exactly did you guys do?"

"Nothing out of the ordinary," Quinn said. "Just teenaged boys horsing around."

"Ha!" said Bernie. "What about the time you convinced Rob it would be a great idea to streak the drama class?"

Quinn grinned. "I'd forgotten about that."

"Streak the drama class?" Christy said. "What exactly did Rob do?"

Bernie chuckled. "He burst into the class wearing nothing but a mask and a red cape as if he was some kind of naked superhero and started to recite poetry he'd written for a song." He paused and grinned. "If you're a SledgeHammer fan you probably know the poetry. It was part of 'Going Down', his first big hit. Anyway, there he is, reciting his song lyrics with the whole senior year drama class gaping at him. Then the principal walks in."

"You didn't plan for that," Quinn said.

Bernie chuckled as he shook his head. "Who could? It was a great life lesson for someone like me who ended up as a city planner. You've got to allow for the unexpected or your system is going to break."

"And break it did," Quinn murmured.

"Yeah. The principal was not amused."

"Probably because he was showing around a school trustee," Quinn said.

Bernie shook with laughter. "We were all caught, not just Rob. We got the lecture to end all lectures and were suspended for a full week. I thought it was great. My parents weren't so thrilled."

"I guess not," Christy said, wide-eyed.

"Trevor gave us his court room stare," Quinn said, "and told us he didn't want to hear about a stunt like this again. I always thought he was fine with the doing, but he didn't like us getting caught."

"So there was more?" Christy asked.

"Lots," said Bernie.

"According to Bernie, the naked poetry reading was just the tip of the iceberg," his wife, Emily murmured, breaking into the conversation. She was dark haired, slim, and several inches shorter than her husband. Her eyes danced as she spoke. "The part you see and know about. Down below there was a lot more that went on. Over the years I've heard about all of their escapades." She smiled at Christy. "If you want to get together for lunch one day I can fill you in."

"I'd like that," Christy said.

As Bernie said teasingly, "Not everything," Christy noticed that Quinn's gaze was fixed on something over her shoulder. She turned to look and saw that Roy was talking to Mitchell Crosier. Standing beside Mitchell, Kim Crosier was frowning as her husband jabbed his finger forcefully in Roy's direction while he talked. Roy was running his fingers through his long, iron gray hair. Since it was tied at the back of his neck some strands came loose. Roy didn't seem to notice, but Christy thought she saw a hunted look in his eyes.

"Hell," Quinn said. "I'd better go over and rescue my dad."

Bernie turned and looked, then he laughed. "The guy—what's his name? Crosier?—is probably suggesting your dad use this great idea he had as the plot for your dad's next novel." Bernie had been friends with Quinn long enough to know the pitfalls his father faced being a famous author.

"Yeah," Quinn said. "Or he's telling Dad how to write a book."

"He certainly doesn't look like an adoring fan the way Aunt Ellen used to," Christy said. "Speaking of Aunt Ellen, I'd better go and make sure she's behaving herself. Lovely to meet you both." She turned to Emily. "Quinn and I are taking my daughter down to Disneyland during Spring Break, but I'll call you when I get back and we'll do that lunch."

While Quinn rescued his father, Christy found Ellen with Trevor standing near the sofa and talking to Vince Nunez.

She spoke with them all for a few minutes, then Chelsea came up to see if they needed anything. As she moved away, Ellen took the moment to say, "Nice young woman. She's Charlotte Sawatzky's granddaughter, you know." Charlotte was the widow of a construction engineer who had become one of Vancouver's premier property developers. After his death, her son had taken over the business. Charlotte was a fixture on the boards of many non-profit organizations. Christy knew her, though not well, but she was a great friend of Ellen's.

"I hadn't met Chelsea before tonight," Ellen said. "But her grandmother thinks the world of her. She's an A student at English Bay University and her family expects she'll go on to grad school once she has her BA."

"How do you know her grandmother?" Vince asked.

"We're on a couple of committees together. She is still very active, even though she's almost eighty." Ellen paused, then said with forced lightness, "She was very supportive of me when I went through some nastiness before Christmas."

The nastiness had been an accusation of murder and a couple of nights spent in jail while Trevor, acting as her lawyer, scrambled to get her released on bail. The real culprit had been found and the charges against Ellen dropped, but it had been a trying time for her. And it hadn't stopped with her exoneration. As Christy had discovered when people thought she was in cahoots with her late husband Frank, embezzling the assets of the Jamieson Trust, memories could be long and people judgmental. Despite having nothing to do with the crime, Ellen had been dropped from committees and friends suddenly were very busy when she called.

The experience had drawn her closer to Christy and Noelle and the budding friendship was helped along by her refusal to return to her downtown condo where a young woman's dead body had been found on her terrace. Ellen was adamant that she'd never live in the apartment again. Now, four months later, she'd begun looking for a new place, but she was still living in Christy's Burnaby townhouse. Trevor, who had a house on Salt Spring Island, had taken over her city condo and was considering buying it so he would have a Vancouver residence once more.

"Ladies and gentlemen!" The words reverberated through the arena, signifying the concert was about to begin. Quinn joined Christy and they found seats together. They were followed by the Oshalls and the musicians. Vince stayed up in the box with Kim and Mitchell Crosier, while Syd Haynes left his seat on the sofa to lean against the eating bar, half in, half out of the box.

SledgeHammer came onto the stage with a profusion of pyrotechnics and opened with their biggest hit, a hard driving song with a pounding beat. The crowd roared, sparks flew, and Christy settled in to enjoy herself.

CHAPTER 3

I *still think you could have smuggled me in.*

Christy's mouth twisted. "It would have been impossible." She was in the townhouse kitchen, stacking the breakfast dishes into the dishwasher after returning from dropping Noelle off at school. "The security guys checked all bags. If they'd found you in my tote there would have been a huge scene. I would have had to take you back to the car and you would have had to spend the evening there."

She was talking to her late husband Frank, who in the form of Stormy the Cat was sitting on her kitchen counter. The cat, an extra large dark gray tabby with a tortoiseshell belly, was watching her work. Frank was arguing with her.

You could have bribed a security guard to let you in without going through the checkpoint.

Christy slammed a plate into its slot with unnecessary force. "I don't bribe security guards." She straightened and stared the cat in the eyes. Stormy's whiskers twitched and after a minute he meowed. She stroked the back of his head and scratched behind his hears. He began to purr. "I know," she said. "It's not your fault that he doesn't listen."

Ha, ha, ha. Seriously, Chris. You know how much I like SledgeHammer.

Yes, she knew. Her fingers slowed as she lost herself in memories. SledgeHammer had just begun their rise to superstardom when she and Frank had moved from Ontario where they met at university, back to his home in Vancouver. They were newlyweds, still very much in love. Frank had bought tickets to SledgeHammer's first arena concert. They were on the floor, in the first row. Awesome seats that cost a fortune, though she and Frank actually spent very little time sitting. SledgeHammer, then as now, played a form of rock that was heavy on the drumbeat. They hadn't been as polished then as they were last night, and they'd played a lot of covers of popular songs because they hadn't yet amassed the collection of number one hits they had today. That didn't matter, though. Energy had pumped from the stage. The evening had been magical. Both evenings. The one ten years ago with Frank and the one last night with Quinn.

Christy sighed. She slid her hand down so she could cup Stormy's chin in her fingers. "Frank," she said gently. "Cats don't go to rock concerts. Stormy's hearing is much better than a human's. He would have freaked and there's nothing you could have done to soothe him."

Stormy purred as if he understood what Christy was saying. She tickled his chin with her middle finger and the purring got louder. She chuckled.

I hate it when you're logical.

"So you'll concede I'm right?"

Huh.

Christy laughed and gave Stormy a final pat before she got back to filling the dishwasher. The task completed, she shut the door, then picked up the cat and placed him on the floor. "I have to wipe the counters and I need to be quick. I've got a ton of stuff to do today." She was wearing jeans and a sweatshirt, her standard morning attire, so one of her tasks was to shower and change for the outing today with Frank's Aunt Ellen.

Since he was on the floor Stormy went over to his bowl to see what was in it. The cat had a stomach that was a bottomless pit. That didn't mean that he ate indiscriminately like a dog. He'd been known to turn his nose up at a variety of canned foods, but he was ever hopeful that the bowl would produce something tasty every time he inspected it.

The bowl was empty. This morning it had contained egg, sausage, and chicken—people food, the best in Stormy's opinion Frank had told her—but Stormy had inhaled the contents and now it was empty because Christy kept feeding to a schedule. Disgruntled, the cat came back to sit at her feet, perfectly positioned for her to trip over.

I'm not sure I like the idea of you and Quinn taking Noelle to Disneyland.

"You just want to come too." She finished wiping the counters and returned the cloth to the basket on the side of the sink where she kept it.

I can't. I'm living in a cat, remember?

"How can I forget," Christy murmured. It was a couple of months shy of a year since Frank had been murdered and he'd taken up residence in the body of Stormy the family cat. At first she assumed he'd move on once she proved he had been murdered, but that hadn't happened. Now she wasn't sure when, or even if, his spirit would ever leave Stormy. In the meantime, she'd gotten used to having her late husband talking to her in mind thoughts and staying in her house while she gradually allowed herself to fall for the gorgeous reporter who lived down the street.

She smiled as she thought of Quinn. She was looking forward to their trip to Disneyland. They'd be away for almost a week and they'd be alone for the first time. Well, Noelle would be with them, but Frank wouldn't. She was pretty sure that his thoughts wouldn't be able to follow her all the way down to California.

What if something happens to her?

"Health-wise, you mean? Like she breaks her arm or something?" Christy was teasing him, hoping to lighten his mood.

She understood what was bothering Frank. Or she thought she did. He wouldn't be there to watch Noelle have fun, or to hold her if she got scared on one of the rides. Quinn would. Frank might be able to communicate with Noelle the way he did to Christy, Roy and Trevor, but there were limits to what he could do.

No, not health-wise. What if someone kidnaps her? She is a Jamieson after all.

"A poor Jamieson. The embezzlers drained your trust fund, remember? There's no point kidnapping someone who can't pay."

Aunt Ellen can pay.

"No one is going to kidnap Noelle, Frank. Quinn and I will make sure of it."

"Christy?"

Ellen's voice. Just outside the kitchen doorway. Christy stiffened. She couldn't see into the living room from where she was standing and she hadn't noticed Ellen's footsteps either. How much had Ellen heard?

"Are you all right?"

There was concern in Ellen's voice. Too much, then. "I'm fine."

Ellen walked into the kitchen. She was wearing a charcoal gray skirt suit, a dove gray silk blouse and a string of lustrous natural pearls that were big, fat and cost a fortune. In her hand she held the iPad Christy and Noelle had given her for Christmas.

"I heard you mention Frank's name." She hesitated. "As if you were talking to him."

Christy was aware of ghostly laughter in her mind. She resisted the urge to look down at the cat. Instead she smiled and repeated, "I'm fine. Have the plans for today changed? I thought we were going apartment hunting this afternoon?"

Ellen narrowed her eyes and examined her in much the same way Stormy inspected his dish. Then, apparently satisfied, she held up the iPad. "There was a murder after the concert last night."

Christy felt her stomach clench. Murder had inserted itself into her life twice in the past year. The mere sound of the word was enough to shoot a chill through her body. "Murder? Who? Where? When?" Then, lamely, perhaps even desperately, she added, "We don't know the person, do we?"

Ellen nodded, slowly. She turned on the iPad, accessed her newsfeed, and found the article she wanted. She handed the tablet to Christy so she could read the account.

After scanning the report, Christy looked up. "The victim was the girl who was our suite attendant?"

Ellen nodded again. "Awful, isn't it? She was so young. So pretty. And to think she died so horribly."

The article said that the victim had been sexually assaulted sometime after the SledgeHammer concert had ended. She had struggled and her assailant had struck her on the head, the blow hard enough to kill her. Her body had been found early this morning by cleaning staff in the blocked off area on the second level, not far from the suites she managed.

"I'm going to pay a condolence call on Charlotte Sawatzky. I think I mentioned last night she's Chelsea's grandmother."

Christy nodded.

"I know she must be devastated," Ellen said. Her eyes, usually sharp and assessing, were filled with sadness. "She was so kind to me last November, when most people were acting as if I was a plague carrier. I want to know if I can do anything for her. And I want tell her how awful I feel about this."

Christy put the iPad onto the counter. "Of course. We can go apartment hunting some other time."

After a young woman was murdered on her terrace, Ellen had moved out of her downtown Vancouver condo into Christy's Burnaby townhouse. Five months later she was still there. For the last six weeks, she had been looking for a new apartment, but in a desultory way, without success. Once Christy would have been chaffing at the delay, but the truth was, she'd gotten used to having Ellen living with them. Noelle loved having her aunt available and Christy no longer butted heads with Ellen at every turn.

"Tomorrow, perhaps," Ellen said.

Christy had planned to go to the mall tomorrow to shop for a new bathing suit and a summer outfit or two for the warm California weather, but it was easy enough to switch days. "I'll call the realtor and see if we can change our appointment. I'm sure it shouldn't be an issue."

Ellen nodded. "Thank you, Christy."

"Where does Mrs. Sawatzky live? Can I give you a lift?"

"West Vancouver. I've already ordered a taxi, but thank you." The doorbell rang. "This will be my cab now."

Christy nodded. "Call if you need anything."

"Of course." Then she was gone, leaving Christy feeling gloomy and not a little unsettled. She thought about clothes shopping and wondered if she was in the right mood. Then she thought about Quinn and decided that yes, she'd be in the right mood if she could coax him into joining her.

With that thought in mind she patted the cat, made sure he had plenty of water, and headed out the door.

CHAPTER 4

"The building was completely renovated three years ago," Shelley Kippen, the realtor, said. She was a chirpy woman, somewhere between Christy and Ellen in age. She smiled a lot without the smile reaching her eyes. Not surprising, Christy thought, noticing how Ms. Kippen clutched her iPad to her chest as if it was a shield. Ellen wasn't the easiest of clients to make a sale to at the best of times. She was impossible when she wasn't ready to buy.

"I remember," Ellen said. Elegant and sophisticated in the simple sea blue A-line dress she wore under a knee length wool coat, she looked around the wood paneled lobby, complete with a sweeping staircase that rose grandly to the floor above. "I assume the renovations included structural work, not just the attractive finishings?"

"Of course!" Ms. Kippen said. She gestured at what had once been the reservations desk when the building had been the Regent Hotel on the edge of Vancouver's Downtown East Side. "The renovations were designed to marry modern convenience and old world charm."

Ellen eyeballed the desk where the building manager and the doorman could be seen. Both were smiling at the potential new occupant. They probably believed it would be an additional enticement to buy, Christy thought.

Clearly, they did not know their client was Ellen Jamieson.

"The condo fees must be through the roof," Ellen said, her gaze drifting over the staff members without acknowledgement.

"This building has excellent security as well as wonderful conveniences," the realtor said. She was sounding a little less chipper now.

"Security is important," Ellen said briskly. "Particularly in this part of town."

The building was, in fact, on the edge of one of the poorest parts of Vancouver. In the early days of the city it had been one of the best hotels in town, but as the city grew and hotels were built closer to the newer areas, the Regent fell on hard times. Its last incarnation was as a flophouse for those an inch or two away from destitution. As land values soared in the rest of Vancouver, the decaying inner city began to look enticing to investors and property developers. Inevitably the hotel-turned-flophouse was bought up. Initially it was slated for demolition, but an energetic group dedicated to the preservation of Vancouver's past managed to have it designated a historic building. Instead of being torn down, the old hotel was made to shine again and was now one of the city's premier addresses.

"As the area around the Regent Building is redeveloped, your condo will appreciate in value," Ms. Kippen said. "More and more projects are coming on line. I think you will be very happy here, Ms. Jamieson. Now, if you will come this way." She gestured across the lobby, toward the elevators.

Christy wedged the brown leather clutch purse she only used for outings like this more firmly between her arm and her body. The long coral-colored cardigan she wore with black slacks and a white silk shell had a pocket she could have slipped the clutch in, but the weight would have destroyed the elegant flow of the wool and linen fabric and spoiled the image of sophisticated Jamieson wealth she was projecting for this meeting. Shelley Kippen was trying hard to find a new residence for Ellen, and Christy appreciated that. Ellen was a difficult client, picky and never satisfied. All that was keeping Kippen on the case was her desire to make a sale to one of the well-known Jamiesons and the fat commission she'd earn when she finally closed a deal. Christy figured she'd bail if she thought she was just dealing with a cranky middle-aged woman and a single mom. Hence the Jamieson princess look.

As they marched toward the elevators, Christy reflected that she could have told Ms. Kippen that she didn't have to bother showing them the actual unit. She knew from a dozen or more site visits that Ellen had already made up her mind that this was not the building for her. She measured every unit against the condo she'd moved out of after the murder had been committed on her terrace. She might not want to live in her former apartment again, but Christy figured she still loved the building and the unit itself. That was why she was camping out in Christy's spare bedroom in the Burnaby townhouse, far away from her usual stomping grounds. And why she refused to put the condo on the market.

They entered the elevator and the doors closed. Ms. Kippen shoved a keycard into a slot and prattled on about state-of-the-art security that would not allow anyone without a card to access the residential floors.

"A nice feature," Ellen said grudgingly.

If there had been a system like that at her building the murder might never have been committed in her apartment, because the murderer wouldn't have been able to get in.

The elevator had been decorated to look like one from the 1920s, but it was a modern unit, silent and swift. It delivered them up to the fifteenth floor before Ms. Kippen had finished talking about the building's security system, then glided to a smooth stop. The doors slid open, revealing a brightly lit hallway, wood paneled like the lobby. Red and blue carpeting that was lush and thick beneath their feet provided a splash of rich color. Opposite the elevators was a console table flanked by two padded wing chairs. On the table was a house telephone and an enormous urn filled with fresh flowers.

"Pretty," Christy said, touching one of the blooms.

Encouraged, Ms. Kippen said, "The flowers come from the green house that is part of the roof garden. I'll show you the area later. The gardens are managed by the condo council. There's a committee dedicated to the care of the space. It's wonderful for people who want to downsize from a house with large grounds and who like to garden. It's one of the building's best selling features." She urged them forward. "Unit 1505 is just down the hall, this way."

"Though I do like to look at a well-maintained garden, I am not one to dig in the dirt," Ellen said.

"No, no of course not! Now, here we are." The realtor made play with the keycard, then she flung open the door to the suite. Ellen and Christy went inside.

A half an hour later they were up on the roof garden. The apartment tour had been an anticlimax. It was spacious, but unremarkable. All the residential benefits were in the building—its history, the elegant lobby, and the restaurant and fitness facilities that could be accessed from it. The suite itself was a large box, portioned off into rooms. There were no balconies or terraces attached to the apartments, so the only outdoor space was the roof. It was a beautiful addition to the amenities of the building and the view was spectacular.

Ms. Kippen smiled at Christy and Ellen, and said, "I'll give you a minute to look around, shall I?" She moved away, pulling her phone out of a pocket in her jacket and checking messages while Christy and Ellen set off down one of the graveled paths.

"Do you remember the fuss that went on when the developers wanted to rezone this building from commercial to residential?" Ellen asked.

Christy laughed. "Of course. Protesters camped on the sidewalk in front of it for weeks."

Ellen nodded. "There were signs too, and demonstrations. It was quite a focused campaign, but in the end the rezoning was approved."

"That happened after the man leading the protests was killed, didn't it?"

Ellen shrugged. "Perhaps. The thing is, the developer of this property, Sawatzky Restoration and Renewal, is owned by Eugene Sawatzky." She nodded at Christy's startled expression. "Yes. Charlotte Sawatzky's son. The father of Chelsea Sawatzky, the girl who died after the concert."

"Oh, my God," Christy said. She glanced around the lovely roof garden, designed to look like the grounds of a great mansion, then beyond to the spectacular view of the North Shore Mountains. "Small world."

Ellen nodded. "Seeing the family yesterday...how broken up they are...It made me think."

Death did that to you, Christy thought. Made you reevaluate, forced you to start again. "Ellen..."

Ellen shook her head. She was staring fixedly at the mountains across Burrard Inlet, their muscular shoulders rising majestically into the deep blue sky. "Their troubles moved me," she said. "The Sawatzkys so desperately want to understand why their daughter was targeted, then taken from them." She drew a deep breath. "They want to know who did this to her. And why. They want closure."

"I can understand that," Christy said in a low voice. The breeze lifted the edges of her long line cardigan and she shivered. She pulled the sides together and held them there with her crossed arms. She had wanted closure too, when Frank disappeared. For her closure had been a beginning. It had brought her Quinn and a new family in his eccentric father and his friends. "Closure is important."

Ellen nodded. The wind picked up tendrils of her short blond hair and blew them across her face. She reached up and smoothed them away, but she didn't shift her gaze from the scenic view before them. "The police won't tell them anything."

"Who is in charge of the case?"

"Patterson." Ellen all but spat out the name.

Christy wasn't surprised by her vehemence. Detective Patterson had been the officer in charge of the murder on Ellen's terrace. She had also arrested Ellen for the murder and that was something Christy knew Ellen would never forgive. "Patterson's a good detective."

"She'll jump to a conclusion. The wrong conclusion."

Ellen's view of Patterson was different than Christy's. In Christy's experience Patterson was thorough, but open-minded. Of course, Patterson had never actually arrested Christy, though she had once suspected her of being involved in Frank's disappearance and the embezzlement from his trust fund.

"She'll find out who killed Chelsea. I'm sure of it."

"I'm not."

"She found out who killed Brittany Day."

"After she'd arrested the wrong person."

"She realized her mistake and—"

"With your help," Ellen said, cutting in. She turned at last to face Christy. "If you and Quinn hadn't been involved, she never would have uncovered Brittany's killer. Or Frank's, for that matter."

"She figured out who killed Brittany all on her own. I didn't have a hand in it."

"Of course you did," Ellen said. She sounded impatient, almost scornful. "You brought her the information about Lorne Cossi and you identified why Brittany was killed. Patterson was so busy maligning me and assuming the poor girl's death was a sexual relationship gone bad that she never thought to look at the other people in her life." Ellen's voice quavered with emotion. She stopped to draw in a deep breath. To regain the cool in-control demeanor that was so important to her. "Without you I would be in jail awaiting trial at this very moment."

"Ellen, I—"

"The Sawatzky family will never have closure unless someone helps them."

Christy stared at Ellen, whose expression was resolute, but also guarded. "Oh no," she whispered.

Ellen tipped her head in just the barest of a regal nod. "I offered them you."

Ms. Kippen chose that moment to rejoin them. "Well, ladies, have you had a chance to discuss your impressions? Ms. Jamieson, would you be interested in putting in an offer?"

"How could you?" Christy said, appalled.

"Is there some kind of problem?" the realtor asked, frowning.

"Charlotte Sawatzky is my friend. I want to help her."

"You need more time," Kippen said. "I understand completely. I'll just wait over by the greenhouse. Come and get me when you're ready."

She scuttled off. Neither of the Jamieson women noticed.

"I'm not a private detective, Ellen. Finding murderers isn't my occupation."

"You're good at discovering clues the professionals miss," Ellen said. She raised an eyebrow. "Quinn can help."

"Quinn and I are going to Disneyland!" In the face of the emotional pain the Sawatzky family must be feeling, that sounded shallow, but it was true. Christy was looking forward to the vacation. There was no way she was going to cancel, not when it was so close.

"Not for another week. There should be plenty of time for you to make a difference."

"That week is part of Spring Break. Noelle will be home. We're going to do things together. I don't have time to solve a murder."

Ellen lifted her chin. "It's important."

Christy glared at her for a moment before she turned away to try to regain control of the temper that was seething through her. When she turned back, she was still angry, but she'd pulled her Jamieson princess persona around her, the mask she'd used for so many years when dealing with Ellen. She said coolly, "I understand your pain, Ellen, and your motivation for what you did, but you were out of line. I'm afraid I can't help your friend or her family." She was rewarded with a glare. She smiled thinly and said, "Shall we put poor Ms. Kippen out of her misery and let her know you aren't interested?"

CHAPTER 5

Quinn circled the block searching for a spot to park. Fairview Slopes, on the edge of False Creek, was a high-density area, redeveloped in the 1970s from land given to the Canadian Pacific Railway the century before. Vehicle parking had not been a priority for the city planners who redesigned the area. They disapproved of cars and wanted people to shift to public transit. As a grudging acknowledgement to modern living, parking was available, but was largely used by those who lived and worked in the area. Visitors, like Quinn, had to struggle to find a space.

By the time he did, he knew he was going to be late for the appointment he'd made with Rob 'Sledge' McCullagh and SledgeHammer's manager, Vince Nunez. As he walked down the steeply sloping street toward West 6th Avenue, he wondered why Sledge wanted this meeting. He'd sounded worried when he called, but he wouldn't say why.

Quinn reached 6th Avenue and turned west. Sledge was an old friend, otherwise Quinn wouldn't have come all this way to meet with him. He had edits on the Jamieson book to turn into his editor and he had to get them completed before he and Christy took off for California. He smiled to himself as he thought of their upcoming vacation. He was as excited about the idea of visiting Disneyland as Noelle was, and not just because of the rides. He'd booked a suite in one of the on-site hotels. Christy and Noelle would share one bedroom, while he had the second one all on his own, but they would have a sitting room where they could mingle, and he was pretty sure Noelle would be tired at night.

Who knew what would happen then?

On that cheering thought he reached the building that housed Vince Nunez Music. It was one of those erected when the area was redeveloped and the architecture was very much in the style of the time. Low rise, like most of the structures around it, the exterior included a lot of glass, framed by wood and concrete. At the time of construction, it was a stylish design, but it hadn't aged well. Now the building looked tired, as if it had come to the end of its lifetime and looked forward to being the victim of a new redevelopment. He pulled open the glass door and went inside.

The lobby was small, carpeted with a hardwearing industrial gray flooring that probably had been installed midway through the building's life. The reception desk was simple and rectangular, and the visitors' chairs off to one side were minimalist style, with hard edges and thinly padded seats. They were rectangular too, possibly as part of a reluctant effort to match the reception desk.

The girl stationed at the desk was, unlike the décor around her, spectacular. Her features were perfect, her smile blinded and she seemed delighted to have the opportunity to speak to him, even though she clearly hadn't a clue who Quinn Armstrong was.

Vince himself came out from an inner office to greet Quinn as soon as the lovely receptionist announced him. He was wearing gray chinos and a black cotton dress shirt adorned with a shadowy spiral design woven into the fabric. His garb was more formal than Quinn's jeans and dark gray sweater, but then he was the owner and had an image to maintain. For this meeting, Quinn did not.

"Sorry I'm late," Quinn said, as they shook hands.

"Not a problem, not at all," Vince said. He ushered Quinn past the reception desk, saying to the girl as they went, "Hold my calls. If there's something urgent pass it through to my secretary."

"Of course, Mr. Nunez." The entry door rattled and the girl's gaze refocused on whoever was had come in. Her voice deepened, became softer. "Hi Braiden. The rest of your band are already in the studio. Just go on through."

Quinn glanced over his shoulder to see a young man wearing dirty jeans, a sweatshirt with holes in it and sporting hair that hadn't been trimmed in years. Braiden shot a broad toothy smile at the receptionist, said, "Thanks, babe." Then, as he passed the desk, he leaned in. His voice lowered and his tone could only be called suggestive as he added, "On for later?"

The receptionist's megawatt smile turned into a blaze and she nodded. The musician nodded back and continued on his way, without so much as a pause. He did cast a wary glance at Vince, however, as he passed.

Vince pointed his index finger at him and said, "She's my next-door neighbor's kid. You mind your manners or I'll never hear the end of it." The musician hunched his shoulders, then nodded. Vince said briskly, "Good. This way, Quinn. We're in here."

Quinn was left with the impression that Vince's word was law in this building, which didn't surprise him. Vince Nunez managed a string of successful bands. If you were a musician serious about your career, working with Vince was the ultimate goal. The girl would have to be pretty special for someone to want to screw up his big break for a one-night stand.

Vince's office was like his reception area. All of the furniture did what it was supposed to, but wasn't luxurious. His window looked out over 6th Avenue, and gave him a great view of the busy road, the railroad tracks beside it, and the housing development beyond. The densely clustered buildings obscured False Creek, and the North

Shore mountains only managed to peek through the downtown high rises on the other side of the water.

Sledge was slouched on an angular sofa that matched the ugly chairs in the reception area. Unlike the night of the concert, his sand brown hair was carefully combed. In fact, Quinn thought he'd had it cut between then and now. The two-day scruff of beard that was a Sledge trademark was gone, somehow making his stubborn chin more noticeable. He was wearing a ratty black T-shirt that was a relic of SlegeHammer's first international concert tour to Australia, New Zealand, and other destinations in the south Pacific. The worn cotton clung to his body, showing off his muscular biceps and chest. He straightened, then stood when Quinn and Vince entered. "Hey, man," he said, his gray gaze sharp and assessing. "Thanks for coming."

Quinn nodded. "What's up?"

Sledge looked at Vince, who shrugged. "Why don't we all sit down," he suggested, gesturing to chairs. Sledge slouched down on the couch again, Vince took his desk chair and Quinn sat on a hard, box-shaped chair that was the cousin of one of the thinner, rectangular ones in reception.

Vince and Sledge exchanged looks. Quinn raised his eyebrows. Clearly Vince was letting Sledge take the lead, but he couldn't figure out what Sledge might have to say to him that would be so difficult that the two men would have rehearsed who should start the conversation.

"I need your help," Sledge said suddenly, on a rush. A tinge of red crept into his angular features and emphasized his high cheekbones.

"Okay," Quinn said. He waited. Nothing was forthcoming. "I can't help if I don't know what the problem is."

Sledge and Vince exchanged looks again.

Quinn had better things to do with his time than to sit in an office with two guys who were having trouble committing. He resisted the urge to snap out a demand. Instead he lifted his arm and checked his watch, sending a signal he hoped they would understand.

Vince did. "Tell him!"

Sledge drew in a deep breath then blurted, "I need you to find out who killed that girl."

There was silence after Sledge finished. So he had become the murder reporter, Quinn thought, rather than the foreign correspondent he'd been through most of his career. Served him right for helping Christy find Frank's murderer and then working with her to discover who had killed Brittany Day. "I'm not a detective or a PI."

Sledge and Vince exchanged looks again. Vince said, "No, but you're good at getting behind the scenes and figuring out motives. That's what we need."

"Hammer thinks the cops are going to arrest his brother Kyle for the girl's murder. He's freaking out," Sledge said, hardly waiting for Vince to finish before he blurted out his problem. "If Hammer's brother gets arrested, SledgeHammer is done."

"Surely not," Quinn said. "It's Hammer's brother, not Hammer, who would be under scrutiny."

Vince was shaking his head. "Mitch Crosier has already made it clear that his label will drop SledgeHammer if anything comes of the suspicion. He says any mud in Hammer's family will stick to Hammer. A lot of fans are women. He's afraid they'll abandon the group in droves if Hammer is seen to be a related to the murderer of a young girl."

"And they'll never come back," Sledge added. He sounded gloomy. "Even if Kyle is exonerated."

Possibly. "Is it true?" Quinn asked. "Did Kyle Gowdy do it?"

"No!"

Sledge's answer was so quick and so heartfelt that Quinn believed him.

"Kyle Gowdy is a decent guy. Even a gentle guy when he's with women. And he's married to a great lady. But he's black and he had a couple of run-ins with the cops when he was a teenager."

Quinn leaned forward in the big boxy chair. It wasn't all that easy. The chair was low and confining. He felt as if he might be stuck in it forever. "What kind of run-ins?"

"One was a situation with a girl he knew. She accused him of assaulting her."

Quinn raised his brow. Sledge held up his hand. "Wait! It wasn't true. She was harassing him. One day she went too far and he pushed her. That was it."

"And the other?"

"He was drunk," Vince said. He had his hands flat on his desktop and the expression on his face was grim. "He came on to a woman at a bar and when her date took exception he threw a punch. There were no charges."

"Who's the cop investigating Chelsea Sawatzky's murder?"

"A female detective called Patterson," Vince said.

Sledge added, "Hammer figures she was assigned the case because she was a woman and she'd be relentless."

"She won't give up," Quinn said. He rubbed his jaw, thinking. "Look, I know Patterson. She's—"

"We know you know her," Sledge said. "That's why we thought you could help." He sounded desperate, even though outwardly he retained his rock star cool as he slouched lazily on the couch.

Quinn shook his head. "In a few days I'm going away for a week. Patterson won't wait around for me to be available again. If you feel it's necessary to investigate the girl's murder on your own, hire a PI." Sledge opened his mouth to say something, but Quinn put up his hand and shook his head. "I'm sorry. I can't help you." He stood up. "Talk to your dad, Rob. He probably has a computer file full of names of people who could help you."

Vince stood and after a minute Sledge followed suit. Vince held out his hand. Polite. No hard feelings. "Thanks for coming, Quinn."

Quinn took his hand and shook. He raised his brows at the distinct chill in Vince's voice. "I'll see myself out."

As he walked away from the office, he felt like the raw recruit who had fumbled the ball and let the team down.

CHAPTER 6

W hen Christy walked out her front door on her way to
pick up Noelle from her last day of school before the
Spring Break holiday, she found Quinn sitting on her porch
steps. Beside him sat the cat.

Quinn's upset. Something's wrong, babe.

"Hi," she said, not acknowledging Frank's comment.
Quinn turned. Though he smiled at her, Christy could see
the shadow of concern in his eyes. Glad that she was still
wearing the fashionable outfit she'd put on for the
apartment visit with Ellen, she smiled at him. Quinn would
tell her what the problem was when he was ready. "I'm on
my way to pick up Noelle. Want to walk with me?"

He nodded and stood up. Stormy didn't move. Christy
stepped around the cat and started down the stairs. Quinn
shot him a look that was somehow defiant, then
deliberately took Christy's hand. Stormy arched, hissed,
then leapt off the stair in one lithe bound.

Quinn looked so smug that Christy had to laugh.
"Vanquished your foe with nothing more than a gesture!"

Quinn's mouth quirked up into a half smile. "I take my
victories where I can, no matter how small they might be."

Christy laughed again. The cat disappeared into the
bushes across the street from Christy's townhouse. Christy

and Quinn went down the steps with a good deal more decorum than the cat had shown.

"Be prepared," Christy said as they headed up the street toward the path through the greenbelt that led to the school and beyond. "The kids are going to be wired."

Quinn's expression lightened. "Last day of school before Spring Break. Not surprising." He looked down at her. "How was your house hunting expedition this morning?"

Christy sighed. "Fruitless. The apartment wasn't big enough. There was no terrace, or even a balcony. The building wasn't in the right part of town. The security was good, but not enough. She'd never use the rooftop garden and it was just an added expense that would bring her condo fees up."

"In other words," Quinn said, "it was the same problem as all the other places she's looked at. It isn't the condo she currently owns."

"I don't think she's ever going to move out," Christy said. Her forehead puckered in a frown. "Sometimes I'm glad she's living with us. But others? She needs her own place."

They reached the top of the street and turned toward the path. Out of sight of both of their houses, Quinn squeezed her hand, then let go so he could slip his arm around her waist and pull her close. Christy slid her arm around him so they were linked securely together. She put her head on his shoulder and enjoyed the soft cotton of his ribbed sweater against her cheek and the masculine scent that was all his own. "Ellen's not talking to me."

"What did you do? Tell her a few hard facts about house hunting?"

"No. She wants us to investigate the death of that poor girl who was our suite attendant at the concert." She wasn't surprised when Quinn tensed. "Apparently, she knows the girl's grandmother. What's worse is that the grandmother was one of the people who's been supportive toward Ellen since the arrest. She feels obligated."

"Hell," Quinn said.

As they walked, the vegetation thickened around them. The deciduous trees were in full bud, some with delicate new leaves already showing. Bright green growth showed on the pine trees. Despite the gray sky that suggested it would soon rain, the woodland felt alive with promise.

"Yeah." Christy lifted her head from his shoulder to look at him. "I told her I wouldn't do it, Quinn. That's why Ellen's so mad at me." She put her head back against his shoulder and sighed. "I feel sorry for the family. I do." She shivered and Quinn hugged her tighter.

"We're going away," Quinn said. "We don't have time. Sounds cold, but—"

Christy straightened. "I said the same thing to Ellen. I also told her Noelle would be home next week and I wanted to spend time with her." She drew a deep breath. "Then there's Joan Shively. I didn't mention her, but Ellen knows the score with Shively and child services. Things have been quiet since Christmas and she's backed off. I'm not going to risk her putting my file back on her active supervision list."

"I have to get the edits on my book finished before we go. The publisher has fast tracked it. If I miss my deadline, they miss theirs and then they miss their pub date."

"Exactly! So why do I feel so guilty?" Christy asked.

"Same reason I do," Quinn said. They came to the point where the path forked and took the branch that led toward the school. Reluctantly, Quinn dropped his arm from her waist and instead took her hand. He said, "I had a meeting with Sledge and his manager that went much the same way your conversation with Ellen did."

Christy looked over at him. She frowned, confused. "What do you mean?"

"They wanted me to investigate the murder, too."

"Why?"

"The cops are looking at Kyle Gowdy, Hammer's brother, for the deed, so Hammer's freaking out. Vince is worried about the optics. Hammer swears his brother couldn't be guilty, but what if he's arrested? Hammer would then be closely related to the murderer of a young woman who was the age of many of their fans."

"Tainted by association," Christy murmured. She knew all about that. It had been a big part of her life for most of the previous year. "What did you say?"

"Same thing you said to Ellen. No. I suggested Sledge talk to his dad. I'm sure Trevor can find him a good PI to work the case."

"A private investigator," Christy said. "That's a good idea. I'll suggest it to Ellen if she brings up the issue again." A rueful smile curled her lips. "And she probably will. She doesn't like to be thwarted."

They walked in silence for a minute, then Christy asked, "Is it bad of me to not want to get involved in this? It's been so peaceful since Christmas."

They were almost at the school, but still within the shadow of the trees. Quinn stopped and pulled her to one side of the path. He lifted his hand to brush the hair back from her temple. She looked up at him and smiled. The gesture was tender, the expression on his face determined.

"You've got every right to want to steer clear," he said. "So do I." A smile twitched his lips. "We'll stick together and it'll be okay."

She nodded. He dipped his head and brushed his lips against hers. She kissed him back. She wished they could do more than share the light caress, but the path was hardly private at this time of the day, and she had her reputation to consider.

When the school bell rang, the kids exploded from their classrooms with the joyous energy that only the anticipation of a holiday could bring. Christy had agreed to pick up Noelle's best friend, Mary Petrofsky, when she collected Noelle. Now the two girls skipped ahead, chattering non-stop all the way home. With every step Christy's mood improved as she caught some of their good spirits. Quinn seemed to be in a better humor as well, but as they neared home she saw Ellen standing outside the house, and her mood tanked again.

"Now what?" Quinn asked, beside her.

"Aunt Ellen! Roy! Mr. Three! It's Spring Break. I'm going to Disneyland!" Noelle shrieked as she neared the little group huddled there, waiting.

Waiting for her and Quinn to get home, Christy thought grimly.

Roy grinned at Noelle's pronouncement. His long iron gray hair was escaping from the tie that kept it bound at the back of his neck and he was wearing his favorite jeans and a casual front button shirt.

Ellen, now dressed in an expensive pair of tailored black slacks topped by a silk blouse, said sternly, "There's no need to raise your voice, Noelle. We were close enough to hear a proper voice."

Feeling grumpy, Christy muttered to Quinn, "Give the kid a break. She's excited."

Quinn laughed.

Trevor McCullagh, also know by the nickname Three, said to Noelle, "Hope Disneyland wasn't supposed to be a secret."

Noelle came to an abrupt stop in front of him, Mary beside her. The two girls stared up at him. Taking his comment seriously, Noelle said, "Roy knows, because Quinn's coming with us."

"Guess it's not a secret then," Trevor said, eyes twinkling.

Noelle nodded. "We don't go till the week after next so Mom's going to take Mary and me swimming."

"And to Science World," Mary said.

Noelle nodded. "And skating."

Mary nodded.

"We've got lots planned," Christy said, as she and Quinn came up to the others. "Lots of time to sleep in and find fun things to do together."

"Yeah!" shouted Noelle and Mary together.

Christy looked at Ellen. "Is the door unlocked?"

Ellen nodded. Christy ruffled Noelle's hair and said, "Why don't you girls go inside and put away your backpacks? I'll be in soon and make you a snack."

"Okay, Mom." Noelle looked over at her friend. "Race you!"

They took off, pounding up the stairs and bursting through the door. Before it had even slammed shut behind them, Quinn said, "Christy and I are not going to investigate the murder."

The other three exchanged glances. It was Roy who answered for them. "Didn't expect you would. That's why Three, Ellen, and I decided to take it on."

CHAPTER 7

Trevor thought they should have a conference that included all the interested parties before Quinn and Christy went away. Saturday was the perfect day, since Rebecca Petrofsky was taking Noelle and Mary swimming in the afternoon, then Noelle was staying for dinner and a sleep over that night. Sledge wanted Hammer included in the discussion, as well as the Burnaby contingent, so Trevor had arranged to have the meeting at Sledge's West Vancouver home.

The house was perched high on the slopes of Cypress Mountain, a modern glass and steel mansion with large grounds and a multi-million dollar panoramic view that included English Bay with Point Grey beyond to the south, the city of Vancouver to the east and Vancouver Island to the west. Access was at the end of a steep, curving road with only a sprinkling of expensive houses. In the winter, when snow fell on the higher altitudes of the North Shore Mountains, the road would be a slip-sliding nightmare, but now, when the daffodils were showing their bright heads and the cherry trees were in bloom, the street was simply beautiful.

Sledge answered the door on Trevor's ring. He was wearing jeans and a T-shirt that advertised a brand of vodka made by one of the sponsors of SledgeHammer's recent tour. His hair was mussed and his expression was grim. "Hi, Dad," he said. As he ushered the Burnaby contingent in, he added, "Thanks for coming."

The interior of Sledge's house was as spectacular as its view. The house hugged the contours of the mountain, so the entry was a gallery that overlooked the living space a level below. Floor to ceiling windows rose high in the great room and provided a view for both the entry level and the main floor.

After he greeted everyone, Sledge said, "Hammer's downstairs." He headed for the curving staircase that descended to the living area. Christy, Quinn, Ellen and Roy trailed behind. "He's freaking out," Sledge said, glancing over his shoulder. "He figures Kyle is in serious sh—" He looked at Ellen, then swallowed the word that hovered on his tongue, substituting, "trouble."

Ellen didn't cut him any slack. She raised her eyebrows pointedly and said in austere tones, "Is his brother here today?"

Sledge glanced from Ellen to his father, who was frowning. Christy well knew that Ellen considered sloppy language an indication of poor breeding. Her experience also told her that when you dealt with Ellen Jamieson you watched your mouth or else. Evidently, Ellen had either converted Trevor to her viewpoint or he'd already been there.

With a shrug and a shake of his head, Sledge said, "Hammer and I decided it would be best if we didn't tell Kyle what we're doing until we were sure it was going to work."

"I see," Ellen said, tone now arctic. "You don't think we can succeed. If Quinn and Christy had agreed to investigate would you have been more positive?"

The cat poked his head out from inside Christy's tote where she'd been carrying him. *Jeeze, Aunt Ellen, this is Sledge! Take a break and give the guy some breathing room.*

Ellen gave no indication she'd noticed anything, but Sledge paused. His brows lowered into a frown as he narrowed his eyes and looked around. He swallowed hard then said, "Lady, I'm hoping you guys will come up with something, but I'm not holding my breath."

"You may be surprised," Ellen said, still disapproving.

"Do you mind that I brought my cat?" Christy said, thinking it was high time someone besides Frank wrestled the limelight from Ellen. "Trevor said you liked cats and he thought it would be okay, but I can leave him in the car if you'd prefer."

Great. You wouldn't take me to the concert and now you're going to dump me in the car. Talk about being marginalized.

Sledge stopped at the top of the stairs and stared. There was a distinct pallor to his skin and he looked worried. Stormy lifted one paw to the edge of Christy's tote and then another so that his shoulders as well as his head were showing. Sledge's gaze fixed on the cat and his frown deepened.

Roy's eyebrows rose. "I think you and Sledge need to have a talk, Three. The rest of us can go down and say hello to Hammer."

The cat wiggled his way out of the bag and out of Christy's hold. He leapt to the floor. *I'll come too.* He strutted forward, tail straight up and waving like a plume behind him.

Sledge's eyes were wide now, his expression incredulous. "What the hell!"

Ellen made a disapproving sound in her throat. Roy took her arm and led her to the stairs as Trevor urged Sledge and the cat toward another wing of the house for their private talk. Quinn caught Christy's hand, slowing her so that Roy and Ellen moved ahead. He said in a low voice, "Am I guessing right? Sledge can hear the cat, too?"

"Looks like it," Christy said. She added thoughtfully, "I wonder why?"

"It's Frank," Quinn said wrathfully. "He's excluding me deliberately."

Christy shot him a mischievous look. "Since Aunt Ellen also can't hear him, I think you're probably right. I wonder if Hammer will be able to hear him, too?"

But later, when Trevor, Sledge, and the cat had rejoined the others, it became clear that like Quinn and Ellen, Hammer was deaf to Frank's comments.

The furniture in Sledge's great room was positioned to take advantage of the wonderful view. At first Christy found it distracting, but as they got down to business she was surprised how quickly her mind tuned it out.

Ellen began the discussions. "While I know you are concerned for your brother, Mr. Gowdy, my concern is for the murdered girl's family. I want to find Chelsea's killer and bring the Sawatzkys peace of mind."

"It wasn't my brother," Hammer said. His dark eyes were narrowed and his expression defiant. He was a big, muscular man with a broad chest and bulging biceps from years pounding a drum kit. Like Sledge, he was wearing jeans and a t-shirt, only his was a blaze of white against his dark skin.

"We'll start with that assumption," Trevor said, breaking in before Ellen, who was frowning, said something more provocative and Hammer responded. "Before we start considering who might have had the opportunity and motive, can you tell us why the police have focused on your brother?"

"Apparently, he doesn't have an alibi for the time of the murder," Hammer said.

Christy frowned. "How can that be? When the concert ended we all went down to the meet and greet together."

Quinn shook his head. "We left the box in dribs and drabs. I think Hammer's mom and dad left first. You and I were somewhere in the middle. We waited outside for my dad and Trevor and Ellen, then we all went down together."

"You're right." She turned to Hammer. "What does Kyle say about where he was?"

"My parents went first," Hammer said, with a nod to Quinn. "They took Kristine, Kyle's wife, and Jahlina, my girlfriend, along with them. Kyle stayed behind to use the bathroom in the suite, but there was a line up, so he decided to find a public one on the way down. He said that before he left Chelsea was still cleaning up in the box. She asked him if he'd had a good time and they had a little chat about what it was like to be my brother. She was still in the box when he headed back stage."

"When he left the box was there anyone else in the corridor outside?" Trevor asked.

Hammer paused to think. "Yeah, there must have been. He said there was a security guard at the top of the staircase." The security guards stayed at the exits until the arena crowd had cleared.

"Did he happen to stop and talk to the fellow?" Trevor didn't sound hopeful.

"Naw. He said he didn't speak to anybody. He just went along with the rest of the crowd headed down the stairs."

"Ah," said Trevor. "So there were people around. Trouble is, a crowd is anonymous. That's why the cops haven't ruled him out. But there's got to be something more they've got on him. Any idea what?"

Hammer shifted on his seat. "He's got a record," he said, after a charged moment. "He was convicted of assaulting a girl when he was fifteen."

"He was a juvenile, then," Quinn said. Hammer nodded. "What exactly happened?"

"We lived in a rough neighborhood. The girls were as tough as the boys. She hung around with a guy who was a small-time pusher. Kyle didn't do drugs, so she was always taunting him. She'd sidle in close and get in his face, then call him a chicken. One day she upped the ante and spat on him." Hammer shrugged. "He lost it and gave her a shove. She ended up on her ass in a puddle and all the guys laughed. She went to the cops and made a complaint against him. He pleaded guilty. His punishment was an anger management course and community service."

"So his case never went up to adult court?" Quinn asked.

Hammer shook his head. "No. It was strictly juvenile. That was part of the reason his lawyer suggested he plead guilty. It stayed in juvenile court."

"It was a long time ago. His record would have been sealed," Trevor said, frowning. "How would the cops know the details before he'd been charged?"

"Beats me," Hammer said.

"Someone told them," Roy said. "Got any idea of who that might be?"

Again, Hammer shook his head.

Roy rubbed his chin. "Okay. Three, you want to take that? See what you can pull out of the cops?"

Trevor nodded.

"Ellen, you know the girl's family. Can you tell us about her?" Roy had evidently decided he'd be the manager of the project. He was busy writing in a small notebook he'd produced from a pocket.

"Her family is well-to-do," Ellen said. She spoke slowly, as if she was gathering her thoughts as she went. "She was a student at English Bay University. She didn't have to work—her parents would have been happy to pay for all her expenses, but Charlotte, her grandmother, said she was an independent child. She insisted on getting a job and paying her own way. Or at least contributing. As a suite attendant at the arena she got good tips, so she only had to take two or three shifts a week to make a pretty good weekly salary. She was proud of being able to work and study at the same time, so her parents didn't pressure her to quit. Now, of course they wish they had."

She paused and in the silence that followed everyone reflected on her last gloomy observation. The quiet was broken by thumps from the gallery above. Christy looked up, but the half-wall that guarded the edge meant it was impossible to see what was causing the sound. The thumps became a steady thud, followed by the sound of scrambling paws. Suddenly, a bright yellow ball appeared on the staircase, bouncing ever more swiftly down the stairs as it gained momentum. It was followed by Stormy, slip-sliding down the uncarpeted hardwood steps. The ball reached the floor and rolled majestically toward the windows, the cat in full pursuit. It dribbled to a stop in front of Sledge's feet. Stormy landed on top of it, grabbed it with his front paws, rolled onto his back and prepared to shred it with his hind claws.

"No, you don't," said Sledge. He bent down, tickled the cat under his chin, then grabbed the ball. "This is my favorite stress ball and I don't mind you playing with it, but I don't want you destroying it." He tossed it up in the air, a bright sunny orb with a smiley face painted into it. Stormy's green eyes followed it up, then down and up again. Suddenly Sledge tossed the ball toward the staircase in a throw worthy of a minor league pitcher. There was a moment when Stormy stood frozen, then he dove headlong after the ball. He skidded along the gleaming walnut floor, all four paws scrambling for purchase as he neared the staircase. The ball landed four steps up, then bounced slowly down again. As the ball reached the bottom of the staircase, Stormy leapt, caught it in his teeth, and landed with perfect cat poise, ready to move. He turned, cast a furtive glance at Sledge, and slunk, mouth full of prize, underneath the staircase and out of sight.

Sledge began to laugh. Quinn shook his head. Roy ignored the cat's antics and continued to scratch notes into his tablet.

"Good shot," Trevor said.

Ellen said with some asperity, "That cat."

Christy sighed and went over to rescue the ball.

She found Stormy in a shadowed corner. He was on his side, front paws clutched around the ball, hind legs poised, ready to rip. When he saw her he leapt up, then hovered protectively over the ball.

"Frank!" she said on an annoyed whisper. "Where are your manners? Sledge said this was a favorite possession. It isn't for Stormy to be playing rough with."

The cat is bored. Frank sounded sulky, the way he did when he knew he was in the wrong and the only excuse he had was a lame one.

"Then the cat can go outside and chase the local wildlife. Give me the ball," she said. Even though she kept her voice low she could hear the annoyance that made the sound almost a hiss.

Stormy put a paw on top of the ball and stared at her unblinking. She stared back, then reached for the ball. At the same time she said, "Let me have the ball or I'm going to take Stormy upstairs and put him out." There was no response for a minute, then the cat sat on his haunches and raised his paw off the ball. He began to clean in between his toes with studious care. Christy picked up the ball. "Thank you." When she turned away to return to the others, Stormy was still carefully grooming himself.

She handed the ball back to Sledge. "Sorry about that."

He shrugged and squeezed the ball. "No harm done."

"I knew we should not have brought the cat," Ellen said.

"We thought he might be helpful," Roy said in an absentminded way, still focused on his notes.

"Good heavens, why?" Ellen asked, astounded.

Roy looked up, blinked, and opened his mouth. Nothing came out.

Quinn came to the rescue. "Every group needs a clown for entertainment."

Thanks a lot, jerk. Stormy trotted out from under the stairs.

"Now, now," Roy said. Christy rolled her eyes.

"Shall we begin again?" Ellen said. "We were talking about poor Chelsea."

Roy pointed his pen at Ellen. "Does her family know if she had any enemies?"

Ellen shook her head. "They didn't mention any."

"Sounds like you're suggesting a premeditated murder, Dad. Whoever did it would have had to know her work schedule, then arrange to get a ticket for the concert, which sold out months ago."

"Or figure out some way to slip into the arena without being seen. Pretend to be cleaning staff, or maybe a delivery person. Could be done," Roy said, refusing to let go of his theory.

"I think it's more likely that someone related to her job killed her," Trevor said. "Another employee who had access to the blocked off area could have found her there when she was getting rid of garbage from the suite."

"Or perhaps someone from the nearby arena seats followed her there," Christy said.

"Doesn't have to be someone from our box. Could have been someone from one of the nearby suites that Chelsea managed. People find ways to hide until it's quiet and they can move about freely," Hammer said. The expression on his round face was grim. "We've had enough situations where fans have discovered a way to stay behind, then get to us, for us to know it's possible. The cops don't agree, though."

"There's not much we can do if it was a random concert goer," Trevor said.

"We need to prove it isn't anyone from our suite. We'll start by building a timeline that pinpoints everybody's location from the end of the concert to when they arrived backstage," Roy said.

"I can do that," Ellen said. "I'm good at organizing material. If you men want to do the digging, I can be the record-keeper."

Christy stared at her in amazement.

Frank was more vocal in his astonishment. *Seriously, Aunt Ellen? Where did you learn organizational skills?*

"Charity work," Trevor said, shooting the cat a disapproving look from under his brows.

Ellen colored. "Of course I do not expect to be paid!"

"I really appreciate your doing this for me, Ellen. Everyone," Hammer said, looking at all of them.

Stormy settled down in front of the floor to ceiling windows and gazed out at the gorgeous view, head on paws.

Roy had been busily writing down a list of the people who had been in their box that night. He tapped his notebook and said, "Trevor, you're talking to Patterson. I'll start with young Bernie Oshall and his wife. Seems to me that they showed up late to the meet and greet. Who else is there? Oh, yeah. Vince Nunez, Mitchell Crosier, the music exec, and his wife, Kim. Sledge, you talk to Vince. I'll take the Crosiers."

"He was hassling the girl," Quinn said.

"Who and hassle how?" Trevor asked.

Quinn shrugged. "Crosier. He'd probably called it flirting with her, but it was pushier than simple flirting."

"That's why I thought I'd talk to him," Roy said. He grinned. "He's a sleezeball. It'll be fun to dig deeper into his psyche."

"He's got a lot of power in our business," Hammer said. He sounded concerned.

"Don't worry. He wanted to talk to me about my books. I can work with that. Get him feeling comfortable, then wham! Go in for the kill." He illustrated this statement with hand motions and a slap on a nearby tabletop that made everybody but him jump.

"Okay," said Hammer, dubious.

Bright-eyed, Roy asked, "Do we have any more suspects?"

"I saw the musician and his girlfriend down at the meet and greet when we got there," Christy said. "But wasn't there someone else in our suite?" She frowned as she tried to remember by visualizing the scene that evening. Suddenly inspiration came. "I've got it. That man who helps people on the Downtown East Side. What was his name?"

Roy nodded. "He told me he'd been part of the band once."

"Oh," Hammer said slowly. "Syd Haynes. Who invited him?"

"I did," Sledge said. His voice was clipped. "I thought it would be a good idea."

Hammer shook his head.

"Anyone remember where he was at the end of the concert?" Roy asked.

"He left the suite before we did," Ellen said. "I don't recollect seeing him at the meet and greet, though."

"Wouldn't have the balls," Hammer said.

Ellen sucked in her breath. There was disapproval in the sound.

Hammer blushed. "Sorry," he muttered.

"He was with the band once," Sledge said, after a quick look at Hammer. "We parted under difficult circumstances."

"Anyone remember seeing him?" Trevor asked, looking around. They all shook their heads. "I wonder what he was up to then."

"He may not have been comfortable attending the backstage part of the evening," Christy said. "He probably just left."

"Still, he has to be added to the timeline," Ellen said. Roy made a note.

"And someone needs to interview him and find out exactly what he did do." Roy raised his brows and looked at his son. "Quinn?"

"Dad."

"He's an interesting character. He's done a lot for the East Side. You might get an article out of it. He certainly wouldn't be suspicious if you were the one to question him. You'd get more out of him than any of us."

Quinn blew out his breath. "Okay, I'll talk to him."

There was the sound of a yawn. *Great we're organized.* Stormy left his post by the windows and leapt onto Sledge's lap, where he sat down. Sledge swallowed hard, then slowly reached out to pat him. Stormy stared up, his green eyes demanding.

The cat's hungry. Got any tuna?

CHAPTER 8

The night was clear, the lack of clouds adding a crispness to the air. Sledge stood on his deck looking out over the English Bay, where moonlight rippled on the dark water, and beyond to the dark shadows of the landmass of Point Grey. His father and his ill-assorted posse had departed an hour ago; Hammer had gone long before that. It had to be close to two, but he couldn't settle. A sense of foreboding had caught him in a chokehold and he couldn't shake it, no matter how hard he tried.

He put his hands on the polished hardwood that capped the glass railing surrounding the deck and leaned forward, hoping that somehow the cool night air would wash away troubles he'd hoped to banish with the strategy session today. For a while it seemed to have worked when everyone agreed to pitch in and they'd made a plan. He believed in plans. You never succeeded in anything unless you had a goal and thought out a way to get to it. With the plan in place he'd felt better, so much so that he'd invited the little group to stay for dinner. Hammer had declined. He had something planned with Jahlina, but the rest stayed.

Dinner turned into a party of sorts. Christy had gone into the kitchen and inspected his fridge, since he was clueless about what was inside. He didn't stock it, his personal shopper did. She'd made a drop the day before, but he'd only looked for breakfast fixings and beer since then. Apparently, she'd provided the ingredients of a decent meal, though, so Christy set about making them something to eat. Quinn decided to help her and the rest of them had cleared out.

With Christy and Quinn in the kitchen cooking, and doing God knew what else, Roy Armstrong had pulled out a packet of weed. Ellen had raised her brows and opted out. To his utter shock, his father had also declined.

Was that what was bothering him? His father interested in a woman other than his mother? No, couldn't be. He was an adult and he understood why it was better that some relationships end. Maybe, then, it wasn't that his father was interested in a woman, but the woman he was interested in. Ellen Jamieson, wealthy socialite with a reputation of being stiffer than a starched shirt, and his tempestuous father? Was it possible?

He grinned to himself. Good thing SledgeHammer had no plans to go out on tour again for another year or so. The next few months could be interesting. It would be a good time to be anchored in Vancouver.

With his father flirting with Ellen in the great room, he took Roy and the cat into his music room to indulge in Roy's weed. It had been an interesting session. The cat wanted to talk. No, not the cat, Frank Jamieson. The cat had absolutely no tolerance to the pot, so it didn't take much to get Frank Jamieson high. And once he was high, he started to chat.

Turned out Frank Jamieson was a fan. Who knew? Sledge laughed softly to himself. He was still bemused by the idea that he'd been communicating with a dead guy. Having the same guy as a dedicated fan should have been disconcerting. Instead it just made him sad.

Frank Jamieson's whole story made him sad. A life wasted, cut short before amends could be made. There were the makings of a song in that life, in the frustration and anger that kept a man's soul here, looking for redemption.

The foreboding that had driven Sledge out to the deck eased as a lyric started to form in his mind. The beginnings of a melody followed. He stood for a few minutes, letting the song seep through him, before he went inside to his music room to work on it.

By eight o'clock on Sunday morning he had it finished. He left his perch on the piano bench and stretched. That was when the sense of foreboding hit him again. He didn't know why. He decided that the song must be causing it. He could hear it in his mind, more than just words and a melody. Sometime in the night harmonies had started to form and he'd felt the beat of Hammer's drums as well, something that usually happened during the collaboration process while they were in the studio recording the song. Even though he'd been up all night, he wanted to be in the studio today. Now.

He called Hammer, who was grumpy because Sledge had woken him up, then Vince, who was even grumpier, and convinced both of them that they had to get the song recorded today. Only when he had their agreement did that eerie sense of problems ahead go away.

Five hours later it was back. The song was in the can, the session musicians had left and it was just him and Hammer sitting in Vince's office on Vince's uncomfortable couch, with Vince sitting behind his desk, looking like a businessman, as he always did.

"Yeah, but should we?" Vince asked.

"We always have a party at the end of the tour." Hammer sounded miserable, as if he was being torn apart by conflicting emotions and not sure how to handle it.

"What kind of spin will the media put on it, if they get wind of the party?" Vince asked. He didn't bother waiting for a reply. He answered himself, his tone harsh. "They'll say that you guys are callous bastards who don't care about your fans."

"She wasn't a fan," Sledge said, quite reasonably he thought.

Hammer nodded. "She worked for the arena where we were playing and happened to be the server for the band suite. That's our involvement."

"The girl was killed not far from *your* suite, after *your* concert." Vince narrowed his eyes, then his finger shot out, pointed directly at Hammer's chest. "*Your* brother is about to be charged with her rape and murder! Of course you're involved!"

"Kyle didn't do it." Hammer's expression was tight. His voice shivered with suppressed anger.

"Doesn't matter!" Vince said. "The media is already all over the possibility that he's under suspicion. If we have the party they'll say you care more about your brother than SledgeHammer fans, which is true."

"If we don't have the party, everyone—including the cops—will figure Kyle's guilty. We might as well throw him in a jail cell now and have done with it."

"If we do have a party we might as well announce that SledgeHammer is finished and not bother with that new album we started today," Vince retorted furiously.

Sledge slid a glance at Hammer. He was leaning forward, his hands clenched, his eyes narrowed. He thrust out his jaw, then let fly. "We don't have to break up Sledgehammer. We just have to get rid of our manager."

Shock froze Vince's expression before he smoothed his features into an impassive mask.

The foreboding that had been tormenting Sledge turned into a churning ball of acid in his stomach. This was what he'd feared, a crisis like this, caused by the danger Kyle Gowdy was in. From the moment Hammer had come to him, worried about his brother, he'd been searching for ways to avoid what was happening now. First, he'd asked Quinn for help, which went nowhere when he refused. Then there had been that crazy session yesterday, which had ended with a plan, but little hope of achieving anything concrete. His father and friends might find out who killed the girl, but not quickly enough, because the crisis was here. He'd have to deal with it, now.

"What if we change the focus of the party?"

Vince and Hammer both stared at him blankly. "Explain," Vince said.

"We sponsor a charity and ask everyone who comes to donate."

Hammer snorted. "The roadies'll love that."

Sledge plowed on. "So the roadies don't have to donate. Or if they do they can throw in a toonie. Everyone can afford a couple of bucks. No one will be counting who gave how much. We'll invite some money people to make it sound real and put the squeeze on them."

Vince rubbed his chin. "Could work. What charity are you thinking of?"

"Something the press and the public can get behind. Something local. What about that charity Syd Haynes runs? Homeless Help."

"Syd! Are you nuts?"

"The Downtown East Side is a big problem," Sledge said. "Homeless Help is focused on giving back to that community. If we announce that we're holding an event to raise money for it we'll get a lot of good press."

"We'd have to invite Syd Haynes," Vince said through tight lips.

"No problem there," Hammer said. He showed his teeth in a shark-like smile. "Syd's a reformed person."

"You didn't have to spend your concert in the same box as him," Vince muttered. He tapped his desk with one finger, his expression now thoughtful.

Sledge knew he was starting to come round to the idea.

"So who are the money people you want to invite?" Vince asked. He leaned over his desk, his shoulders hunched, his expression wary.

Sledge grinned. "Mitch and Kim Crosier for starters."

Vince reared back. "I knew you were going to suggest them. I knew it! Damn it, Sledge. Bad enough that I had to entertain them in the box, but Mitchell is a windbag and Kim always comes on to me."

Hammer snorted. "Like you mind a foxy chick like Kimmie Crosier putting her hands all over you. Get off it. We know you better than that."

Vince shot him a hard look. "It's not that I'd mind getting into her pants, but she's married to Mitch and he's a possessive bastard. If he thought someone was screwing his wife, he'd destroy the guy. No broad, foxy or not, is worth losing my business over."

Neither Hammer nor Sledge picked up that one. Finally Vince said into the silence, "Okay. If we invite Mitch we invite Roy Armstrong."

Sledge frowned. "Quinn's dad?"

Vince nodded.

"Why?" Hammer asked.

He sounded truly puzzled. Siblings and friends were often invited to the end of tour party, because the more people who came, the better the vibe, but parents and parents of friends weren't usually on the list. Even if they were cool dudes like Roy Armstrong.

Vince cast him a look as if to say *duh, it's obvious, you dope*. "Great PR. He's a bestselling author, a tree hugging activist, and I'll bet he'd be willing support Syd's charity. Besides, he can play with Mitch."

"I get the author and activist stuff," Sledge said, "but you lost me on the Mitch thing."

Vince's expression was smug. "Crosier is a huge fan of Armstrong's. He buttonholed him at the suite and wouldn't stop talking to him until the concert began. Then Armstrong had an excuse to escape. And he did. That's when Mitch started entertaining himself with the poor kid who got killed."

"So you're setting Armstrong up," Hammer said, with a sneer.

Vince shrugged, then nodded. He didn't look at all bothered by the thought.

A laugh bubbled up in Sledge's chest. "Better let him bring his cat then."

Vince frowned. "His cat? What are you talking about?"

"The cat's cute," said Hammer. "I've got no objection."

Since Vince still looked baffled, Sledge said, "Armstrong has this big old tom called Stormy who's a traveling cat. Likes to visit and make new friends."

"That's right," Hammer said. "He brought the cat to the meeting we had yesterday." He shot a pointed look at Vince. "The one where my friend Sledge and I asked Quinn Armstrong and Sledge's dad to keep my brother out of jail."

"Roy takes the cat everywhere," Sledge said. He figured he'd better steer the conversation back onto the cat before Vince and Hammer came to verbal blows again.

"He was stoned, right? I've heard about Armstrong. He was pretty wild in his younger days."

Sledge shrugged. "Could be."

Vince contemplated this, then he nodded. "Okay. We'll invite the cat too. Maybe it'll—"

"He," Sledge said, interrupting. Amusement bubbled through him. He was still tickled to think he'd been communicating with a cat. Or rather the dead guy living in the cat.

"What?"

"He. The cat's a he."

Vince eyeballed him for a minute to see if he was serious. To prove he was, Sledge nodded a couple of times. Vince shrugged. "Maybe the cat will pee on Mitch's shoes."

That broke the ice with Hammer. He grinned and said, "Shed all over those fancy dark suits he always wears."

"Scratch him where he lives," Sledge said. He liked the way the conversation was finally going. So did that nasty lump of foreboding that had been churning in his stomach. It had finally started to ease.

They all chortled as they envisioned the cat persecuting Mitch, then they got back to business.

"Better invite my dad, then," Sledge said. Vince raised a brow in silent question. "Give Roy someone to talk to. And he can save him from Mitch."

Vince nodded, then rubbed his chin thoughtfully. "If we're inviting the senior set, what about that old broad with all the money who's friends with your dad and Armstrong? What was her name? Your dad invited her to the suite."

"Ellen Jamieson?"

"Yeah, that's her. Starchy old broad. She probably won't come, but maybe she'll donate to Syd's charity anyway."

"You mean like if you're invited to a wedding you have to buy a present, even if you don't go?" Hammer asked. He looked dubious.

"Something like that," Vince said.

"Could work," Hammer said. He didn't sound like he expected it to.

"Right. Who else?" Vince's expression brightened, as if he had just had a brainwave that delighted him. "How about inviting Quinn Armstrong? He's well known. And he's media. He could spin the party for us, heavy on the good deed stuff."

"He won't be in town," Sledge said. "He's going to Disneyland."

Vince reared back as if he'd just been bitten by an adder. "Disneyland? What the hell's he doing there?"

Sledge grinned wickedly. "Playing dad."

Vince pondered that with a frown, then his brow cleared. "The hottie he was with has a kid."

Sledge nodded. The wealthy, high society Jamiesons, and the scandals that had plagued them, meant nothing to Vince. If you weren't part of the music business, or you weren't someone who might be useful, he didn't notice you. Though, from what Sledge had seen of Christy Jamieson, she was a down-to-earth woman who didn't play the rich bitch card.

"Kyle comes to the party," Hammer said. His expression had tightened, the goodwill of moments ago gone.

Before Vince could reply, Sledge asked, "Would he and Kristine come?"

"They always come," Hammer said impatiently.

"Yeah, but they both know Kyle is under suspicion. They probably don't feel much like partying."

"Kyle needs to know that people believe in him. That his family—" Hammer paused to glare at Vince. "His family and friends are behind him."

"Kyle comes," Sledge said. He stared at Vince and hoped the man got it.

Vince caved. "Fine," he said. "Moving on. I'll connect with the media and get the promo going. Who invites Syd?"

"I do, I guess," Sledge said slowly.

"Great, as long as it isn't me," Vince said.

Sledge didn't blame Vince for sounding irritated. He and Syd had never gotten along, mainly because Vince thought Syd was a mooch and Vince liked people who were doers. But Syd was Syd. They had to deal with him, or else there could be problems. "We need to involve him somehow. Like Mitch, he needs someone to play with."

"Doesn't he have a girlfriend?" Vince asked.

Sledge shrugged and shook his head.

Vince brightened. "Maybe Kim would like to play with him."

Hammer looked horrified and Sledge couldn't hold in a laugh. "Christ, Vince. Are you serious?"

Vince sighed. "Wishful thinking. If she was chasing Syd she wouldn't be bothering with me."

Now that the issue of his brother had been dealt with, Hammer could laugh. "The man has a point. Mitch couldn't blame us if his missus went after a good deeds guy."

"He'd try," Vince said gloomily.

"I'll tell Jahlina to talk to him," Hammer said. He was clearly feeling magnanimous now that he'd forced Vince to agree to have Kyle attend the party. "She can introduce Syd to the money people and he can do his pitch. That'll satisfy him."

Vince thought about this, then he nodded. Jahlina worked as an events planner at EBU. She was good with people. "Right then, I'll send out the invites and get a press release prepped and out."

"Anything you want us to do?" Sledge asked.

"Show up," Vince said, already firing up his computer.

"Not hard. The party's at my place."

CHAPTER 9

Quinn dressed carefully for his interview with Syd Haynes. He thought that presenting a professional image would lower the man's guard and get him talking, so he wore a gray sports jacket, front buttoned blue shirt, and black slacks. He realized his mistake the moment he entered the small windowless office in the back of Homeless Help. Haynes was wearing serviceable no-name jeans and black T-shirt that advertised the name of his non-profit. What had he been expecting, Quinn wondered? Haynes dressed for his audience, in a way Quinn had not.

He shrugged off his discomfort. At least he hadn't worn a full suit and a tie and made himself look like a complete establishment hack. "Thank you for agreeing to do an interview, Syd." He held out his hand. Syd took it. His grip was limp, his hand swiftly withdrawn, the handshake of a man who didn't like the touch of others.

When did that happen, Quinn wondered? As a young adult, Syd had a cocky, in-your-face self-confidence. At the concert, the confidence has been muted, with an underlying caution, but to Quinn's mind, still there. So why the lackluster greeting now? He stashed the question away for reflection later and focused on digging whatever he could out of Sydney Haynes.

The formalities over, Syd sat on an executive style desk chair, deeply padded and covered in black, butter-soft leather. This was positioned in front of a beautifully worked teak desk that wouldn't be scorned in any CEO's office. Since the room was small and the desk large, it had been pushed against the wall. Beside it was an old wing chair, upholstered in what had once been a fine silk brocade. Now it was threadbare and the stuffing was popping out in places. Syd gestured to the wing chair. "Have a seat."

Quinn eyed the chair. He suspected it had been rescued from a refuse dump somewhere and wondered if he was going to head home after the interview with bedbugs or lice stowed away on his person. Not something he relished at any time, but just before going on vacation the mere thought made him grimace internally. As he moved to sit down, he happened to glance at Syd. The man was watching him with amusement. Evidently he expected Quinn's reaction. Quinn wondered if he had placed the chair here deliberately to disconcert anyone who headed into his lair.

Not one to back down, Quinn raised his brows and said, "I take it from your smile that the chair isn't home to a small army of parasites?"

Syd laughed and shook his head. A lock of thick golden hair flopped onto his forehead and he combed it back with his fingers. "The chair looks run down, but the springs are good and it's wonderfully comfortable to sit in." He gestured to a floor lamp positioned to one side of the chair. "I often use it when I have to read long documents. It's much easier on the back than hunching over my desk." As Quinn was lowering himself into the chair, he added, "Oh, and yes, the chair did come from someone's garbage, but I had it fumigated before I brought it into the office." He flashed a smile that was wicked. "So you're safe."

"I'm glad to know that," Quinn said. "I've had body lice before and it's not an experience I'd want to repeat." The chair was, as Syd said, very comfortable, despite its disreputable appearance. He sank back into the cushions and pulled out his phone. He gestured to the beautiful desk. "Mind if I tape the interview?"

Syd shrugged. "Go ahead."

He leaned forward to place the phone. "Nice desk."

"It and the chair are discards from a multinational company located downtown." Syd patted the leather on the arm of the chair. "There's a tear near the bottom of the seat. It was repaired and you can hardly see it, but the head of the company knew it was there and it bothered him. So the guy asked us to take it away for him." Syd shrugged. "He wrote off the cost of a new executive suite and I got a great desk and chair."

"You didn't think of selling it?"

"I did, but that pesky tear kept people from paying the price I felt the chair deserved." His smile flashed, the cocky grin Quinn remembered.

"Do you get finds like this often?" He kept the question light, the focus on Homeless Help. Syd had been reluctant to talk to him until he mentioned a national newsmagazine was interested in a story on Homeless Help and Syd's work with the hard hit east side community. He convinced Syd the focus of the story would not be on Syd himself, but on his organization. Syd had given him a cautious agreement. Now the trick was to get him to open up and find the information he'd really come for.

Syd nodded. "More often than you'd expect. A lot of the stuff businesses dispose of can be reused. It's not usually as fine as this, but it does happen."

Quinn finished setting up the recorder, so he settled back into the chair, crossed one booted ankle over the other knee, and slipped into interview mode to get Syd talking.

Forty minutes later Quinn had the core of an article about an organization that was providing hope and opportunity for people in one of the poorest areas in the city. Syd was talking freely, his pale gray eyes sparkling with enthusiasm and his hands moving expressively. Time to see what made the inner man tick. "You started Homeless Help to provide a new way of life for the people you knew when you were on the street."

Syd nodded, then leaned forward, his expression earnest. "I didn't do it alone. I couldn't have! I came up with the idea, but I faltered. Who was I, a homeless guy myself, to think that I could start a business?" He paused, then deliberately corrected himself. "Not just a business, but a *successful* business. I talked about the idea endlessly, then one day, Reverend Wigle told me to make it happen." Syd's expression took on the inner glow of a person lit by faith. "He wouldn't let me think of failure. He believed in me in a way no one else ever had." His voice softened as he spoke, his devotion obvious.

"Not even your family? You father?" Quinn asked, watching him closely.

Syd's lip curled. "Especially not my father. My biological father, that is. The Reverend Wigle was more of a father to me than Tate Haynes ever was. He pulled me out of the gutter and rebuilt me to be a better man than I'd been before my fall. What did Tate Haynes do when I lost my way? He abandoned me, left me to my fate. I was desperate and he didn't care."

Angry tone and grandiose terms, Quinn thought. It was almost as if Syd saw his life as a chronicle of the death and rebirth of a hero. He decided to push further. "Reverend Wigle was something of a crusader, wasn't he?"

The glittering light faded from Syd's eyes, replaced by affection and amusement. He nodded. "The perfect description. Reverend Wigle believed passionately that the downtrodden and poor deserve as much respect as the fat cats in the big office towers on West Georgia Street. He fought for all of us and thought nothing of facing down a bully when he had to. He was fearless."

"He organized the protests that shut down Hastings over the repurposing of the old Regent Hotel, didn't he?"

Syd's expression darkened. "The protests that were used as an excuse by the oligarchs to murder him, you mean?"

It wasn't exactly what Quinn had meant, but he nodded anyway. This was more interesting stuff than the official corporate story Syd had fed him earlier in the interview.

"Yes, he organized that protest. The city called the Regent a flophouse and a blight on the area. They were happy when a group of fascist developers came to them and asked to have the block rezoned." Syd fairly spat out the words as he leaned forward, one hand flat on the teak desk, the other curled tightly around the luxurious leather of the desk chair. His body was tense, his expression angry. "Reverend Wigle didn't want to do a sit-in. He wanted to talk, to discuss with the city ways the building could be saved for the people of this community! Not so that it could be redesigned as expensive housing for rich bastards looking for fancy digs in the city."

Quinn kept his expression neutral. He'd broken through a barrier and the angry words were flowing out in a flood of emotion he bet Syd usually kept carefully hidden. Not only was the man tossing out terms loaded with anger, but with pain as well. The protest the Reverend Wigle had organized must have been a turning point in Syd's life, a time filled with opportunity and regret.

"The protest wasn't just a short term sit in," Quinn said. "It turned into a tent city that blocked a major artery into downtown. I'm not sure it was only the municipal officials who weren't ready to talk." Quinn hadn't been in Vancouver when the protest went down. He'd researched the incident for this conversation with Syd. Away from the emotion of the moment, it seemed to him that there had been grandstanding on both sides as they each struggled to spin the story so it favored them.

"Reverend Wigle didn't deserve to die." Syd snarled out the words, his lips drawn back from his yellowed teeth, fury in his voice.

"No." They could agree on that at least. "Everyone has the right to protest government decisions, but at some point common sense should take over."

"Common sense." The curl of Syd's lips was derisive now. "The excuse of the fat, stupid, majority."

Quinn shrugged. "Self preservation, then. Reverend Wigle must surely bear responsibility for his own actions and some for the actions he pushed others into doing."

Syd sat back. "Reverend Wigle died a saint," he said, his voice flat.

The Reverend Wigle's church had deplored the violence that led to his death, but they had also apologized for his actions, saying that he had taken his protest too far. The press release had stopped short of stating that he got what he deserved, but the implication was there. "You miss him," Quinn said.

Some of the tension leached from Syd's shoulders. "I and everyone else on the East Side. He was a light for all of us and I can't tell you how many, like me, he saved from themselves. How many he was a father to, because their own had abandoned them."

Syd Haynes clearly had daddy issues. Was it worth looking into before he wrote the story? Maybe. He'd let the idea percolate in the back of his mind while he and Christy and Noelle were at Disneyland. "What do you think about the redevelopment now that it's actually happened? I passed the building on my way here and I noticed that the façade has been restored as close to the original as possible. I hear the lobby is lovely and that there is a fantastic roof garden." The description was courtesy of Christy, who'd given him a thorough briefing before he came down today.

Syd glowered at him. "I wouldn't know. They don't let the riff-raff from the area inside."

"You didn't continue Reverend Wigle's struggle after he died?" The tent city had come down after the riots. It was as if Wigle's death had taken the heart out of the movement.

"Reverend Wigle couldn't be replaced," Syd said. He made it sound as if there was a virtue in doing nothing. He moved his beautiful executive chair back, a sure sign that he was planning on ending the interview.

Quinn took the hint and uncrossed his legs. As he leaned forward, reaching for his phone, he grinned at Syd in a friendly way. "Did you ever think way back when we were teens that we'd end up here?"

He'd meant the question to be an unthreatening way of referencing their shared past and keeping the door open for follow-up interviews. It backfired.

"You mean back in the day when Rob and Graham and I were creating SledgeHammer? When they were leaning on me for my business sense? Before Vince Nunez stole them away from me with his promises of fame and success? You mean back in those days?"

Quinn didn't usually argue with those he interviewed. He let them talk and he didn't impose his views, in the questions or in the article that he wrote. But this? He couldn't let this pass. "You were into Ecstasy and coke before Rob met Hammer. You got into heroin and dropped out before SledgeHammer had been around long enough to have a sound or a presence."

"I was the brains behind SledgeHammer," Syd said. "I developed the sound, the image. The style! Rob and Graham left me behind because Vince seduced them with his promises. But not me. I had integrity. I stood my ground."

Quinn frowned. "I'm surprised. You sound angry, but when I saw you at the concert last week, you seemed to be at peace with the past."

Syd gestured toward his desk. "I'm sorry. My phone is blinking. I'm afraid I have to get back to work."

He'd morphed in a moment from an angry, bitter man to one who was in charge of his world and comfortable with it. The abrupt change had Quinn rising from the wing chair, leaving his phone recording for the moment. "Of course. A pity about that girl."

"What girl?"

"The one who worked our suite, who was killed after the concert." Quinn shoved his hands into the pockets of his slacks and hitched his hip onto the beautiful desk. He shook his head. "The cops have been all over it. They've questioned everyone in the suite as if we were all potential killers."

"The detective did speak to me," Syd said grudgingly. "I told her the girl was still in the suite cleaning up when I left."

"You didn't come backstage to the meet and greet." Quinn curled his mouth into a sympathetic smile. "Now I understand why."

"No," Syd said. His tone was curt. "I joined the rest of the audience and left through the front doors. Now," he pointed to his desk. "I do have to get back to work."

"Of course." Quinn held out his hand. "Thanks for seeing me, Syd. I'll let you know when the article will appear."

For a moment Syd stared at him blankly and Quinn thought the man wouldn't shake his hand or accept the polite end to the interview. Then Syd smiled and this time his handshake was hearty.

His eyes were cold though, as he ushered Quinn out of his office.

CHAPTER 10

"**B**athing suit, shorts, tops, jeans…" Christy ran through her packing list, mentally ticking off each item as she said the word. "…sunscreen. Okay, we're done. Noelle, have you got your carryon packed for the plane? Paper and pencil crayons? Felts? iPad? Sleeper for tonight in case our luggage is delayed?"

"Got it, Mom." She held up her backpack and shook it enthusiastically so that Christy would be sure to hear the rattle of moving parts inside.

"Good." Christy smiled at her daughter. They were in Christy's bedroom. Her suitcase was open on the bed, its contents neatly stacked, the lid ready to be closed. Noelle was hopping from foot to foot in anticipation. If they didn't get started soon, she'd shift from excitement to panic and by the time they got to the airport she'd be frantic that they'd miss their plane.

The doorbell rang. "It's time!" Noelle shrieked and bolted for the stairs.

Christy took a moment to peak out the window. Below her she saw Roy leaning against the side of the Armstrong car. As she watched, Ellen came down the walk and stood by Roy. She said something and Roy replied. The sound of their voices floated up, though Christy couldn't make out the words. Noelle was right. Since Roy was driving them to the airport, it must be Quinn at the door, here to pick them up. She went back to the case, did her quick mental run through again, then started to close the lid.

At that moment, the cat jumped onto the bed, then hopped into the suitcase. *Time, babe.*

"I know," Christy said. She picked up Stormy and lifted him out of the case and on to the bed. "I saw Roy through the window." She shut the lid. The cat jumped up on the top of the case as she zipped it shut. He crouched down and dug his claws into the surface, as he looked at her with mournful green eyes.

"Frank."

Stormy doesn't want you to go.

"Right." She took a moment to sit down beside the case and stroke the cat's soft fur. He began to purr and rolled onto his side to give her access to his belly.

You'll look after Noelle, won't you?

"You know I will." She kept her pats slow and soothing. Stormy might be possessive about family, but it was Frank who was worried about the trip. "Noelle knows the drill. She'll stick close. And there are two of us, Frank. Quinn's going to look out for her too."

There was a mental grunt at that. Then, *I was looking forward to Noelle growing up so we could do stuff like this. Disneyland. Paris when she's sweet sixteen. London. New York.*

The trips would never have happened. Even if most of the assets of the Jamieson Trust hadn't been embezzled, Frank's drug usage meant that he had been drawing further and further away from his family in the years before his death. She doubted he would have been capable of father-daughter travel, no matter what Noelle's age. "I don't think Noelle minds, Frank. She's closer to you now than ever before. I think she's happy."

The cat nipped her finger, though he didn't break the skin, then rolled and stood upright. He shook himself before he jumped from the case to the bed.

"Ow. What was that for?" The nip was the old Stormy, the cat who had put Frank first, Noelle second, then her dead last after mice and spiders when they lived in the Jamieson mansion and Frank had been alive.

Stormy jumped off the bed, head and tail up, the picture of disdain. *You don't understand.*

Annoyed, Christy said, "Try me."

I'm dead, Chris. Another man is taking my kid to Disneyland. Another man will harass her first boyfriend. Another man will walk her down the aisle. Another man will hold my grandchild. The cat paused in the doorway. He looked over his shoulder, green eyes hard and unwavering. *Another man has you.*

The cat disappeared out the door. Christy flopped down onto the bed as if someone had stuck a knife in her and she'd deflated. "Way to take the fun out of a vacation, Frank," she muttered. She heard footsteps, then a cat hiss. Moments later Quinn appeared in the doorway.

He smiled at her. "I've come for your suitcase. All packed?" His good cheer quickly turned into concern. "What's the matter?"

She shook her head as Quinn came toward her. "Nothing distance can't solve."

He reached out and caught her hands, then he drew her to her feet. "Frank's upset we're going away." Christy nodded. He slid his arm around her waist and brought her against him, so that she cuddled into him. "Bound to happen," he said, stroking the hair at her temple in a soothing way.

He didn't add that Frank would get over it. Christy appreciated that, because she knew it wasn't true. Frank might deal with his current situation, but he couldn't just brush it away and move on.

"I'd be pretty upset, too, if I was in his place. Let's get going. If we leave quickly and don't draw this out it will be easier on him."

Christy sniffed and nodded against Quinn's chest. He gave her another hug, then he let her go. She rubbed the heel of her hand against her eyes to wipe away moisture she hadn't expected to be there. Quinn hefted the suitcase and said, "Noelle's case is in her room?"

Christy nodded. He collected it, then they both headed downstairs, Christy first. By the time they reached the front door, Noelle was outside. Her best friend Mary Petrofsky had come to see her off, so she and Mary were rushing here and there, squealing, giggling, jumping, and generally expending nervous energy. Ellen was standing by the car, observing this with a frown, while Roy ignored it completely. Stormy was sitting on the porch, tail tucked neatly around his paws, watching the girls.

While Quinn loaded the suitcases into the car, Christy sat down beside Stormy. "You be good," she said.

The cat slid her a look.

"Listen to Aunt Ellen and mind what she says."

Another long look. *Shades of my unlamented childhood.*

"We'll be gone a week. That's all."

Stormy tipped his chin up and looked away.

Roy came over and gave him a quick scratch behind the ears. "Stormy will be fine. I've got some excursions planned."

Ellen came over too. She frowned at the cat. "Excursions? What kind of excursions?"

Mischief twinkled in Roy's eyes. "Stormy's going to help me interview suspects."

Ellen gaped at him. "Interview—how?"

The cat yawned and cleaned a paw. *Don't confuse the old broad. She doesn't listen. To me, especially.*

The twinkle in Roy's eyes deepened. "Cats are icebreakers. A cat on a leash is a showstopper."

Stormy leapt to his feet and hissed. *A leash! Not in your lifetime.* He turned, shot Christy a furious look. *See what you've caused?* Then he bolted back into the house.

Christy stared after him. She didn't want to part with Frank this way. She consoled herself with the thought that it was only a week. When she got back he would be fine.

Ellen frowned as the cat's tail disappeared into the house. "You would almost think the animal understood what you were saying, Roy."

"I wouldn't be surprised," Roy said. "He's a smart cat."

"Cases are in the trunk, Dad," Quinn said, coming up to them. "Come on, Christy. Let's round up Noelle and get this show on the road. We don't want to have to rush at the airport."

Ellen went off, calling Noelle to say good-bye. Roy winked at Christy. "Don't worry, he'll settle down."

"A leash, Roy? Really?" Christy said.

"Sounds like a plan to me," Quinn said.

"Can you imagine Stormy on a leash?" Roy shook his head. "Not going to happen."

Christy laughed and gave him a hug. Quinn said, "Too bad. It was a sight I wanted to see."

Christy rolled her eyes, laughed again, and focused on getting her daughter and herself into the car.

Ellen stood on the walk as the car drove up the hill. When it disappeared around the corner she turned back toward the house. She should have gone with them to the airport to see her family off.

The thought had her pausing in the doorway. Her family. She hadn't consciously identified herself with Christy and Noelle before now, and the thought shocked her. Frank was her family, certainly. He was her brother's son. Her parents' grandchild. He was family. By that yardstick, Noelle was also family, she supposed. Christy, however, had always been an interloper. As such her flaws were to be accentuated and her good points ignored.

Until Brittany Day's murder had sent Ellen to Burnaby. She'd claimed sanctuary that morning when she showed up at the townhouse and Christy had given it to her. Not many people who had been as put upon as Christy had would do that.

The cat came down the stairs, moving slowly, hopping stiff-legged down one step at a time. *Are they gone?*

Ellen closed the door. "I watched the car drive away and I felt sad. That was so unexpected."

The cat stopped two steps from the bottom. *Can you hear me?*

Ellen stared down at him. "Christy is a good woman."

Yeah, well, I know that.

"She's been treated badly by this family."

You can hear me!

She started up the stairs, moving around the immobile cat, heading for the kitchen. As she put a coffee pod into the brewer, she said, "She was very patient teaching me how to use this machine so I could fend for myself. I'd turned into something of a princess, I think. Stupid of me."

How long have you known? Did I say anything that, well, insulted you?

The machine gurgled as water boiled and coffee began to drip into her cup. "She's a good mother. Firm, but reasonable. Noelle does chores!" Ellen shook her head and picked up the now full mug. "I do chores!" She laughed at that as she circled the counter and went over to the table.

There were no servants here in Burnaby, even though Ellen had the money to hire as many as the household needed. Christy had told her quietly one evening after Noelle had gone to bed that the child wouldn't have the Jamieson fortune behind her as Frank had, and Ellen too for that matter. Noelle would have to fend for herself and that meant knowing how to wash her laundry, keep her living quarters clean and tidy, and cook her own meals.

Ellen sat down at the table and set the cup in front of her. The best way for Noelle to learn how to do all these things was to have adult role models, Christy had said. As Christy smiled pointedly at her, Ellen realized that Christy considered her to be a role model. "So I learned to do chores along with Noelle."

Ellen shook her head, still mildly surprised that she didn't mind vacuuming the carpet, or taking her turn with the laundry and cooking. A couple of weeks ago she'd even washed windows along with Christy, Noelle, and Quinn as part of Christy's spring cleaning rituals.

"I've been domesticated," she said. The cat hopped onto the table. She shook her finger at him. "And so should you." She picked him up, holding him just behind his front legs, then put him on the floor. "No jumping on the table while I'm here on my own."

So you can't hear me. That's a relief. I think.

The cat sat where she'd put him and stared up at her through unblinking green eyes. The look was unsettling, almost as if the beast was taunting her. Daring her to do something. She shook her finger at him again, and said, "Bad enough that I'll have to clean out your litter box."

The cat yawned. Ellen drank her coffee and told herself that she didn't miss Noelle's energy and Christy's quiet kindness. "He's in love with her, I think." He being Quinn. "And she with him. I'm not sure how I feel about that." Frank was dead and Christy had a right to get on with her life, but she'd raised Frank and if Christy moved on, it would make Frank's death more final somehow.

You're not the only one. The cat licked his paw and contrived to look uninterested in what Ellen was doing and saying. *I should be happy for her. Quinn's a better guy than I ever was. But…I don't want to let her go.*

Ellen sighed and drank her coffee. Stormy gave himself a complete body wash. They both jumped when the telephone rang.

Ellen stared at the handset parked in its charger on the counter, then she got up to answer. One of the new behaviors she'd learned while living here in Burnaby—answering the house phone if you were nearby, because somebody in the family had to do it. The call was from Trevor. He'd spoken to Detective Patterson and he wondered if Ellen would like to have dinner with him tonight? They could discuss the case while they ate.

Ellen's flagging spirits rose and she agreed to be ready for six o'clock. She headed up to her room to inspect her closet and decide what to wear.

CHAPTER 11

Having dropped Quinn, Christy, and Noelle at the airport, Roy was at a loose end. He could head home, but he didn't feel like working on the story that was his current project. It had reached the revision and polish stage and, since he'd now read it at least a dozen times, he was totally bored with it. He could do some household chores. Someone had to clean the toilets after all and since he'd be the only one using them over the next week, it was clearly up to him.

The idea of cleaning toilets didn't light a fire in his belly. Briefly, he considered smoking a joint, *then* cleaning the toilets, but even that didn't entertain. He turned the car onto Boundary Road and headed up the hill from Marine Drive. He realized he was already half way home and he was driving on autopilot. If he kept this up, he'd be turning onto his street still without a plan for the rest of his day.

Gloom settled over him. He'd end up cleaning the damn toilets.

A SledgeHammer song came on the car radio. He turned it up for maximum audio impact and his mind drifted to the concert and the tragic aftermath. He'd been cornered by that pompous idiot, Mitch Crosier. Even then, having just met the man, he had realized that Crosier was one of those people who talked you into agreeing to things you didn't want to. He'd made sure to stay focused on what the guy was saying, so he'd missed a lot of the action before the concert.

He *had* been aware of where people were, though. Hammer's parents had drifted out to the arena seats, probably anxious to get the best location for the show. Syd Haynes parked himself on the sofa close to the veggies and dip, and didn't move. Vince hovered near Mitch for a bit, then circulated. Quinn and Christy were sitting near Emily and Bernard Oshall. Quinn was catching up with Bernie, he supposed. Unmarried guys tended to lose contact when a single friend became part of a couple. Roy grinned. Christy and Emily seemed to get along well. Could be Quinn wouldn't be losing contact with Bernie again this time.

The two couples had been sitting at the eating bar that ran behind the seats. Quinn had his back to the wall and Christy had moved her stool so that she was beside Quinn, facing toward Emily and Bernie and, incidentally, the suite, not the stage. The few times he'd noticed, Bernie had been focused on Quinn, but he must have looked around at the action happening inside the suite from time to time. Say when some interesting or unexpected movement caught his eye.

Bernie's observations might prove useful. Roy had always liked Bernie and Trevor had maintained that Bernie Oshall was a good kid. Though he had been involved in whatever mayhem Sledge and Quinn got up to at the school, to Trevor it was high spirits, not meanness that motivated him.

Trevor wasn't one of those fathers who excused everything his kid did because he knew the law and he could get him off. When the boys raised hell they got punished, but they didn't get nagged about being forever well behaved. Trevor expected them to overdo it. So did Roy. As long as their excesses were exuberant, not malicious, he was fine with that.

For that reason, Roy would be surprised if Bernie Oshall had committed the murder. Trevor had planned to be the one to interview Bernie, to find out why he didn't walk down to the meet and greet with the group that included Quinn and Christy, but Trevor had gone downtown to see what he could pry out of Detective Patterson. Roy had the afternoon free, though. He could drop by, have a chat.

The afternoon was starting to look up. When he got home he'd find Bernie's address and phone number, then give him a call. But wait. It was Wednesday. Bernie, and maybe Emily too, would probably be at work. His mood tanked.

Still, there was the evening. He had nothing on tonight, except a solitary dinner and the opportunity to work on his book. Maybe the Oshalls would agree to see him. If they did, he'd grab Stormy and they'd go. He had a suspicion that Frank would be missing Christy and Noelle as much as he was missing Quinn. A road trip would be just the thing to perk them both up.

Roy didn't have Bernie Oshall's cell number, so he looked the name up in the phone book and got the house landline. He ended up connecting to voicemail and left a message, asking if Bernie would mind speaking to him about the night of the concert, then hung up and waited. About five o'clock he caught sight of Stormy through the window chasing a big black squirrel up a tree. He went out and stood beside the cat at the bottom of the tree, looking up as the squirrel scolded them both in a non-stop stream of chittering squeaks. Stormy's green eyes stared up, unblinking. The squirrel was his archenemy, but the only sign that he was annoyed was the restless flick of his tail.

"I may be going out to do a little sleuthing after supper. Want to come along?" The squirrel bounded along a branch that got more and more spindly the further he got.

Sure. Why not? Can you tell Ellen? She's going out to dinner with Trevor.

Stormy crouched, muscles tensing, gaze glued to the busy squirrel.

The squirrel's going to fall, the cat's sure of it. He's not going to let that wretched little beast get away this time!

"I'll leave you to it," Roy said. The squirrel reached the end of the branch. It sagged down under the animal's weight, then bounced back up. The squirrel used the momentum from the branch's swing to launch himself across an impossibly wide divide to a branch on another tree. As the squirrel flew through the air, Stormy took off after him, streaking along the ground with precisely the right amount of speed to have him where he needed to be if the squirrel missed his target. Unfortunately, the squirrel landed with acrobatic ease on the new branch. He raced along it, away from the danger Stormy represented, still chattering, though now Roy thought he heard a distinctly gloating tone to the sound. On the ground, Stormy crouched, tail lashing, as the squirrel disappeared into the canopy.

Roy called Ellen and told her Stormy was busy chasing squirrels. Ellen made disapproving noises, but mentioned she was going to dinner with Trevor. Having an appropriate opening, Roy offered to look after Stormy for the evening. Ellen thanked him and said Trevor was picking her up in a half an hour. Roy told her to have a good time and not to worry about the cat. That duty completed, he got on with putting together dinner fixings.

He was out on the deck, barbequing a steak, when Bernie called and suggested Roy come over at eight. The timing was perfect. He could finish his meal and still have time to put on a clean shirt and comb his hair before he started the twenty-minute trek to the suburb where the Oshalls lived.

"Hi, Dad. How's it going?" Quinn had decided to call home and let his father know they'd arrived safely while he waited for Christy and Noelle to dress for dinner. He'd already replaced his shorts and a T-shirt with slacks and a front button shirt. With time to spare, he was lounging on the sofa in the living room of the two-bedroom suite they were sharing.

"Quinn!" On the other end of the phone line Roy's voice sounded pleased. "I was just getting dinner ready. How was the flight?"

Different, Quinn wanted to say. He'd logged hundreds of hours in the air, in all sorts of aircraft, but he'd never had a flight quite like this one. He, Christy, and Noelle had changed seats three times before the plane took off, as Noelle tested out the middle, aisle and finally the window seat, where she settled. Christy sat beside her, in the middle, so he'd been beside her in the aisle seat, but her attention for most of the flight had been on Noelle.

The hell of it was his attention had been on Noelle too. She'd prattled on about what she was seeing through the window, what she expected to see at Disneyland, what the people in the other seats were doing, and how many flight attendants there were. He knew the kid was wired because they were going to Disneyland, but the flight, which was less than three hours, had felt longer than a non-stop to Europe.

"Uneventful," he said to his father.

"Really?" said Roy. There was laughter in his voice, damn it.

Quinn persevered. "We took off on schedule and landed on time. No bumps on the flight. We checked into the hotel mid-afternoon, then headed down to the pool. It's gorgeous here."

By the time they'd retrieved their baggage and found their way to the car rental kiosk, it was well past lunch. Everyone was hungry, so as soon as they finished the negotiations for their rental car, they piled in and headed off to find a place to eat.

Not so easy. L.A. was a city of freeways and high volume traffic. Figuring out where places were before the exit was upon them was tougher than he'd expected. Christy sat beside him, handling the map the car agency had given them, a guidebook she'd brought for the trip, and the GPS, but they still got lost. In the backseat, Noelle fell asleep when they were halfway to Pasadena. At that point

Christy had suggested they check in, then have an early dinner at the hotel. Relieved, Quinn had focused on getting them there in one piece.

Traveling with a family was far different than going solo or even with another adult. The basics were the same, but the patterns were different. He hadn't realized it before, but his dad had, which was why Roy was laughing at him, of course.

"We're off to dinner at one of the theme restaurants in the resort. Noelle picked it," he said. He thought his tone had that obnoxious sound of deliberate cheerfulness in the face of impending disaster and mentally cursed himself. Just because the damned restaurant had a princess theme and was the size of a baseball field didn't mean the food wasn't good. Besides, food wasn't always key to enjoying a meal; the experience was also part of it. He'd eaten combat rations in Afghanistan and enjoyed every bite, simply because it was proof he'd survived another day. He could manage mega restaurant food just fine.

"Really?" Roy said again. He chuckled this time. "Family fare. Make sure you chase it down with a bottle of wine. That's what your mother and I always did when we were traveling with you."

"Good advice," Quinn said lightly. He didn't know why he was so edgy. He'd been the one to suggest the trip. He wanted to travel as a family with Christy and Noelle.

"Frank and I are going to see Bernie and Emily Oshall this evening," Roy said, apparently tiring of teasing his only child.

"You're taking Frank? Really?"

"Yeah. He's feeling a bit blue since Christy and Noelle left. I've also got an appointment to meet with Mitch Crosier tomorrow."

"I'm not worried about Bernie, but Crosier might be the killer. Be careful when you talk to him, Dad. Okay?"

"Of course," Roy said amicably. "I'll take Frank with me. No one takes a guy who visits with his cat seriously."

Quinn closed his eyes for a moment, then said, "Good idea."

Roy chuckled and switched subjects abruptly. "Haven't heard how Three did with the cops yet. He planned to pick up Ellen right after he finished talking to Patterson. They're having dinner together tonight."

"Really?"

"Yeah," said Roy. "At Seasons in the Park."

Quinn grinned. "Wait till I Christy. Maybe she won't have to worry about Ellen buying a new condo. Maybe she'll move back to her old one." Trevor was renting Ellen's condo where Brittany Day had been murdered, the one Ellen had so far refused to return to. Things could change though.

Roy laughed. "Don't get her hopes up. Three always was catnip to the ladies. That's why he ended up getting divorced from Sledge's mom."

"I thought it was pressures of work."

"That was the excuse they told Sledge. There was an issue of several women on the side as well."

Interesting how a person perceived things at different points in his life, Quinn thought. At fourteen he couldn't see Trevor as an attractive male. He could only imagine him as an overworked lawyer and an underachieving dad. And yet he'd evidently been something of a rogue as well.

The door to the room Christy and Noelle were sharing opened and they emerged, hand in hand. Quinn's breath caught at the sight of them. Christy was wearing a sleeveless dress of marine blue silk that hugged her body and stopped somewhere mid thigh. On her feet were heels that made her legs look long and slender. Noelle also had a dress on. It was a bright, primary yellow, and sleeveless like her mother's. The skirt was full and when she saw Quinn looking at them, she twirled energetically to show him how the fabric belled out.

"Gotta go, Dad. My dates for the evening are here."

"Enjoy," Roy said, and hung up.

Quinn disconnected more slowly. He was still trying to deal with the surge of pleasure and pride that was washing through him. Christy smiled, a little shyly, he thought. He needed to say something, the right something, to let her know how glad he was they were all here together.

He went over to them and extended his hands, first to Noelle, then, with a special smile, to Christy. "Miss Jamieson. Mrs. Jamieson. Would you do me the honor of joining me for dinner tonight? I have a table reserved at a special restaurant, one where only princesses are welcome."

Noelle giggled. "I'm not a princess."

Quinn grinned at her. He raised their joined hands to touch her lightly on the nose in an unconsciously affectionate gesture. "Sure you are. You're a Jamieson princess, just like your mother."

Christy laughed. "Now I know you're teasing."

He wanted to tell her that she was wrong, that she was his princess, his brave and sexy princess, but he couldn't say the intimate words in front of Noelle. Someday, maybe, but not yet. Something must have shown in his eyes, though, because he heard Christy's breath catch and saw her eyes darken.

Elation lapped through him, slow, steady and sustaining. He smiled again and said, "Come on, you two. Let's go find the restaurant and show everyone in the hotel what a lucky guy I am."

Noelle giggled and did a little skip, tugging at his hand. "Tonight I'm a princess and tomorrow I go to Disneyland. Yea!"

Christy laughed at her daughter's enthusiasm and smiled up at him. In that moment he thought that dinner at the princess restaurant would be the best meal he'd ever had.

CHAPTER 12

"**P**atterson has a source," Trevor said. "But she won't tell me who it is."

Ellen frowned. She and Trevor were walking in Queen Elizabeth Park, a large green space on the residential west side. In the early days of Vancouver, it had been the stone quarry for the fast growing city. The old stone works had been reclaimed and turned into gorgeous quarry gardens, with flowerbeds designed to bloom all season long. Now, in the spring, the cherry trees were in flower, and spring bulbs brought bright color to the plantings.

The park was one of Ellen's favorite places to walk and think. Trevor had brought her here an hour before their dinner reservation at the nearby Seasons in the Park, so that they could meander through the delightful paths while they discussed the murder. It made her think that he loved this place as much as she did, and that warmed her in ways she wasn't sure she wanted to investigate. Focusing on the murder was a good way to keep their leisurely stroll impersonal.

Ellen didn't have a high opinion of Detective Patterson, so she wasn't surprised that the woman wouldn't be willing to share information with Trevor. "If Kyle Gowdy's records are sealed, she can't use them against him, can she?"

"She can get them unsealed if she has enough proof to convince a judge to do it," Trevor said grimly. "For that, she has to have a solid case against Kyle Gowdy."

"In the meantime, she knows the crime he was convicted for, so that is going to influence her clue gathering."

Trevor's lips quirked. "That's the polite way to describe it."

"The person who told Patterson about Kyle's record must have been in our suite."

Trevor nodded. "My thought exactly." He was wearing a well-cut dark suit. His shirt was a pearl gray and his tie marine blue. The colors enhanced his silver hair and the suit his trim waist and hips. To Ellen he looked as polished and sophisticated as the restaurant he was taking her to for dinner.

Their shoes clicked on the path as they wandered along. Ellen had chosen navy blue heels, not quite stilettos, for the evening. She told herself it was because they matched the feminine navy lace sheath over a shimmering silk liner she'd decided to wear, not that they made her legs look long and slender. She'd noticed Trevor looking at her legs earlier when he helped her out of the car. The look had sent a little rush of pleasure through her and made her glad she'd chosen the ultra feminine dress. The sheath was quite stunningly beautiful and it made her feel beautiful too, even now, when it was hidden by the coat she was wearing.

She said thoughtfully, "If he was with us in the suite, it narrows the field."

"Considerably. I can't believe Hammer or his parents would provide the details. By my reckoning there were only a few people who would have that information. Like Bernie Oshall, for instance."

"I thought he was Sledge's friend." As soon as she said the words Ellen gave herself a mental headshake. She couldn't believe she was talking about people called Sledge and Hammer in such a normal everyday way. Really, she should be calling both by their given names, Rob and Graham. But with everyone else, including Trevor,

Sledge's father, calling them by the ridiculous nicknames, it was almost impossible to remember the more appropriate designation. She would have to try harder.

"He is," Trevor said. "But Bernie was around when Sledge and Hammer got together and started SledgeHammer. I'm not sure how much he knew about Hammer and his family, but I don't think Kyle's situation was ever a secret."

"So we have one possibility. We can eliminate Quinn and Roy, of course."

"And me!" Trevor said.

Ellen laughed. "And you. Who does that leave us?"

"Mitch and Kim Crosier, and Syd Haynes."

"A rather short list," Ellen said and Trevor nodded.

They descended a set of rock-hewn stairs into one of the reclaimed quarry gardens. The scent of freesia was heavy in the air. Ellen breathed deep, letting the beauty of the place sink into her. They walked past a middle-aged couple dressed casually. Probably tourists. The thought was confirmed when the woman, smiling, asked in broken English if Trevor or Ellen would take a picture of her and her husband in front of the flower bed.

"Of course!" Trevor said, friendly and accommodating in a way Ellen had never been, and probably never would be. Had she been alone she would have walked past the couple without acknowledging them. As she watched the woman and her husband, too, instruct Trevor on the workings of the camera, all of them laughing, she wondered if perhaps she should rethink some of her basic behaviors.

Trevor lifted the camera; the couple posed and he snapped the picture. He took two more shots, then let the couple check the results and offer enthusiastic thanks before he caught Ellen's elbow and moved on. "I doubt Crosier or his wife knows about Kyle's record. That leaves Syd."

"So it was probably Bernie or Syd. That makes sense. They were both involved in Rob and Graham's lives prior to their becoming famous."

Trevor raised his brows at her use of the formal names, but he didn't comment. "I suppose I should check out Crosier too. He might have heard about it somewhere."

"And Vince Nunez, their manager. He knew them early on. Surely he'd know about Kyle's record."

"Good point. I'll ask Sledge—" His mouth quirked into a half smile. "Rob—what Vince knows about Graham's family."

Ellen became aware that she was smiling—smiling!—simply because Trevor had followed her lead and used his son's proper name. It made her realize how much she liked the way his attention made her feel.

"Thank you for suggesting we come early to walk through the gardens before we went in for dinner," she said. "I was amazed at how empty the house seemed without Noelle scampering around." She smiled faintly. "I found myself talking to the cat the way Christy does, almost as if I expected the creature to talk back." She looked over at Trevor as she spoke and wasn't surprised to see amusement in his eyes, though it was carefully hidden in his expression. His reaction wasn't unexpected, but she thought it was kind of him not to laugh at her over her silliness.

"This is my favorite time of year," Trevor said. "It makes me believe anything is possible."

"Yes! I feel the same way," Ellen said. They reached the end of the garden and the path, bordered by grass and plantings of mature cherry trees, wound up hill. The trees were in full, glorious, bloom, with masses of small pink blossoms that created a fragrant canopy overhead. As she admired the scene, Ellen wished she had a camera with her, or had brought her phone, so she could capture a memory of it. She understood why the tourists were so busy snapping pictures. This was an image she wouldn't want to forget. Mentally she shrugged and told herself she was being sentimental. She would be able to return next spring and see the cherry blossoms again.

"Hope is important," she said. "The last six months have been difficult, filled with betrayals and changes in my life I would not have predicted a year ago."

"You're talking about the trustees and Frank."

"I forget that you didn't know us when Christy was searching for Frank, and as it turned out, his murderer. Yes, the trustees betrayed all of us—Christy most particularly—but me as well, because I worked with them for years and had no idea they each had a base nature they indulged, but kept hidden. The changes, well you know why I feel so negatively about Patterson."

He nodded at that. "Being accused of murder puts a stain on your soul, particularly if you aren't guilty. It's why I became a defense attorney. The police work hard to find solid evidence and figure out the culprit. Usually they get it right—but sometimes they don't. It's the mistakes that motivated me and kept me going."

"I'm glad you were on my side," Ellen said, and meant it. She flashed him a smile. Trevor smiled back. "That horrible situation shook up my whole world so thoroughly I still feel unsettled. I don't know how many apartments I have viewed, but I can't seem to commit to any of them. There is always some flaw about the place, that later, when I think back about it, wasn't all that important. Yet, at the time I feel it is so huge that I couldn't bear to live in that particular unit because of it."

"Change takes a while to adjust to," Trevor said. "When I was diagnosed with cancer, I had all the prescribed medical treatment. Then the disease went into remission and I decided I needed to live life instead of living to work. So I retired and moved to Salt Spring Island. Slower lifestyle. Fresh air. Worked in the garden. Read a lot of books. Traveled to China and India and South America, too." His lips twitched. "South America was because of Sl…Rob. I followed the band on one of their tours, for a while at least. I couldn't handle the pace they set, though, so I gave up in Argentina and went back to Salt Spring. When Roy called and asked for my help, I was ready for a new challenge."

He looked down at Ellen, his expression grave. "If your crisis had happened a year earlier I wouldn't have been. I'd have referred Roy to someone here and gone back to my garden."

"I'm glad you didn't do that."

"I am too. The thing is, Ellen, when the time comes for you to make a change, you'll know. It will seem right and you won't be filled with doubts."

"I'm sure you're right," she said. Her tone sounded dubious to her. She hoped that Trevor wouldn't notice. She didn't want him to think that she didn't appreciate his pep talk. She did. But…she wasn't ready to accept it. Inner amusement at her silliness brought a smile to her mouth even as she changed the subject back to the reason he'd invited her out in the first place.

"There's another suspect we haven't considered, because he wasn't a member of our party."

Trevor accepted the change of subject with equanimity. "Someone who worked with her?"

Ellen nodded. "Charlotte Sawatzky mentioned that the general manager of the arena has a reputation for chatting up the female staff."

Trevor raised his eyebrows. "Just chatting up? Sure it isn't something more?"

"That's just it," Ellen said. "Chelsea told Charlotte he'd propositioned some of the girls. Not her, she said, but she was warned it might happen."

"Interesting. So you think that he made a pass? Then when she turned him down, he got rough?"

She nodded. "And things went further than he wanted or expected." When Trevor stared ahead without responding, she said, "It's a possibility, isn't it?"

After a minute, he nodded. "It is, but—" He broke off, shook his head, then began again. "This is the kind of thing the cops get wind of pretty quickly. My guess is they've focused on Kyle Gowdy because they've looked at, and discarded, guys like the general manager as viable suspects. Still," he added, sounding a little more enthusiastic, "it's worth adding him to our list. You never know, we may find something Patterson's overlooked."

"That would not be difficult," Ellen said in a tone that had the edge of a disdainful sniff to it.

Trevor laughed. He glanced at his watch. "Our table should be ready, fair lady. Would you care to join me for dinner?"

He gestured in the direction of the restaurant. Ellen realized that he'd guided them along a path that led directly there. She smiled at him, feeling freer and younger than she had in years. "I should be delighted, kind sir."

"Then we are away," Trevor said with a flourish, and swept her off to the elegant, and expensive, restaurant.

CHAPTER 13

——◆——

The Oshalls lived in Port Coquitlam, a suburb about twenty minutes from Roy's Burnaby Mountain home. They were halfway there when Frank said, *I'm not sure I like the idea of my aunt dating.*

Roy glanced over at the cat.

Stormy was standing on the shotgun seat, paws on the door's armrest, staring out through the passenger window, watching the passing scenery. He appeared to be enjoying the outing. Frank sounded as if he was sunk in gloom.

"Trevor's a good guy," Roy said. There was the sound of a grunt in his mind. Roy wasn't sure if it was a disbelieving grunt or a disapproving one, but he got the picture. Frank was jealous. Ellen was, after all, the closest thing to a parent he'd had through most of his life. "People move on," he said.

Stormy's tail flicked. The cat abandoned the window, circled the seat, then stood stiffly, again facing the window. His ears went back and his tail twitched in an agitated way. Roy had the sense that the cat and Frank were having an argument. He waited for the outcome.

After a minute, Stormy's ears straightened and he went back to staring out the window. Roy wondered if his comment about people moving on had struck a nerve with

Frank, so much so that he'd wanted to climb into the back
seat to sulk. He thought about telling Frank to grow up, but
decided it would be better to have a conversation about the
issue instead. "Ellen ever date when you were a kid?"

Always. She was very social. There was a moment's
hesitation before Frank continued. *Her relationships never
lasted very long. There was a time, soon after my parents
died, when I wished she'd settle down so I could have a dad
again. Then she sent me to boarding school and it didn't
matter anymore.*

Christy maintained that Frank was still here because he
was dealing with issues from their marriage. Roy thought
there was a lot more going on and it wasn't all related to the
Trustees trashing Christy.

He wondered what Ellen had been like as a young
woman. Had she, like Frank, had a relationship that the
authority figures in her life disapproved of? Frank had
married Christy. Had Ellen given in and ended an
unsuitable romance? "What were your Jamieson
grandparents like, Frank?"

*I don't remember much about them. My grandfather died
before I was born. My grandmother flitted in and flitted out
until she died.*

"When was that?"

*A couple of years after my parents were killed in the car
accident. About the same time I was sent to boarding
school.*

Interesting. If this were a novel, he'd make it a tragic love
story. As a young woman, with the Jamieson good looks
and a pile of money behind her, Ellen would fall in love
with a sexy young stud who was completely unacceptable
to her parents. They would use some sort of coercion or
blackmail to force her to split with the fellow. After years
mourning the end of her tragic romance she would learn to
live again, but would never commit to another. Then her
father died, and later her brother and his wife. She took on
the care of her nephew and tried to find a partner, but
wasn't willing to settle for a practical marriage that would

never have the emotional element she'd lost in her youth. With her mother's death she had a fleeting opportunity to relive the relationship from her past, but it was not to be.

The plot was rough, of course, and there were holes, but the storyline at least explained some of Ellen's issues. It also suggested that Ellen might be open to a deep emotional relationship in the future. He wanted to believe that was possible. Trevor had been showing considerable interest in Ellen since he'd come over from Salt Spring to help prove she wasn't guilty of murder. He'd survived cancer. He didn't deserve to have his heart broken, instead.

The GPS beeped. A canned voice he'd nicknamed Jeeves, because of its snooty British accent, told him to turn right in eight hundred meters. He abandoned thoughts of Ellen and Trevor to refocus on driving and prepping Frank for the upcoming interview. "Bernie and Emily have little kids. I don't know if they'll still be up, or if they're cat trained. Tell Stormy to be good. He can't scratch, or bite. If the kids annoy him, he should run away or jump up where they can't reach him. I'll try to intervene, but little kids like cats, so we need to be prepared."

There was a brief silence. Stormy's tail flicked and he turned his head to look at Roy, his green eyes cold. *Stormy knows the drill. He was a little offended that you would think he'd hurt a kid.*

Jeeves' plummy voice sounded again with new directions, saving Roy from replying. When they reached the Oshall house, Stormy leapt out of the car through the driver's door and followed Roy up the front walk. *Nice house,* Frank observed as Roy rang the doorbell.

The Oshall's home was in an older area of Port Coquitlam. The property was larger than that found in more modern developments, and the trees and rhododendron bushes had grown large. The house itself was two-story, angular in design, and filled with windows to take advantage of light and shade. Emily answered the door, wearing black trousers and a white silk blouse. The smile on her lips warmed her eyes. "Hi. Come on in."

She stood aside to let Roy enter. He cleared his throat and said, "My cat stowed away. Do you mind if he comes in too?"

Emily looked down, her expression dubious. "Well, I…"

Stormy slithered past her ankles, rubbing against her as he went. His purr drowned out whatever she had meant to say. Her expression changed to delight and she reached down to pat the cat. The purr became louder. She glanced at Roy. "Can I pick her up?"

"It's a he and sure." Roy stepped into the house.

Emily lifted the purring Stormy. "What a lovely cat."

Roy shut the door and Emily led the way into the interior of the house, still cuddling the cat. "Bernie! Roy's here and he's brought his cat."

Bernie greeted them in the living room. "Good thing the dog is down in the basement watching television with the kids," he said.

Stormy's purr died off. *Dog?*

Maybe including Frank hadn't been such a great idea. Arriving with your cat and bringing it inside was a bit odd, unless you knew that there was more to the cat than normal. And it appeared that Bernie and Emily weren't among those who could hear Frank talk, so they didn't know. "He jumped into the car without me noticing. I can put him back now…"

No way!

"No!" said Emily, still patting Stormy, who started to purr again.

Bernie, looking amused, said, "Emily loves animals of all kinds. I don't mind if he stays." He went on to offer coffee or a drink. Roy chose coffee and chatted with Emily while Bernie organized the coffee and checked to make sure the dog was safely focused on the kids.

Once they were all together, Bernie passed around the coffee mugs and offered cream and sugar. "You mentioned on the phone that you wanted to talk about the evening of the concert."

Roy nodded. "The cops suspect Kyle Gowdy, Hammer's brother, of causing that poor girl's death. That's got Hammer and Sledge upset."

"Such a sad thing," Emily said. Her attention was focused on Roy, but her fingers were still busy rubbing and stroking the cat. Stormy's purr vibrated through the room.

Roy nodded. "Trevor promised to do what he could to help Kyle," he said. Then he shrugged. "And I promised to help Trevor."

Bernie laughed. "Sounds reasonable. What do you want to know?"

"When you and Emily were talking to Quinn and Christy did you happen to notice what other people were doing?"

Bernie frowned. He looked over at Emily, whose expression was thoughtful. "I noticed Kyle and his wife by the food table. Jahlina, Hammer's girlfriend, came up from the seats and joined them," she said.

"I saw Vince talking to them at one point," Bernie said, nodding. He grimaced. "Vince had his back to Syd Haynes as if he was studiously ignoring him."

"Syd was sitting on the couch by the round table, right?"

Bernie nodded. "Stayed there the whole time, eating vegetables and staring at people."

Fun guy. Did he actually talk to anyone?

"Just after the band was on, I heard a sound behind me," Bernie added. He was frowning. "It sounded like a slap, though I have no proof it was. I turned to look and noticed that Chelsea was glaring at Mitch Crosier. Vince was standing inside the suite at that point, looking at the stage like the rest of us. I saw him glance around to see what had happened, I guess, and then he rushed over to separate Mitch and the girl. She looked really upset and so did Vince."

"I noticed too," Emily said. "Mitch was beet red. I'm not sure if he was embarrassed or furious, though."

"Could be either," Roy said. "Where was Kim? Did she know what Mitch was up to?"

Bernie shook his head. "She was down in the front having a great time dancing to the band. Syd, though, was watching. He just sat there, taking it all in, not getting involved."

"Did you see him talking to anyone?"

Emily looked at Bernie, then said, "Kim spoke to him at one point, and Bernie introduced me to him. We exchanged greetings and he mentioned Homeless Help, but he didn't say much else. He wasn't rude, but I got the impression he didn't think we were worth bothering with because we weren't likely to provide a donation for his charity."

Bernie nodded. "I think he was uncomfortable. Kyle Gowdy told me Sledge invited him because he thought it was time to bury the past, but it was clear that Vince didn't like Syd and Mitch wasn't interested in him. Or in Homeless Help for that matter. Hammer's family was reserved toward him, too. Trevor was friendly, and Syd was friendly back, but I think he accepted the invitation because he thought there was a networking opportunity that wasn't happening and he regretted coming."

"I remember him being rather shy as a teenager," Roy said. "Not good at asserting himself. That's why he turned to drugs."

"Not shy," Bernie said. "Self absorbed. He was never in the wrong back then. When Vince told Sledge and Hammer that Syd had to go, he blamed them, not himself and the drugs."

"It's tough getting straight," Roy said. "He's changed since then."

Bernie drank coffee. "Yeah, I suppose."

There was a moment of quiet, filled by the purr of the cat. "Why are the cops looking at Kyle for the murder?" Bernie asked finally.

Kyle Gowdy's juvenile record was his own affair, so Roy wasn't about to mention it, but the question provided him with the perfect opening for a question of his own. "There was a delay between the end of the concert and his arrival at the meet and greet. He says he was using one of the public washrooms. The detective isn't buying that." He raised his brows and said reflectively, "I have to admit, it does seem odd when there was a perfectly good private washroom in the suite."

Emily laughed. "And a line up. Bernie did the same thing as Kyle. While I waited to use the one in the suite, he went out to the public ones."

"Yeah, and they were busy too," Bernie added with a laugh. "Took me longer than Em."

Well that explained the delay for the Oshalls, and maybe for Kyle as well. "Have the cops interviewed you two?"

Emily nodded. "The day after the murder a Detective Patterson came to see us."

"We told her the same thing we just told you," Bernie said. There was sympathy in his eyes. "So she knows about the line ups for the bathrooms and the delay they caused."

Roy grimaced. "Too bad. I thought we were on to something there."

Did they tell her about this guy Mitch and the slap?

Roy barely resisted the urge to say, "Good thought." He caught himself and changed the beginnings of a word into the clearing of his throat. "Did you mention what you told me about Mitch?"

Bernie looked at Emily, who frowned. It was she who said, "No, I don't think we did."

Roy brightened. "It could be nothing, of course, but it might be worth following up." He stood. "Thanks for talking to me."

Emily and Bernie stood too. Emily put Stormy onto the ground and he pranced beside Roy as they left the house. "Nice couple," Roy said as he let the cat into the car, then slid into his seat and buckled his seatbelt.

Didn't help much.

Roy tapped the steering wheel. "Odds are that it's not one of our group who killed the girl. Kyle Gowdy is a suspect, but he may not be the only person Patterson is looking at." He started the car. "Let's hope so, anyway."

CHAPTER 14

N *ice house.* It was the next day and once again Stormy stood on the passenger seat, this time with his front paws on the dashboard as he stared out the windshield.

Roy stared out the windshield too. He tended to agree with the cat. It was a nice house, if you liked big houses that had gates, three stories, and were constructed of red brick in a neo-Georgian style. Add in some ivy snaking its way up the brick and you had a traditional appearance that proclaimed old family wealth. Roy preferred something smaller with a lighter look, but that was him. Big houses were hard to maintain and gates were a pain in the ass.

The little box on a pillar just before the gates squawked. "Roy Armstrong for Mitchell Crosier," he said, as someone inside the building demanded his name and reason for being at the gate.

There was some static, then the voice said, "Enter," as the gates slowly swung open.

"What does Crosier have that he has to go to so much effort to protect it?" Roy said, eying the gates critically as he drove through the widening space. He kept the pace slow in deference to the cat, who was still on his hind legs, paws on the dashboard, taking in everything he could.

We had gates at the mansion. They gave the place a nice cozy feel, because you knew you were safe in your own space once they were closed behind you.

"Huh," Roy said. "I never thought of it that way." He was both pleased and wary about this visit. He had been trying to figure out a way to arrange a meeting with Mitch Crosier that wouldn't make the man suspicious about his motives, or worse, hostile at being questioned, but nothing he came up with had that note of authenticity he needed. Then Crosier himself had called last night while he'd been out in Port Coquitlam talking to Bernie and Emily Oshall. He left a message asking if Roy would like to come over to his house for drinks about five the next day. Roy had called him back this morning to accept and here he was.

The drive curved as it neared the front of the house, then widened to allow parking. He mulled over the concept of locking yourself into a walled compound and how that might influence characterization as he pulled the small car into a spot between a Ferrari and a Mercedes and parked. "Okay," he said, wagging a finger at the cat. "Remember, you're a stowaway. And you're claustrophobic. You'll wreck the interior of my car if I leave you inside, so that's why I want to bring you in the house."

The cat stared at him with unblinking eyes, then his front paws flexed, his claws came out and he began to knead. *Got it.*

He shook his head. "Tell Stormy he doesn't have to show me. I'm on it." He opened the door and climbed out. Stormy followed, leaping past him, so that he pranced ahead as they walked toward the imposing front door.

Roy rang the bell. Stormy sat on his haunches and cleaned a paw, the picture of detached boredom. The heavy redwood door opened with more force than appeared to be strictly necessary. The person manipulating it was Kim Crosier and in Roy's well-informed opinion, she was high as a kite.

"Roy Armstrong!" She opened her arms wide, as if she was about to embrace him. Roy took a step back. "So delightful to have you visit us!"

Roy thought she'd be delighted if a bylaw officer showed up at her door, there to complain her gates were encroaching on public property. He told himself he was being uncharitable, so he smiled and said, "Hi Kim. Thanks for inviting me."

"Come in. Come in," she said, abandoning the thwarted embrace and instead swinging her arms in a sweeping motion to usher him inside.

"Sure," Roy said, and stepped cautiously into the house. Stormy slipped past his ankles and made it into the hallway as Kim was flinging the door shut.

"Oh," she said. Her eyes lit up, even brighter than before, if that was possible. "What a sweet kitty. Is it yours, Roy?"

I belong to myself.

The voice was annoyed. Roy thought there was even a sniff to it.

"Of course you do," Kim said, looking chagrinned. She turned and headed into the house. "Mitch is on the deck. We thought we'd have drinks there as it's such a nice afternoon."

Roy looked at the cat. Wide green eyes stared back at him. "Well. I didn't expect this." He thought he heard the ghost of a laugh in his mind.

The Crosier's backyard was a vast expanse of green, manicured and regimented. A swimming pool, still covered for the winter, sprawled across one quarter, while a hedge hid the fencing that surrounded the compound. Mitchell was seated on a cedar deck that ran the length of the building. A wooden portico, made of unstained cedar, extended from the house. Designed to keep off the rain, but leave the space open to the air, it covered the seating area. The patio furniture, as comfortable as any found in an inside room, and a built-in barbecue with a table that seated eight, was nearby. Beyond this the deck was open to the elements before steps descended to the lawn and garden.

Roy rather grudgingly decided it was a nicely designed space, though more manicured than he liked.

Mitch smiled and stood when he saw them step onto the deck. "Roy, good of you to come by." He shot out his hand.

"My pleasure," Roy said, shaking it.

"What's your poison?" Mitchell gestured to one of the luxurious couches that surrounded a built-in fire pit. A fire was burning there, creating welcome warmth against the cool of a spring afternoon.

Roy sank into soft, yielding cushions. He felt as if he had been swallowed up in a great enveloping cloud. It was disconcerting. "I'll have a beer, if you've got it."

"Of course. Kim, honey, can you get Roy a beer?"

"Sure." Kim smiled happily and drifted off toward the cooking area, which apparently sported a refrigerator as well as the enormous barbecue.

Stormy trotted off behind her. *I'll help.*

"Why, thank you, sweetie."

Mitchell frowned, but all he said was, "Where did the cat come from, honey?"

"Roy brought her," Kim said, looking back over her shoulder. Her expression was mischievous.

Him. I'm a him.

She giggled. "Oh, I'm sorry. Him, Mitch. It's a boy cat."

Mitchell's frown deepened. Roy said hastily, "Stormy likes to go for car rides. I didn't notice when I left, but he must have hopped in when I wasn't looking. I hope you don't mind, but if I leave him in the car he'll destroy the upholstery."

"As long as he doesn't destroy my upholstery, I couldn't care less," Mitch said with a shrug.

On the other side of the deck they could hear Kim talking chattily to the cat as she organized drinks. Roy could also hear Frank, and knew that she wasn't just talking about nothing. He was interrogating her about the evening of the concert, and he was having a lovely time doing it.

Mitchell started talking about books, so Roy had to focus on what he was saying. When they spoke this morning

Mitch had been vague about why he was inviting Roy over, but as the conversation unwound, Roy discovered the reason.

Mitch wanted to do a deal. He was a man who liked to think big. He had envisioned a multimedia empire where a convergence of music, words, and film would create the ultimate cross platform marketing opportunity and he was looking for properties to fuel it.

Kim brought a tray that included Roy's bottle of microbrew beer, a bottle of scotch, and glasses for both the beer and scotch. There was also a basket lined with a linen napkin and filled with small vol-au-vent pastries stuffed with some kind of creamy mixture. She handed out the drinks and glasses, set the basket on a side table between Roy's cloud-soft seat and her husband's, then said, "I'm going to show the sweet kitty the bird feeder."

Any squirrels in the area? The cat prefers them to birds.

Kim giggled. Mitchell didn't seem to notice. His gaze was on the vol-au-vents. "Sure, honey," he said, reaching for one of the appetizers. Kim and Stormy wandered off while Mitch ate a vol-au-vent with evident enjoyment that ended with a sigh. Then he splashed scotch into his glass, took a swig and continued, earnestly explaining to Roy that his novels would fit perfectly into the new arts and entertainment model he envisioned.

Roy listened, drank his beer, and let him talk—in between moments of eating and drinking. The vol-au-vents were gone and the scotch in the bottle had lowered by a considerable amount when he finally wound down.

"What do you think?" Mitch asked.

"I'm overwhelmed," Roy said. He thought his mind was devious, at least when he was plotting, but Mitchell's thought processes boggled him. The man seemed to have no scruples at all. If there was a way to manipulate an audience and quadruple profits at the same time, he'd be there.

Mitchell beamed. "I thought you'd like it."

Not much, Roy thought. At the far end of the yard, he saw Stormy sitting at the base of a tree. His head was tilted up. Beside him, Kim was sitting cross-legged. Her head was tilted up too. Apparently Stormy had treed a squirrel and they were both waiting patiently for it to surrender and meet its fate. Time to get a move on.

"I'm tied up in contracts," Roy said.

"Most of the good ones are," Mitchell replied, looking glum.

"I leave the business stuff to my agent."

Mitch brightened. "Tell you what, why don't you let me have your agent's particulars? I'll give him a call."

"Sure," said Roy. He'd send a text as soon as he was out of the house and tell the agent to blow Mitchell off. No way did he want to be involved in the man's convergence empire.

"Great opportunity meeting you at the SledgeHammer concert," Mitchell said, after he had typed contact information into his phone. He shook his head. "I go to these events all the time, but usually I'm bored out of my skull."

"A real shame about the girl's death," Roy said. He was relieved they were finally talking about the real reason he was here. He'd begun to think he would have to take off without broaching the subject. "I hate to think of it."

Mitchell leaned forward to pour another slug of scotch into his glass. He waved it at Roy a little blearily. "The cops were on to me about it. Can you believe it?"

"No! Really? Why?" This was too easy. He'd expected Mitchell would be cagier.

"They wanted to know what I did after I left the suite. Someone told them that I'd been flirting with the girl all night and they wanted to know if I'd taken it any further. As if I'd be so stupid." He snorted and for a moment his face contorted. "It was probably that little shit who does good works down on the east side."

Sydney Haynes. How intriguing. "What makes you think that?" Roy asked. He couldn't see any connection, but

Mitchell did. Why he did would give Roy further insight into the way the man's mind worked.

Mitchell stabbed his forefinger in Roy's direction. "Found God, didn't he? I heard tell he used to be a drugged-up punk who didn't have what it took to make it in this business. He dropped out and disappeared. Then suddenly he's a big man in the homeless crowd and full of righteousness. Guys like him want to stick it to guys like me."

Possibly. Fascinating, but not what Roy wanted to know. He grinned at Mitchell and said, "I don't remember you going backstage with us, but since you're here and not in jail, I guess the cops were satisfied with your explanation."

Mitchell downed the last of the scotch in his glass. He gestured defiantly with the empty glass, then put it on the table so he could top it up. Once it was full again, he took a drink before saying, "You bet. When we left the box, Kim and I went down to Erik's office. That's Erik Freeman, you know? The GM at the arena. I wanted to talk to him about my convergence ideas. Kim left when we started to chat, like she always does, and went down to the meet and greet. Erik and I talked for awhile, then his wife showed up and the three of us went down as well." He cackled. "I had impeccable witnesses for the whole time I was in the building."

Roy wasn't sure Detective Patterson would be quite so positive about one of those witnesses if she could see Kim Crosier sitting at the base of a tree communing with a cat and a squirrel, but he nodded and said, "Awesome, man," even as he stood up. "Well, thanks for the drink and the discussion. It was...enlightening."

"My pleasure," Mitchell said. They shook hands, then he bellowed, "Kim! Bring the cat and come say good-bye to our guest."

"Coming, Mitch!" She scooped up Stormy and trotted back to the deck. "So glad you could drop by," she said as she neared.

I had a great afternoon.

She handed Stormy to Roy. "So did I. It was fun."

"Took the words right out of my mouth," Roy said, because Mitchell was frowning again. Though he had a feeling Crosier had consumed enough scotch that he wouldn't remember anything important about the visit, he thought it would be a good idea to keep the conversation as normal as possible.

"Come back soon," Kim said, with a sweet smile that looked remarkably sincere.

"Absolutely," Mitchell said heartily, ushering Roy and the cat toward the front door.

They almost made it out without a further incident, but as Mitchell opened the door, Kim paused to scratch the cat under the chin. Stormy tilted his head up and purred. She winked and said in a conspiratorial tone, "Gotta keep those squirrels in line!"

You bet!

Speechless, Roy could only nod.

Once they were in the car, he said, "Frank, you're going to kill me. What the hell was going on with that fruitcake?"

She's not a fruitcake. She's bored, lonely, and way smarter than her husband.

"Wouldn't be hard," Roy said. He started the car. He wanted to get out before the Crosiers locked down the gates and trapped him here forever.

She doesn't like the way he does business, so she zones out.

"What do you mean?" he asked as backed out of his parking spot.

He schmoozes with the guys, flirts with the women. It's always sell, sell, sell. He doesn't know when to stop.

"Why is she with him then?" He could see the gates opening ahead and he increased his speed to reach them.

When they're alone he's different. He lets her be who she wants to be, not what people think she should be.

Roy thought about that. About Kim Crosier's abundant good looks and the expectations they roused. Compassion curled in his stomach. As he drove through the gates, they were already closing behind him. He wondered if Kim Crosier felt trapped in her opulent home with the well-oiled gates or if, like Frank, she found them comforting. "Did she tell you what happened that night?"

They went to the admin offices to find the General Manager of the arena. She says Mitchell called it a courtesy call.

"What does she call it?" Roy asked, intrigued.

Hounding him. She says Mitchell has this stupid idea he wants to use to take over the world. She says it won't work, and everyone but Mitchell knows it, but she can't convince him to drop it.

Roy grunted. He was with Kim on this one.

So she stayed in the office and listened to him babble— her word—about his pet project until she couldn't stand it anymore. Then she went down to the meet and greet.

"Fits with what Mitchell said. He bent the GM's ear until the guy's wife arrived, then they all went backstage."

One down. Who's next?

"Not sure," Roy said. "I need to talk to Three and Ellen and see how they've done." He paused at a light, then did a quick right onto a side street so he could pull over and send a text his agent, telling him not to do business with Mitch Crosier. He looked at the cat. "Good work today, Jamieson." He grinned. "A little unorthodox, though."

Stormy yawned at the same time Frank spoke. *My pleasure.*

CHAPTER 15

"**B**ring the cat."

As she hung up the phone, Ellen looked down at Stormy, who looked back up at her with wide green eyes. "Roy just invited me for dinner, along with Trevor McCullagh. He says I should bring you too. Why would he want me to bring Christy's cat to dinner?"

Jeeze, Aunt Ellen, of course I'm going over there for dinner. What's the problem?

The cat's gaze didn't waver. She felt as if she was being stabbed by a jagged shard of bottle glass, allowing guilt and regret to overcome her. "This is crazy," she muttered to herself. She went down to the basement to check the cupboard under the stairs where Christy stashed her meager wine collection. If she was going to Roy Armstrong's house for dinner, she did not intend to arrive empty-handed.

She found a reasonable vintage that must have come from the mansion. Not her first choice, but at least presentable. She pulled it out of the wine rack and turned to head back upstairs. And almost had a heart attack when she saw the cat standing in the doorway, hackles raised and tail lashing. A low growl rose in its throat.

What are you doing? Put that back! That bottle belongs to Christy and she's keeping it for a special occasion. Choose another or go buy your own!

Ellen looked at the cat, then at the bottle in her hand. There was no way a cat would care about a bottle of wine, especially a specific bottle, but still, she turned and replaced the bottle in the rack. She snuck a look at the cat. The wretched beast was now sitting down, cleaning a paw as if it had never acted like an attack cat. Cautiously, she pulled out another bottle, this one a popular everyday brand. The cat looked up, then once again began to clean itself, ignoring her. Hugging the bottle to her chest, she stepped over the animal without incurring any scratches.

She sighed with relief. Living with Christy's cat these past few days had been surprisingly difficult. The creature either ignored her or hissed at her. There didn't seem to be any happy medium without Christy here to arbitrate.

"Arbitrate," she said to no one in particular as she entered the kitchen and put the bottle on the countertop. She turned and saw that the cat had followed her in. "Cat…"

His name is Stormy. Why can't you use it?

"You will behave when you go over to Roy's house. No jumping on tables. Sit on the floor and be a proper cat."

Typical! Always nagging me about the rules. I'll do what I want.

The cat—Stormy!—stared at her with a coldness in its green eyes that made her uneasy. She knew it was just a cat, though apparently a very loyal one, since it had protected Christy from a burglar. She knew, too, that Noelle loved it. Perhaps she was being too hard on the beast. She sighed with a guilt she didn't understand and turned to leave the kitchen. Roy wanted to discuss their next move over dinner, so she went up to her room to collect the list she had made itemizing what they had discovered so far. The cat, she noticed, did not follow her.

While she was in her room, she changed into a slim fitting dress with three quarter length sleeves that showed off her still-trim waist. The V-neck plunged just enough to make a certain man's eyes sparkle, and the horizontal pleats in the skirt made her feel fashionable and feminine. She redid her makeup, then slipped on a pair of heels. After a final glance in the mirror, she picked up some pens and her leather portfolio with its precious list, then headed back downstairs.

The cat was no longer in the kitchen when she went to collect the wine, and she couldn't see it in the living room either. She went down to the front door and called. "Stormy! Time to go." She heard scratching in a litter box and wrinkled her nose. Christy expected her to clean out the box while she was away. The task was not one she looked forward to. If Christy hadn't been specific that it had to be done daily, or at least every two days, she wouldn't have done it at all.

She opened the front door. The cat trotted up the stairs from the basement, then slid out the opening. It glared at her as it passed.

The toilet needs cleaning! Don't you know cats have ultra sensitive noses? Don't you care?

She felt vaguely guilty for absolutely no reason that she could fathom, and followed the cat out the door.

At the Armstrongs' she was relieved to have people around her again. Roy had concocted some kind of chicken dish, which he served them all, including the cat, after they downed a round of drinks. The chicken had a sauce loaded with heat, so Ellen wasn't surprised that the cat's portion consisted of chicken and rice only.

Over dinner they shared a bottle of wine with their food as they chatted about things other than the murder investigation. Ellen had a sense that Roy wanted to prolong the evening, and wondered if he, like her, was missing the vacationers. The cat, thankfully, remained politely on the floor, where it should be.

They retired to the living room with glasses of brandy for Trevor and Roy and a Grand Marnier for Ellen. Roy took his favorite chair, while Ellen and Trevor shared either end of the sofa. She thought she saw amusement in Trevor's eyes when the cat hopped up onto the couch and settled between them, but that was ridiculous. She reached out and stroked the creature's back. Stormy began to purr.

Roy cleared his throat. "I've been thinking about what we've found so far, and none of it adds up to much."

Ellen leaned forward to picked up her portfolio. She'd placed it on the coffee table when she arrived, along with her three favorite fountain pens, each filled with a different color ink. With the leather folder in hand, she straightened, then pulled out her list. It was precisely designed, with categories and groupings that provided the most clarity for the information they had discovered. She had gone through a dozen drafts, weighing the information, putting it together into a structure, then tearing that structure apart and beginning again. It had been much work, but this, the final result, was an informative document and it pleased her. She might not be much use searching out clues and interviewing people, but she was organized. She considered herself a vital member of their investigative team.

"There were sixteen people in the box on the night of the concert," she said. She looked up from her papers and glanced from Roy to Trevor. "Would you like me to itemize them?"

This could take all night.

"Why don't we consider groups rather than individuals," Trevor said. He looked down at the cat and frowned. "For instance, you, Roy, Quinn, Christy, and I stayed together after we left the box. There's no way we could have harmed the girl."

Ellen nodded. "Good point. All right, we can break everyone in the box into four groups. Us—" She glanced at Trevor and then Roy.

She's flirting with you guys! My aunt, in front of me!

Trevor turned beet red and Roy tossed down the contents of his glass. He poured himself more brandy.

Ellen continued. "The second group would be invited friends. I put Bernie and Emily Oshall in this category, as well as Jahlina, Graham's girlfriend, and the former band mate, Sydney Haynes. What do we know about them?"

Roy rubbed his nose. "The Oshalls are okay. After the concert Bernie left the suite to find a washroom. Emily said he was gone for awhile."

Trevor's gaze sharpened. "Kyle Gowdy did the same thing. Why?"

"Ladies are slower than gentlemen," Ellen said. She made a note beside Bernie's name with a bright orange fountain pen that was filled with a neon orange ink. "He may have been doing exactly what he said. Or he may not. Obviously, Emily and Jahlina are not suspects, so that leaves us with Sydney Haynes."

"He's overcome some serious issues since he became a drug addict in the early days of SledgeHammer," Trevor said. "He was quiet all evening and I didn't see him saying or doing anything disrespectful to Chelsea Sawatzky when she was in the suite." He turned to Roy. "Didn't you tell me that Bernie Oshall saw her slap Mitch Crosier at one point?"

"We'll get to the Crosiers in good time, gentlemen. Right now we're assembling data on the Oshalls and Sydney Haynes."

Rules, rules, rules! It's always rules. Can't you go with the flow, Aunt Ellen?

"Yes, ma'am," Trevor said.

Ellen smiled at him. "What did Mr. Haynes do after the concert was over?"

"He didn't go down to the meet and greet. Quinn said he had a skewed view of the past," Roy said. "Not surprising, I suppose. People always see themselves as the hero—or antihero—of their own lives."

"Another one with no alibi," Ellen said, making a bright orange note. "Why don't we move on to the professionals now. Vince Nunez, Mitchell and Kim Crosier, and those two musicians whose names I can't remember. The ones who are managed by Mr. Nunez."

"The musicians beat us backstage. They were there when we arrived." As he said 'us' Trevor made a sweeping gesture to indicate the people in the room.

"Good," Ellen said. She capped the orange pen filled with the orange ink and picked up a white one adorned with sky blue swirls. The ink inside was a lovely azure blue. "I'll make a note and cross them off as potential suspects," she said, doing precisely that. "Why don't we discuss Mitchell Crosier now?"

Trevor nodded. "If the girl slapped Crosier, he was bound to be angry. He struck me as the kind of guy who'd hit back. I'm not sure, though, if he'd be angry enough to kill."

"He's out," Roy said gloomily. "His wife has given him an alibi."

"Pity," Trevor said.

Ellen shook her head. "Not a nice person. I so dislike seeing men in positions of power taking advantage of a woman, particularly a young girl like Chelsea. Her grandmother told me that she was having similar problems with a Mr. Freeman, the manager of the arena. He propositioned her, as well as other employees, and was not above making suggestive touches." She shook her head. "I have put him into the professional category, as an extra, even though he wasn't at our suite."

Roy was shaking his head before she finished speaking. "Mitch and Kim met up with Freeman in his office. Seems Mitch bored the poor sod with the same pitch he made to me. They can all provide alibis for each other."

Ellen fiddled with her pen. "That is disappointing."

"What about Vince?" Roy asked.

"He went straight down to the meet and greet. Patterson told me he was seen backstage before the murder took place, and was there long after the body was found," Trevor said.

"That leaves us with Hammer's family. His parents, and his brother and sister-in-law," Ellen said. She raised her brows and looked from one man to the other. "Thoughts?"

"The parents are clear. They went backstage with Vince. Kyle?" Trevor shook his head. "Like Bernie Oshall, he exited the suite looking for a washroom. He has no alibi for the time of the murder."

"Which is why Patterson is looking at him," Roy said. "What I don't get is why she isn't more interested in Bernie Oshall, who was also missing around the same time."

"Kyle Gowdy has a juvenile record," Trevor said.

Roy frowned. "Still…"

Trevor shook his head. "It counts."

"What about DNA?" Ellen asked. She hesitated, then said, "Wouldn't there be some if she was raped?"

Roy raised his brows. "Good question." He looked at Trevor. "Patterson say anything about that, Three?"

Trevor shook his head. "If they retrieved any DNA, they haven't processed it yet. I do know Kyle hasn't been asked to give a sample, but then he hasn't actually been charged, so Patterson may not want to tip her hand."

That was disappointing. Ellen looked at her list. "We don't have a lot of suspects, do we? Just Bernie Oshall and Kyle Gowdy. What if poor Chelsea was murdered by a stranger? Someone who had a seat in the stands and who hid until it was quiet after the concert, then attacked her? Maybe the goal was the rape, and her death was an unfortunate accident."

Interesting thought, Aunt Ellen. I'm surprised.

"You could be right," Roy said. He glared at the cat.

Trevor nodded. "The size of the potential suspect pool is probably the only reason Kyle Gowdy isn't in a jail cell right now." His expression was grim. "A random act of violence is the hardest crime to solve. If that's what happened, the police may not be able to lay charges against anyone. It's possible Kyle will always have the shadow of suspicion hanging over him."

CHAPTER 16

"Catch me, Mommy!" Noelle shrieked, at the same time as she leapt off the side of the hotel pool.

Christy wrapped her hands around her daughter's waist just before she hit the water and allowed Noelle's weight to topple her backwards, so they both submerged. Quinn dove beneath them like a seal, and hauled them to the surface. They all came up spluttering and laughing, Noelle most of all.

It was the end of their second day at the theme park. As with the previous day, they'd had dinner at the park, then came back to the hotel afterward. Last night they stayed for the fireworks. Tonight they switched up their plans and came back early so they could make use of the pool before bed.

Bed, Christy thought, as Quinn dove beneath Noelle and came back up with her on his shoulders. The water sluiced off him, making his skin gleam. The muscles in his arms flexed as he lifted Noelle high and tossed her back into the water. She shrieked, then came up giggling. Quinn grinned, then dove again.

Their first night in L.A. Noelle had been so excited about their vacation Christy couldn't get her to settle. She had planned to spend some time with Quinn in the suite's living room—and maybe beyond—after Noelle went to sleep, but it was not to be. At least not that night. She finally had to say good night to Quinn and settle into her own bed before Noelle would quiet.

Last night Noelle slept fitfully, exhausted from a long day full of experience overload, but still excited by the prospect of a second day at the park. That day—today—had been as full as the first one, but Christy was hoping that some of the glamour of the first couple of days had worn off and Noelle would sleep through the night. Because she had plans. This wasn't just Noelle's holiday; it was hers too.

Noelle paddled in her direction, then shouted, "Look, Mommy! Look what Quinn taught me!" She proceeded to dive down and kick up her legs in an attempt to do an underwater handstand. Her legs flailed, water splashed, and she came down on her back, doing something that looked more like an underwater somersault.

Christy looked at Quinn. He was watching Noelle with an affectionate, almost tender, expression that made Christy's stomach knot. He must have felt her gaze on him, because he looked over at her. A smile quirked his lips and he headed toward her. Christy wanted to reach out to him, to run her fingers through his wet hair, and ruffle it until it was no longer plastered to his skull, then pull him to her so their lips could meet in a kiss.

She couldn't do that, of course, but she could look, she could imagine, and she could hope that he would guess what she was thinking.

He was standing beside her when Noelle came up for air. She was pouting, probably because the handstand had failed so spectacularly. Quinn held up his hand for a high five. "Aced the somersault, kiddo."

Noelle frowned. "I did a somersault underwater? Really?" She didn't sound too sure, but she high-fived Quinn anyway.

"Really," Christy said. "I was impressed."

"I'll try again!" She ducked into the water, this time doing a better handstand than a somersault.

Quinn took advantage of the moment of public privacy to slip his arm around Christy's waist and lean in close to whisper in her ear, "Is she always this energetic?"

Christy laughed at the amazement in his voice. "Always," she said as Noelle surfaced again.

They played in the pool for another half hour. While they were in the water Noelle's energy levels continued at full blast, but by the time they were in the elevator and on their way to the suite, she was beginning to flag. Back in their room, Christy made her take a shower, then blow dried her hair. Noelle was yawning before Christy was even half finished. Once in bed, she curled on her side as Christy opened the book to read to her.

She was asleep before Christy finished the first page.

Christy continued to read to her for another five minutes before she closed the book. Her heart was pounding. Out in the living room she could hear Quinn moving around, then the low tones of the television. This, then, was it. Decision time. Commitment time. Very carefully, she put the book on the bedside table, then she went into the bathroom to do a quick check. Her hair was still damp, so she flicked on the blow dryer and risked waking Noelle. Well, not a risk really. If she woke up from the sound of the dryer, she wasn't asleep enough for her mom to go out into the living room and meet her lover.

Her lover. Saying the word, even in her own mind, made her feel guilty and aroused at the same time.

She switched off the dryer and listened. Not a sound from the bedroom. She took a deep breath, then went to her suitcase and pulled out the nightgown she'd bought right after Quinn suggested they come down to L.A. It wasn't a garment meant to be slept in, but one designed to be taken off. A rich, emerald green, it was silk with diaphanous lace inserts in some very strategic places. It had fueled her fantasies from the moment she tried it on in the store, but now, as she held it up before her, she had to swallow hard as she looked at it.

Was she reading Quinn right? Did he want to take the next step as much as she did? Or would he think she was coming on too strong? She took another deep breath. She could fold this beautiful garment up, then hide here in her bedroom and never know what might be.

Or she could put the gown on and take a step into her future.

She stared at the shimmering fabric for a long moment, then pulled it over her head and draped it down her body. She went over to the bed and kissed Noelle tenderly on the cheek. Her child didn't stir, even though Christy watched her for a minute, just in case.

She opened the door to the living room.

Quinn was sprawled on the sofa, watching a hockey game on TV. At the sound of the opening door, he looked up and the expression on his face told Christy everything she needed to know. He was on his feet in an instant. She closed the door quietly and stood as he came toward her, her hand still on the knob. With his every step her heart pounded harder, until she couldn't have spoken even if she wanted to.

As it was, she didn't know what to say to him when he reached her. She wanted to tell him how often she thought about this moment. The number of times she had played this scene out in her mind. She could see approval in his eyes and a wicked, dangerous look that called out to her. He threaded his fingers through her hair and bent his head, capturing her mouth at the same time as he wrapped his arm around her waist and drew her against him.

She gave herself into the pleasure of the kiss, of the strength of his body against hers. He lifted her and she let go of the doorknob to grab his shoulders for balance. When he put her down again, he released her mouth and she realized they were halfway across the living room.

His teeth grazed her earlobe. Her breath caught and she tilted her head as he nibbled. "I went to the doctor," she said.

His head shot up and his gaze sharpened. "Are you okay?"

She was still clinging to his shoulders because right now her body felt boneless. She nodded. "I mentioned it because—I wanted to tell you. I…"

He continued to watch her, but he was frowning now.

"I'm on birth control again," she burst out, feeling like an idiot and cursing herself for ruining the mood.

His expression cleared and that lazy, devilish look warmed his eyes again. "Good to know," he said. His voice was husky and she thought there was more than a hint of laughter in it. "Now I can seduce you properly and not worry about the consequences." His hand drifted down her side, lingering on those lace inserts to tease and tempt. "Because one daughter," he said, his voice rough with affection, "is about all I can handle just now." Then he kissed her again.

Christy lost herself in his touch and when he scooped her up to carry her into his bedroom with its king-sized bed, she was more than ready.

CHAPTER 17

———◆———

Sprawled on a sofa in Sledge's roomy great room, Roy took a puff of the joint Sledge had supplied as part of his party consumables. Roy was more than a little stoned as he contemplated the smoke rising from the glowing tip, his mind drifting lazily. The end of tour party was in full swing. People were everywhere, including the kitchen, though Chef Rita, who was catering the party, kept chasing them out. Even the bedroom wing seemed to have become part of the venue. Roy suspected that each of Sledge's four bedrooms was currently occupied with couples who were not discussing the weather.

He hadn't been to such a rocking party as this for a very long time, since his hippy radical days, pre-Vivien, in fact. It took him back, made him nostalgic. Though that might be the weed, come to think of it. Still, there was no getting around it. He wasn't twenty any more. He wouldn't want to do this on a regular basis, but occasionally…He grinned at nothing and no one. Letting go once in a while had a lot to recommend it.

He took another puff and breathed deep, exhaling slowly. The cushions moved as Stormy leapt up onto the couch. With typical feline disregard for anyone's comfort but his own, he hopped onto Roy's lap and walked up his chest so that his nose was close enough to the joint for Frank to enjoy some of the smoke. Roy stroked Stormy's head absently, and the cat began to purr and knead with pleasure.

Awesome. Damn, but Sledge gives a good party. I can't believe some of the people who are here.

Frank was right. Half of Vancouver's music scene was here tonight. They'd drift in, jam with Sledge and Hammer, then drift out again. Or maybe they'd just disappeared into one of the bedrooms. Trevor had told him that the end of tour party was a tradition for SledgeHammer. A time for the road crew, the band, the backup singers, and everyone else involved—including their accountant—to get together to mourn the end of the tour and celebrate its success.

The murder after the last concert had put a crimp into tradition, though. No one wanted to plan a celebration when a girl had died, so they'd compromised and made the party in honor of Homeless Help, Syd Haynes's charity. Everyone had been asked to donate. Sledge had announced earlier, just before Syd left, that they'd raised nearly a hundred thousand dollars.

Trevor needs to lay off my aunt.

That roused Roy out of his happy stupor. "What are you talking about?"

They're out on the deck. Huddled together. It's creepy.

There was something surreal about the way Stormy purred and kneaded lazily while Frank bitched about Ellen's behavior. If he hadn't already been aware of it, this alone would have told him that there were two different creatures living in the cat's body. "Are they necking?" He didn't want to think that Trevor and Ellen might be waiting for a spot in one of the bedrooms. Best not to go there.

They're talking! Get your mind out of the gutter, Armstrong.

Roy resisted the urge to point out that he wasn't the one who had brought up the subject. Instead, he took another puff and hoped the residual smoke would turn Frank's thoughts elsewhere and stop him ruining the vibe with his disapproval.

"Go to hell, Vince!" The angry voice belonged to Hammer and from the expression on his face as he stomped through the glass doors that opened onto the deck, he was furious. Stormy stopped purring and kneading, then hopped off Roy's chest to perch on the back of the sofa for a view of the action.

"Be realistic, Hammer. He's a liability."

That was Vince as he trailed into the great room behind the angry Hammer. Roy noticed that Sledge was just behind, a frown on his forehead.

"He's my brother, damn it! I'm not going to dump him so I can give the band better optics."

The conversation in the great room died off as the angry voice of Hammer and the milder, but still loud, one belonging to Vince, dominated.

"He's got a record, Hammer. Mitch told me his company is going to—"

"Mitch Crosier doesn't care about anyone but himself," Sledge said. His tone was even, carefully controlled, but Roy thought he could hear anger simmering below the surface. "The band sticks together."

"Since the media got hold of the info that Kyle was a suspect in the murder of a decent kid from a good family— and that he has a history of violence against women—our record sales have tanked! Do you know what that means?"

"I don't give a f—"

"I won't be a billionaire before I'm forty?" Sledge asked, raising an eyebrow. His tone was ironic, his expression amused as he broke in on Hammer. If he was trying to defuse the situation, though, it wasn't working.

"Get serious!" Vince said, his tone scathing. "It means no radio play. And no radio play means no sales. And no sales means no recording contract. And no recording contract means no tour. And no touring means no SledgeHammer!"

"I don't give a sweet fu—" Hammer said again. He'd been drinking steadily and had gone out onto the deck to look for Jahlina, who had disappeared about a half an hour before. His brother Kyle was on the deck as well. Clearly something had happened out there to trigger this very public argument.

Vince rounded on Hammer, furious. "You should! SledgeHammer is at the top of the heap right now, but there are plenty who want to take your place and they'll do whatever they need to get there. If the gossip media links you to Kyle, SledgeHammer is done!"

Hammer curled his lips into a sneer and said, "My name is already linked to Kyle's. We share the same surname, in case you don't remember."

"Sure, make fun of me. Go ahead. You were in the arena that night, just like Kyle was. If a rumor starts that you came on to the girl, or that you disappeared for ten minutes at one point, it won't matter that you have fifty people who will say that you were in a room with them the whole time. You'll be condemned and if you try to defend yourself, it will only make it worse." Vince stopped, drew a deep breath. "Cut him."

"Oh, this is bad," Roy said, to himself and to Frank. The mellowness of a few minutes ago had disappeared. He was glad to see that Trevor and Ellen had come in from the deck. As they edged around the two combatants, he made space for them on the sofa.

Hammer's eyes glittered as he stared at Vince, and his hands curled into fists at his sides. Tension stiffened his shoulders and his chin jutted dangerously. "I'll cut you first."

"This isn't about me," Vince said impatiently.

"I don't think we want to go where this is headed," Sledge said. His eyes were watchful and his voice had that same level tone, but his expression was hard. The argument was way past the flippant diversion stage.

"It's not?" Hammer said, ignoring Sledge. "I think it is. You've done this before. Remember Syd? Remember back then? We cut him, because you said he was a liability. Well, maybe we were wrong to do it then. And we'd be wrong to cut Kyle now."

Vince swore under his breath, then he turned to Sledge. "I'm not suggesting forever. This is a short-term fix until Kyle is cleared and the killer is found. Once that happens it won't matter that Kyle has a record."

"He's my brother!" Hammer bellowed. Rage glittered in his eyes as he turned to Sledge. Pointing at Vince he said, "He goes or I go. Your choice." He stomped up the stairs from the great room to the gallery, his footsteps echoing in the sudden quiet. Moments later, the sound of the front door slamming was loud in the shocked silence.

"I'll go talk to him," Vince said.

Sledge shook his head. "Let him cool off." He shot Vince a hard look. "Then go and apologize. And make it good. Otherwise, SledgeHammer will be looking for a new manager." He turned away and deliberately went over to talk to the lead singer of a popular local band. Vince was left standing alone in the center of the room.

Hammer's brother won't be cleared, because there's a good chance that he was the guy who did it. Looks like Vince is out of a job.

"Hey," Roy said. "I don't believe that."

Everything points to Kyle Gowdy. Stormy hopped off the couch and onto the floor. *The cat wants to pee. Can somebody let him outside?*

Roy did the honors, opening the front door Hammer had so recently used. There was no sign of the man in the front yard, so Roy figured Hammer was walking off his temper. Back downstairs, he slumped down onto the couch. "What happened out on the deck?" he asked, looking from Trevor to Ellen.

"I didn't notice anything at first," Ellen said. Roy thought he detected a blush on her cheeks.

"Kyle was on the deck when we first went out," Trevor said. "He was talking to Syd Haynes. After Syd left, Kyle stood for a long time, leaning against the railing and staring out over the water."

"He looked very isolated," Ellen said, nodding.

Kyle had come alone to the party, leaving his wife at home, and he'd spent most of it out on the deck, lingering in the shadows. Roy had thought it unwise of him to attend, but Trevor told him that Hammer had pressed him to show up.

"Hammer went over to Kyle and told him he should come inside and join in," Trevor said. "Kyle was reluctant. They had a bit of an argument, which Kyle ended by saying he wished he hadn't come."

"Then Vince joined the conversation. He agreed with Kyle. He even suggested Kyle leave by the deck and not go back into the house." Ellen shook her head. "Voices were raised. People started to stare."

"Hammer was furious," Trevor said. "Not surprising, I suppose. Sledge heard the commotion and came outside. He urged both inside. I think he had an idea that they could find a more private space to finish the argument. They didn't stop, though." He shrugged. "Well, you saw the result."

Ellen said, "Kyle looked more and more miserable as the fight went on, poor man. I think he would have been happy to take Vince up on his suggestion and slip away."

Roy looked from Trevor to Ellen. "What do you think? Was Vince out of line?"

"Reputation is important," Trevor said. "Social media opens doors, but it also closes them." His forehead wrinkled. "I don't think several hours into a party where everyone is drinking or taking one form of drug or another is the best time to broach the subject, though."

Since Trevor had offered himself up as designated driver, he'd be aware of the level of intoxication in the people around him. "Was Vince drunk, then?" Roy asked.

Trevor nodded. "He holds it well, but yeah, he's loaded."

Roy nodded. He suspected Vince was soberer now. If the fight had blown away the mellowness Roy had been feeling, Vince must have been blindsided. He was about to say as much when he realized that Frank was talking to Stormy. The conversation was one sided, but he gathered that Stormy was on the prowl and the object of his desires was a sleek Siamese. Frank wanted Stormy to come inside. Stormy was having none of it.

Roy looked over at Trevor. His color was rather high, so Roy figured he wasn't imagining the situation. When Sledge broke off his conversation with the other singer and came over, Roy's assumption was confirmed.

"That's Mrs. Tam's Siamese. She'll never speak to me again if he gets her pregnant," Sledge said. He looked at his father as he spoke.

Ellen stared at him, her eyes wide and her lips parted.

"What do you expect me to do about it?" Trevor said.

Sledge looked at Roy.

"I could go and get him," Roy said.

"Please." He turned, about to move away.

Kim Crosier appeared at his shoulder. She beamed at all of them. "So cute. The kitty's in love."

Ellen looked at Trevor, then Roy. "What is going on here?"

Inside his mind Roy heard a groan, then a sigh. Kim put her hand over her mouth and giggled. Trevor blushed. "Okay," Roy said, wanting to get away before Trevor tried to explain the situation to Ellen. "I'm gone." He stood.

"I thought this night couldn't get any worse," Sledge said. He looked and sounded gloomy.

Roy decided that he'd go find the cat anyway. He was halfway up the stairs when panic struck.

Help! I need help! Stop that! Stop now. You bastard! NOOOO!

Roy ran up the rest of the stairs two at a time. He was at the front door and was about to wrench it open when he heard the howl. It wasn't in his mind, but was the anguished sound of a tormented cat. He wrenched the door open and dove outside.

The front yard was a mosaic of light and shadows. Roy paused to get his bearings. Sledge had spotlights strategically located around the house to provide security against marauders, but outside of their range, shadows lurked. The eerie sound a keening cat was coming from the shadows to the west of the drive.

"There," Sledge said behind him. "Toward Mrs. Tam's house."

Roy looked over his shoulder and realized that not only was Sledge behind him, but also Trevor, Ellen, and Kim Crosier. They followed Sledge's directions and the mournful howl grew louder. The little group had almost reached the sound, when he noticed that Hammer was beside Sledge.

Odd. He thought Hammer had left the house. When had he joined the group? Roy shrugged and went on. His gut was telling him that something bad had happened and he had an urgent desire to find the cat. After that desperate cry for help, Frank had fallen silent, and Roy was very much afraid that something had happened to both Stormy and Frank.

When he saw Stormy crouched over a mound, his green eyes glittering in the dark, he heaved a sigh of relief. He slowed down, not wanting to startle the already agitated cat. That was all that kept him from falling over the little heap where Stormy crouched. "Hey cat," he said. "What's the problem?"

Stormy put his head back and yowled again, more loudly this time. The sound had adrenaline pumping through Roy, clearing away the last fumes of his earlier indulgence. He bent to look more closely at what the cat guarded.

"Oh, my God," he said, shocked to his core.

Behind him, he heard Trevor say, "Ellen, don't look. Go back to the house and call the police. There's been a murder."

CHAPTER 18

Detective Szostalo of the West Vancouver Police Department was a large man. Despite the lateness of the hour, he was neatly dressed in a well-cut dark suit, a white shirt, and a sober, navy blue tie. After viewing the crime scene and discovering the basics of what had happened, he corralled everyone in the great room and told them he would have to interview each of them before they could leave. As the party had been going strong when Vince's murder happened, there were at least three dozen people crowded into the space and the great room didn't look so large anymore. There were protests, groans, and not a few rude comments about Fascist police tactics. Szostalo paid no attention and had his constables get on with compiling names and personal details while he set about finding a suitable space for an interview room.

As Sledge's house was designed on an open concept layout, there weren't many non-bedroom spaces that were closed and private, so his options were limited. He finally settled on Sledge's music room.

Since the room was where Sledge wrote music and practiced, furniture was limited to the chair he sat on when he played the guitar, a baby grand piano where he wrote his melodies and a couple of easy chairs for people he invited in while he worked. There were a dozen guitars, all carefully placed, but there was no desk for Szostalo to sit behind while he interrogated his suspects. He'd rectified that by bringing in Sledge's kitchen table and several of the wooden chairs that matched it.

Rearranging the furniture to provide for Detective Szostalo's comfort—or perhaps to appease his dignity—turned into a major effort that included moving the baby grand into a corner and stacking the guitars underneath and on top of the piano. When thumps from the room indicated the contents were being rearranged, Sledge protested. He was ignored. As the kitchen table was lugged to the room, Sledge's temper peaked and erupted. The music room was his refuge, the place where his creativity flowed freely, and he didn't want it tainted by the murder. He certainly didn't want his precious instruments shoved around like put-it-together-yourself disposable furniture to make the space fit the table. He shouted at Szostalo and demanded the detective stop. Szostalo simply returned him a flat stare and told him he had no choice in the matter. The muttering in the great room, which had paused during the argument, resumed louder than before.

With his fussy nesting instincts satisfied, Szostalo started interviewing suspects. He began with Sledge. Roy waited for his turn with the rest of the partygoers in the great room. He had resumed his place on the squishy sofa and was patting the still tense Stormy, hoping it would help the cat relax, and trying not to let the angry undercurrents in the room affect him. Ellen, sitting beside him, was as tense as the cat. On Ellen's other side, Trevor was watching the proceedings narrow-eyed. As a potential witness, Trevor couldn't act in a legal sense and Roy figured his defense counsel instincts were giving him grief.

Sledge was still being interviewed when Stormy finally curled into a ball on Roy's lap. Roy looked at him hopefully. Frank hadn't yet said anything and Roy was getting a little anxious. "Feeling better?" he asked the cat, conscious of Ellen sitting beside him.

She looked over at the cat. "Poor creature. I guess even cats are affected by death."

She put a tentative hand on Stormy's back and stroked. The cat looked up at her, unblinking, then put his head down again and closed his eyes. Frank made no comment. Roy began to worry.

His thoughts were interrupted when Sledge, released from the interrogation room, stormed into the great room. On the way, he pushed past the constable stationed at the entrance to the hallway to ensure that no one left the great room who wasn't supposed to. He paused dramatically in the opening, catching the attention of the crowd in the big space.

"Listen up, Hammer," Sledge said. Loudly. He indicated the music room by pointing over his shoulder with his thumb in a jerky movement. "You're next on Szostalo's hit list. You know why?"

"Sir," said the constable. "Please sit down and refrain from discussing the case with the others."

His temper at full boil, Sledge paid no attention. "I'll tell you why."

"Sir, please!"

Angry, shaken by Vince's death and furious that the sanctity of his house was being violated, Sledge said, "It's because Vince was our manager. In that idiot Szostalo's uninformed opinion, that means Vince ordered us around and we didn't like it. Why did he order us around? Because in Szostalo's ignorant point of view, rock bands are made up of guys who never grew up, and the manager's job is to treat us like naughty teenagers and keep us in line."

Hammer, who was threading his way from the window where he'd been standing beside his brother, stopped a few feet from Sledge. "That's bullshit," he said.

"Move along, sir," said the constable, now tight-lipped and scowling. "The inspector is waiting."

"It gets worse," Sledge snarled, ignoring the cop. Frowning, Hammer didn't budge. "The idiot thinks that because we're drugged up, immature teenagers, we don't know how to discuss our issues, so we're more likely to use our fists—or in this case, a rock—to deal with the problem."

"That's enough!" shouted the constable. He lunged toward Sledge and grabbed his arm.

Trevor sprang to his feet. "Unhand him," he bellowed in his best courtroom voice.

In the commotion that followed Trevor joined the fray, Ellen shrank closer to Roy, and Stormy did his best to depart to other locales. But Frank didn't make a comment, even when the constable threatened to arrest Sledge and Szostalo had to come out to arbitrate.

When peace was restored, and Hammer led off to the music room, Sledge and Trevor sat down on the couch with Roy and Ellen. Sledge looked over at Roy. "So who did it?"

Roy shook his head and shrugged.

Sledge stared at Stormy, his brows raised. "How can you not know?"

Trevor looked pointedly at Ellen. "Probably someone from outside, same as the poor girl at the arena."

"Not likely," Sledge said. He rubbed his forehead. His expression was gloomy. "I live here because the place is secluded. No one just drives by. You have to come here on purpose." He looked at Stormy. "If we had a witness who knew who the killer was, we could tell the idiot cop who did it and get this fu…fiasco over with."

Stormy, now settled quietly on Roy's lap, stared back at Sledge. Frank said absolutely nothing.

Hammer was in the interview room much longer than Sledge had been. When he came back to the great room, his jaw was set and his hands were bunched into fists. He went straight to the windows where Kyle still stood.

"This doesn't look good," Trevor murmured.

"You're next," Hammer said, loudly, to Kyle. "Because you're my brother. That means you must have helped with the planning. So you're a key suspect."

The constable guarding the room surged forward. "I told all of you not to discuss the interviews!"

Sledge jumped to his feet and headed for the windows. Trevor followed.

As angry as Sledge was earlier, Hammer glared at the constable. "Back off."

"You tell him, Hammer," said one of the musicians, who had been sitting in the jamming area strumming a guitar. He punctuated his statement with a discordant swipe across the strings.

Kyle put his hand on Hammer's shoulder. "It's okay, man."

"It's not okay," Sledge said. Another of the guests sat down at Hammer's drum set and did a roll. The first musician played a riff and someone else began to clap.

"I advise you not to say anything without representation, Kyle!" Trevor shouted over the din.

"Quiet!" the cop yelled. The clapping stopped, the guitarist did one last strum, then fell silent, but the drummer started to lay down a beat, punctuating each of the constable's words.

His color high, the policeman pointed to Trevor. "Sit down." He indicated Sledge with a nod of his head. "You too. After you stop the noisemakers. It's disrespectful."

"Most of my guests didn't see Vince's body," Sledge said quietly. "There's no disrespect intended. They're just blowing off steam."

The cop stared at him for a minute, while the drummer idly pounded away, then he nodded. Sledge turned to the musicians and asked them to take a break. In the silence that followed, the constable's voice was authoritarian and harsh. "Mr. Gowdy, please come with me."

"Listen to Trevor, Kyle," Hammer said, as Kyle was led away. "Don't let the creep bait you."

With so much going on, Roy figured Frank wouldn't be able to resist making a comment, but he was silent as Kyle disappeared down the hall and the room settled into an uneasy calm.

Kim Crosier came over. "How's the kitty?" she asked. She scratched behind Stormy's ears, then began to stroke him.

Roy looked at Ellen, then back at the cat. "He's very quiet."

Kim frowned. "He's not saying anything?"

"After all of that howling, I am glad the cat is being quiet," Ellen said. She shuddered dramatically. "That sound was horrible. It will be with me till my dying day."

Kim cocked her head. She said to Roy, "She doesn't hear?"

"I hear perfectly well," Ellen said tartly. Roy shook his head.

"Poor kitty. He must be so upset," Kim said. She reached for the cat. "Let me hold him for a bit."

Frank didn't say anything as she picked him up.

Now Roy was really worried. With Kim cuddling Stormy, Roy hauled out his phone. He looked at Ellen. "Excuse me a minute. I have to call Quinn."

Midnight in L.A. Quinn dug his fingers into Christy's thick hair and savored her kiss. Since the first night they made love, she was always on his mind.

Strike that. She had been in his mind since she'd moved into the townhouse two doors down. This vacation, though, this combination of family retreat and adult playtime, had shown him a side of her he'd never expected. Practical mom by day. Siren by night. The combination had him on edge and aware, even when they were hurtling through space on the Magic Mountain rollercoaster ride and he felt like he'd left his insides behind.

He slid his hand along the smooth silk of that sexy nightgown she was wearing and enjoyed the way she quivered under his touch. She was always wearing it when she came out of the room she shared with Noelle after her daughter had gone to sleep and she always put it back on after they made love, and before she went back to her bedroom. In between she loved letting him take it off and everything they got up to after he'd done it.

He hadn't been sure that she would come to him tonight. Today had been their last day in L.A. They'd filled it to overflowing with a day at Universal Studios, then back to their hotel for a final dinner with the princesses, followed by a visit to the pool. Noelle was tired, but restless when they returned to the suite. Christy had let her watch some TV to help her settle, then sat with her and read to her once she was in bed. While he was waiting, he'd checked his e-mail, caught up on the news and watched some sports. He'd been considering going to bed when his patience was rewarded by the sight of her in the alluring green gown.

His hand found the lace insert that covered her breast. He skimmed his fingers over the fabric, rubbing it against her sensitive skin. She gasped and tilted her head back. He put his lips against the vein throbbing in her neck and kissed her until she began to quiver. She murmured a demand that he give her more and he laughed. She laughed too and he forgot about being logical and trying to rationalize how she made him feel. He scooped her up from the couch and carried her into his bedroom. There he could shed his clothes and tease that sexy gown off her, and claim her once more.

They both fell asleep afterwards. The sound of a ringtone woke him up. He looked blearily at the bedside table where he'd dropped his phone. The hotel had an alarm clock there. The red numbers said it was just before two in the morning. Quinn frowned as he reached for his cell. He was becoming more alert by the second, because the ringtone was his father's. Roy kept odd hours, so it wasn't unusual for him to be awake now, but he wouldn't phone unless there was a problem.

Beside him, her head on his shoulder, her body tangled with his, Christy stirred. "What's up?" she asked, as she yawned sleepily.

"It's my dad," Quinn said, and answered.

"Did I wake you?" Roy asked, sounding worried.

Something was wrong, Quinn thought. But what? "It's late, Dad. Is there a problem?"

"Yeah," Roy said. "You could say that."

Though Quinn hadn't put the phone on speaker, the agitation in his father's voice came through loud and clear. Christy eased away and reached for her slinky green nightgown.

Quinn watched her, feeling the disappointment he had felt every night she'd done this, but still enjoying the sexy way she twisted her body to allow the gown to slide down her. Other nights she would have kissed him good-bye and slipped away to her own room. Tonight she hiked up the skirt and eased back into bed with him.

He banked his pillows and sat up. She curled against him, clearly listening. When he slid his arm around her waist she moved closer and rested her head on his shoulder. "Out with it, Dad. What's happened?"

"We're at the SledgeHammer party. All of us." Roy paused.

"Yeah," Quinn said, trying to be encouraging. He didn't want to say 'spill it!' to his father, but that's how he felt.

"Trevor, Ellen, Frank, and me."

"You took the cat to the SledgeHammer party?" Had something happened to Stormy? Was that what Roy was calling about? Had some intoxicated party guest, who shouldn't be behind the wheel of a car, run him down?

Beside him, Christy stiffened. Clearly she was thinking the same way he was.

There was a little hesitation, then Roy said, his tone now belligerent, "He wanted to come. He liked Sledge's house and he's a big fan of SledgeHammer."

Quinn resisted the urge to sigh. He was pretty sure where this was going and he didn't like it. Not that he really cared about what happened to Frank Jamieson if his host body expired. But he did care about Christy and from her expression she expected the worst and had already started to grieve.

"What happened to the cat?" Quinn said, wanting to get the issue out into the open.

"What? Nothing! The thing is, he found the body. Saw the murder, that is." Roy broke off and there was the sound of voices in the background. Then Roy said, "I'm just talking to my son. I'll be with you in a minute." Additional voices, more urgent now, with an edge of demand in the tone. "He's got nothing to do with this. He's out of town. In L.A. No, he's not my lawyer. Do I need a lawyer?"

Christy sat up straight, her eyes wide. "What the hell?" Quinn said to no one in particular, because although Roy hadn't disconnected, he wasn't on his phone at the moment.

There was more background talk and Quinn thought, with some relief, that one of the voices belonged to Trevor McCullagh.

"Probably telling the cops that he's Roy's lawyer," Christy murmured, indicating that she could hear as much as Quinn was.

"Great, but if he is at the party, he might be a suspect too," Quinn said.

"What's that?" said Roy, suddenly back on the line.

"I was talking to Christy, Dad. I woke her up when you called and she's here now. I'm going to put the phone on speaker."

"Don't do that! It's—"

"Why not? I'm going to tell her anyway."

"I know, but…Better if you break it to her gently. Later. I don't have time to put everything that's happened into a nice package. There's a pompous ass of a West Van cop who wants to question me. Trevor bought me a couple of minutes, so I'll have to be quick."

Quinn glanced at Christy, who was sitting up straight now, tense and wide-eyed with fear.

"Who's dead?" he said.

"Vince Nunez. SledgeHammer's manager."

"You said Frank saw the murder. Who did it?"

Roy's voice lowered. "That's just it. We don't know. We heard Frank demanding that someone stop and then the cat howling, so we all rushed out to see what had happened. There was Stormy, sitting with his paws on Vince's chest and yowling, but no one else was around."

"Was it a stranger who did it? Someone Frank didn't know?"

"No. I mean, I don't know. Yes, yes, I'm coming!" The last must have been to the officious detective from the West Vancouver police department.

When he spoke again, Roy's voice was even softer than before. "Here's the problem. Frank hasn't communicated with any of us since he saw the murder being committed. No words. No visions of what happened. Nothing."

He hesitated and Quinn had a sense that his father was about to tell him what he wanted to Quinn to shield Christy from.

His voice almost a whisper, Roy said, "I think he's gone, Quinn. I think Frank has left Stormy's body behind."

CHAPTER 19

T he call to Quinn had made Roy's worries real. Stating
his fears aloud gave them weight and importance. By
the time he went to make his witness statement, his heart
was heavy and he was grieving for more than the man
whose body he'd so recently found.

He took Stormy with him into the music room, carrying
the cat in his arms. He told himself that Frank had not
passed on, along with Vince, that he was simply
traumatized by the experience of seeing the SledgeHammer
manager murdered. He hoped that being part of the
interview would get Frank involved in the deduction side of
the murder and help him deal. He also thought that having
Stormy with him would annoy Szostalo and perhaps cause
him to let some information slip, like how his suspicions
were coalescing and who he had set his sights on.

He was right about Szostalo. The detective focused on
Stormy, limp and huddled in Roy's arms, and frowned.
"What the devil is going on here, Constable?"

The uniform cop who had escorted him into the interview
room shot Roy a look of loathing. "I tried to get him to
leave the cat behind, sir, but he refused. He said if the cat
didn't come, he wouldn't either."

Szostalo's frown turned into narrowed eyes and a glare. "The choice isn't yours, Mr., ah, Armstrong."

Roy didn't bother answering that. He sat down on one of Sledge's kitchen chairs and settled Stormy on the table so that he crouched between the detective and Roy. "The cat saw the murder, Detective. I think he deserves to be part of what's going on."

"It's a cat," Szostalo said impatiently. "It can't talk so it isn't any use to me."

"He was traumatized," Roy said. "I want to give him closure." He thought perhaps he was still a little stoned, despite several cups of the coffee someone had produced, and the adrenaline rush caused by finding a dead body. He didn't want to admit to anything he'd later regret, so if the detective thought him both stoned and off his rocker, that was all to the good.

Szostalo stared at Stormy and the cat stared back, green eyes wide and very cat-like. He looked over at Roy, who smiled and did his best to appear vacant. "Fine," he said. "The cat stays. Now, Mr. Armstrong, tell me exactly what you saw when you found the body." He paused then raised his eyebrows and added, "Just the facts, please. Not the kind of embellishments you use normally."

The constable had already collected personal data—address, email, phone, occupation, driver's license and all the rest—so Szostalo clearly knew who Roy was. He grinned. "Read some of my books, Detective?"

Szostalo stiffened. "I've read the articles you published lambasting our police forces for upholding laws you disapprove of. And yes, I read the novel you wrote after your incarceration for civil disobedience. I am well aware of your views on the value of the laws that govern this land and of the justice system I serve."

Roy sat back. This was going better than he expected. "Don't like me, do you, Detective?"

Szostalo stared back at him, that flat, unemotional stare, and refused to rise to the bait. "I don't know you, Mr. Armstrong. I am here to find a killer and you are amongst the group of people who found the deceased. I need your input. Please answer my question calmly and succinctly."

Stormy sat up and stretched, distracting Szostalo. Roy let his thoughts drift back to the moment and visualized the scene in his mind's eye. "Vince was sprawled on his back on the ground. There was a wound on his temple. Lots of dark goop on the grass. Blood, I guess, pooling around his head and matting his hair. He wasn't moving and he wasn't breathing. Stormy here, was crouched over the body, with his paws on Vince's chest. He was howling. Horrible sound. Trevor told the ladies to stand back and not look." Roy shrugged. "I wish he'd told me not to look, too."

"You were the first to see the body, were you not?"

Roy shrugged again. "I'm responsible for the cat. I heard him howling, so I came out to see what the problem was."

"You went outside because of the cat?"

Szostalo sounded incredulous. He was clearly not a cat person. "Yes," Roy said.

Szostalo huffed. He didn't sigh like any normal person would when he was dealing with a difficult interview. No, he huffed like the self-important SOB he was. "There was no other reason you went out?"

"None," Roy said. He wondered if Kim, who hadn't been interviewed yet, would tell the detective that Stormy was a talking cat and if she did, how Szostalo would take it. He wished he could be an unseen eavesdropper on that conversation.

The detective shot Roy a look that said he didn't believe him. In Roy's experience, his next question would be on another subject, but he'd circle back to the answer he didn't like and ask the same question a different way. Guys like Szostalo were like that. Crafty, prepared to entrap you with your own words. Roy had his own ways of dealing with the pompous asses who blindly upheld the law. He leaned forward and plunked his elbows on the pine surface, taking possession of his half of the kitchen table. He scratched Stormy behind the ears. Stormy started to purr.

"Mr. Armstrong!" Szostalo said.

"Just tending the cat," Roy said, smiling at the detective as innocently as he could, which wasn't easy given that all of this was meant to be a sass and a distraction. Not innocent at all.

"Describe your movements prior to going out to, er, tend to the cat."

Roy put his chin on his upraised palm and thought back, visualizing again, while he continued to pat the cat. "I was sitting on the white couch, talking to anyone who stopped by."

"Were you drinking?"

An easy one to answer. "No."

"Did you indulge in any other substances?"

Roy sat up. "What's that supposed to mean?"

The detective huffed again, before he said, "I don't care what you were taking, Mr. Armstrong. I'm here to investigate a violent death. I need to know how valid your recollections of the time around and before the murder are."

"Ah," said Roy, and subsided into his slouched position again and resumed patting the cat with one hand. Chin on the palm of the other, he inspected the detective. "I was smoking." He deliberately didn't say what. Szostalo could draw his own conclusions. He was admitting nothing.

"Were you in the great room when Hammer and Sledge had their argument with the deceased?"

"Yes."

"Describe it, please."

"It was three guys who knew each other well sounding off."

"So nothing much. A tiff, as it were."

Roy nodded. Szostalo stared that flat stare of his, and as he continued to question Roy his voice wasn't any more expressive. He guided him through the aftermath of the fight—Hammer storming out, Vince disappearing from the great room a few minutes later, and then the search for the cat.

"And you decided you had to go after the cat why?"

They'd circled back to the finding of the crime scene again, just as Roy had expected. He sighed. He was a regular, decent person, not a pompous ass of a policeman, so he didn't huff. He wanted to, though. A good huff at this point would have been very satisfying. "Sledge was worried about the cat's amorous intentions toward Mrs. Tam's Siamese."

Stormy rolled onto his back and splayed his legs so his belly was exposed. Roy scratched it absentmindedly. The cat purred loudly.

Szostalo stared at the purring cat, then checked his witness list and frowned. "There's no Mrs. Tam at the party. Why would Sledge worry about this woman's cat?"

Roy scratched Stormy's belly. Stormy continued to purr. "Neighborly relations. She lives next door and she has a Siamese female. Apparently, Mrs. Tam is very protective of her cat."

"But why would he think the Siamese would be out at night for your cat to encounter?"

Roy moved his fingers up so he was scratching behind the cat's ears. Stormy opened his eyes and gave a little cat yip of protest. Szostalo frowned. Roy moved his fingers back to Stormy's belly and the purr began again. "Some cats like to roam at night, Detective. I guess the Siamese, like Stormy, is one of them."

Szostalo considered Roy's answer for a moment, then he nodded. Roy thought that his answer must have tallied with Sledge's. "Thank you for your assistance, Mr. Armstrong. That will be all for now, though I may have to contact you again."

Roy nodded. He stood, then scooped up Stormy. Or tried to. Stormy hissed, did a boneless cat twist that had him leaping out of Roy's arms, then landing back on the kitchen table inches from Szostalo face. Szostalo reared back and the constable who had been taking notes, jumped up, prepared to defend his chief.

Did Stormy's action mean that Frank was still in the cat and wanted to stay in the music room to hear more? Hope unfurled in Roy's chest and with it relief and not a little elation.

Stormy ignored Szostalo, brushing past him as he hopped off the table. Then, tail high, he strutted for the door.

Roy sighed, his hope dashed. It was Stormy who had hissed his annoyance when the patting ceased, not Frank expressing irritation because he was being removed from the center of the action. Roy nodded to the detective, then turned and opened the door for the cat.

CHAPTER 20

━━━◆━━━

Sledge was sitting on the most uncomfortable sofa he had ever had the misfortune to use. The back was straight, so a person couldn't slump comfortably the way he ought to be able to. It met a hard bench seat at a ninety-degree angle that allowed no flex. There was a minimum of padding on the back and seat. He thought the padding was more to plump up the green velvet fabric that covered the whole, than for the comfort of the unfortunate souls—like him!—who had to sit on it.

The sofa was an antique from the Victorian era, according to Ellen Jamieson who was sitting opposite him on a chair that had thin spindly legs, a seat covered in yellow silk and an oval shaped back, covered in the same fabric. If anything, her chair looked even more uncomfortable than the sofa. Sledge thought longingly of the deep squishy cushions on his chesterfield in West Van. He could stretch out on it, snooze, watch TV or eat his dinner, if he felt so inclined. Hell, he'd made love on it more than once and neither he nor his partner had complained.

He wouldn't be sitting on his sofa for a while, though. Not only was his house a crime scene, but news of Vince's death had got out and caused a media sensation. News trucks and paparazzi had started to assemble before dawn and every departing guest, already strung out from an interview with the annoying Szostalo, had to run the gauntlet of the media frenzy. The cops were all over his house looking for clues—though what they expected to find, since Vince was murdered outside, Sledge didn't know—so he was restricted to rooms they'd finished with. As the night had greyed into dawn, they gave him access to his bedroom. By that time his guests had all been interviewed, Szostalo had departed, and the only people who remained were the meticulous crime scene techs. He had crashed for a few hours, hoping they'd be gone when he woke up, but they weren't.

He spent the afternoon avoiding the techs and peeking out his windows at the ever-growing crowd of media at the end of his drive. Many were snapping pictures using super long lenses on high-end cameras and they all clamored for interviews every time someone moved in or out. He couldn't live like this. He knew it was part of the cost of the fame he'd worked so hard to achieve, but faced with this feeding frenzy at a time when he just wanted to grieve, it was too much.

He had snuck out in the small hours of the morning. He didn't attempt to breach the media barricades. Instead, he'd slipped through the trees that separated his property from Mrs. Tam's, then crossed her lawn to the next house. Waiting for him at the base of the driveway was his father. Which was why he was now sitting on Ellen Jamieson's antique sofa, wishing last night hadn't happened yet and it was the day before yesterday. Vince would still be alive, he'd be looking forward to the party and maybe, just maybe, everything would happen differently.

But it wasn't the day before yesterday. It was today. Vince was dead and he was homeless, living in Ellen Jamieson's downtown condo as a guest of his father. He shifted on the Victorian monstrosity. Thank God Ellen's condo had a spare bedroom. He couldn't imagine spending a night on the sofa. His back would seize within an hour.

His father, who was sitting on the other end of the Victorian monstrosity, didn't appear to find the sofa uncomfortable. He wasn't sitting upright, though; he was leaning forward, his elbows on his knees, his expression intent as he listened to what the others were saying.

Ellen and Roy had arrived about a half an hour ago to join his father and him in a brainstorming session to figure out who killed Vince. Across from him was Ellen, perched on her pretty little lady's chair. Beside her, Roy lounged in a high-backed chair, all wood, with not a hint of padding to be seen. It was constructed of walnut and beautifully carved, with a wicker seat and back. Ellen had said proudly that it was Jacobean, whatever the hell that meant. Sledge thought, with some considerable admiration, that Roy had aced the damn Jacobean antique. He looked as if he owned it, sitting on it with an easy confidence, like a lord presiding over a gaggle of serfs. Crouched under Roy's Jacobean throne, and still not talking, was Stormy. The cat had taken up a position there when Ellen had chased him off the Victorian monstrosity. Sledge thought the cat might have the better of the seating arrangement.

Trevor said, "Szostalo hasn't arrested Hammer yet, but he will."

That roused Sledge from his introspection. They'd been talking generally about the situation, allowing him to tune out and do a little wallowing. It looked like they were finally getting down to business. "Why?" he asked, unable to hide his hostility. "Hammer didn't kill Vince."

"So he says," Trevor said.

That made Sledge mad. His father often said stuff to prod people into looking at situations in a different way. Maybe that was what he was doing now, but if so Sledge was having none of it. Hammer was his friend. His ally. As close to a brother as a man could be. "Yeah. He says. And if he says it, it's true."

Roy rubbed his chin. "He did leave the house just before Vince left. He could have been waiting for him outside. Maybe he didn't want to cool off. Maybe he wanted to go at Vince in private. They got into another argument and it got out of hand."

The anger that had made Sledge snarl at his father boiled up into a rage that was fueled by worry and grief. Vince had been more than their manager, he'd been a trusted friend, as much a member of SledgeHammer as Sledge and Hammer were. He'd been there at the beginning. His energy and his belief in them had brought success and made them all wealthy. He couldn't believe Vince was gone. He knew Hammer would never kill him, any more than Sledge himself would. "Vince was family. Families disagree, but they come together again."

Roy cocked a brow. "Even when the quarrel is about a brother? A real brother?" He paused for a minute, then added, "Vince was telling Hammer he had to dump his brother for the good of the band. He was forcing Hammer to choose. Sounded to me like Hammer did before he rushed out."

"I know Hammer. He wouldn't kill Vince." Sledge's voice rose, hardened.

Roy shrugged.

"And I know Vince." The words came out with a snap. He swallowed, fighting his temper. This was a brainstorming session, after all. Everything laid out on the table. "Once he and Hammer both cooled down, they would have talked it through and worked out a compromise."

"What if Kyle Gowdy is charged with the murder of the girl? Then what?" Trevor asked. "Hammer must have known that Vince would push him that much harder to disown his brother." He tapped on the inlaid coffee table between the sofa and the chairs. It looked like an antique, too. "Maybe Hammer decided to silence Vince now, before his demands started to make sense."

"You think Hammer would dump his brother because he was framed by the cops?" Sledge asked tightly.

"Not framed, charged, because of the body of evidence made a case against him."

"Framed," Sledge said. Anger burned through him and made him bite out each word. "Framed, because he's no guiltier than Hammer is."

His father flicked a glance at Roy, who flicked a look at him. Roy then closed his eyes once, slowly like a cat, and Trevor nodded. Fury engulfed Sledge. They were managing him, the bastards, like he was a little kid having a temper tantrum.

Ellen's quiet voice broke through his outrage and had him quickly looking her way. "There were so many people at the party, wandering in and out of the house, moving from room to room. Is there any way we can figure out who heard the argument, and who was where? Besides us, I mean."

"You're right," Roy said. He sounded chirpy, as if this was all a game that was hugely entertaining. "Since we were in the great room, we were center stage, as it were. Let's try visualizing." Ellen frowned. His father looked intrigued. Roy continued. "Close your eyes."

Between the party, the cops, and the late night flit, Sledge hadn't had much sleep. If he closed his eyes he'd probably doze off, even on this dreadful sofa. Then he'd wake up with a crick in his neck and a headache.

"Imagine yourself in the great room," Roy chanted in a soothing monotone. "Feel what you are sitting on."

His chesterfield, a hell of a lot more comfortable than this God-awful Victorian monstrosity. He wished he was home again, not here.

"Listen to the voices around you. What are they saying? Can you hear one voice? Who does it belong to?"

"Hammer saying that he just saw Sydney Haynes leave," Ellen said. She sounded as if she was in a trance, or at least on the edge of one.

This was ridiculous. "Too early," Sledge said, trying to keep his voice as mellow as Roy's. He didn't succeed. There was an edge to it as he said, "I saw Syd slip out before the argument ever started."

"How long?" Trevor asked. His voice was sharp. He wasn't zoned out in some meditative trance.

Sledge shrugged, but the question made him look back on the evening. "Long enough for him to get into his car and be gone before either Hammer or Vince left the house."

Roy nodded. "Sledge is right. Syd came late, had a few words with everyone who counted." He snorted. "That means everyone who gave big donations, like Mitch Crosier. Early on, I saw him and Vince talking, but I don't know what they said." He pointed at Sledge. "Getting back to the time in question. That chef—what was her name?"

"Rita. Rita Ranjitkar," Sledge said. He decided he wasn't going to be pissed about the finger pointing. He wondered where Roy was going with this.

"She came out after Syd left and whispered something in your ear."

"She was asking me when I wanted her to bring out the celebratory cake. I was about to tell her we had to round up all the guests, so in about fifteen minutes, when I heard Vince and Hammer out on the deck, voices raised. I went out to see what was up. Rita went back to the kitchen. At least that's what I think she did."

"But you don't know for certain where she went?" Trevor asked.

Sledge thought back, then shook his head.

"Now we're getting somewhere," Roy said. "Who else was in the great room when Vince and Hammer came in from the deck?"

"Kim and Mitchell Crosier," Ellen said. She sounded a little more with it, but she still had her eyes shut.

"Kim was with us when we heard Stormy howl," Sledge said. He addressed his comment to Roy and his father. Ellen's serene, spacy expression was creeping him out.

"Mitchell wasn't, though," Trevor said. He shot Sledge a penetrating look. "Crosier and Vince did business together. Were there any issues between them that might have been contentious? Contract problems, that sort of thing."

"Crosier had a crazy scheme he wanted me to buy into," Roy said. "Was he pushing it at Vince too?"

Sledge shrugged. "Could be, but if he was, Vince wouldn't care. He kept his focus on the band and our interests."

"Any concerns, then?" Trevor asked.

"He was negotiating a new contract. He told me he was asking for better terms and more perks, because SledgeHammer was at the top of the charts and a hot commodity."

"Money and profit, then," Roy said, satisfaction in his voice.

Sledge could imagine him rubbing his hands together with glee and he had the thought that if Quinn were here, he'd shake his head and say his father was plotting a novel again.

"What about that musician? The guy who plays guitar when you're on the road? He was talking to Vince earlier, I think," Trevor said.

"He asked if Vince had talked to Mitch about something," Ellen said.

Sledge frowned. "You mean Brody, Brody Toupin?"

Ellen smiled at him, proving she wasn't in a trance, but she still looked very relaxed for someone who'd witnessed a murder and was now discussing suspects. "Could be," she said. "Dark hair, wearing a leather jacket and a black T-shirt, with jeans. Black boots on his feet."

The damn woman was uncanny. "That sounds like Brody. He wants a chance as a solo artist and I know he'd talked to Vince about it. That was one of the reasons he came on the tour with us. Vince was testing him out, trying to see if he could handle the pressure. I doubt Vince had decided yet, though. He usually takes a couple of weeks off after the tour ends before he picks up the pieces again."

"I saw a young man emerge from the corridor that leads to your music room just as you all came in from the deck. I don't think he knew anyone was looking at him. His expression was…" Ellen paused, thought. "I don't know.

Fierce. As he listened to the argument it changed and became almost…gloating."

"You're talking about Hank Lofti," Sledge said. "I saw him too. He was one of the roadies on the tour. Stoned half the time and snarky the rest of it. Undependable. Vince wasn't going to hire him for the next tour. He wasn't happy about that."

"Then, of course, there's Kyle Gowdy," Roy said. The cat slipped out from under his chair and began to paw his leg, claws sheathed. Roy picked him up and absently settled him on his lap. "He was the cause of the argument. He would obviously want his brother to side with him. What if he thought Vince would keep at Hammer until Hammer ditched Kyle and left him to the mercy of the Vancouver cops? He's probably afraid of being charged with poor Chelsea Sawatzky's murder."

"So any number of people had a good reason to dislike or be angry at Vince," Trevor said. There was approval in his voice. "Our job, then, is to dig up what we can on everyone but Hammer, because I don't think Detective Szostalo of the West Van PD is going to bother doing it."

"What about Chelsea?" Ellen said. There was no relaxation in her expression now. If anything she looked upset. "We were searching for her killer. Are we going to abandon that project in favor of this one?"

Trevor drew a deep breath, his expression thoughtful. "The murders don't appear to be linked, except that Kyle Gowdy is a featured suspect in both. I think that's happenstance, though."

"I'm sorry the girl died," Sledge said, "but this is personal. I need to know who killed Vince."

Slowly the others nodded, one after the other. Stormy yawned, then began to knead Roy's leg. "I think he's hungry." Roy said.

"Maybe he wants to use the litter box," Trevor said, frowning.

"He probably wants attention," Ellen said, with a sniff.

It was easier, Sledge thought, when the cat could talk.

CHAPTER 21

———◆———

"Thanks for coming, man," Sledge said, as he waved Hammer into Ellen's apartment.

Hammer looked around curiously as he followed Sledge from the entry foyer to the large living-dining room. Sledge had to suppress a grin. The apartment was in a modern building that was mostly glass and steel, creating expectations of sleek, simple furniture with clean modern lines. Ellen's antiques, designed for another era and a more formal generation, came as something of a shock.

"Can I get you anything? A beer? Scotch?" Sledge asked as he gestured toward the Victorian monstrosity. He could no longer stifle his grin as he saw the dismay on his friend's face when he realized where he would be sitting.

"Beer," Hammer said. He perched gingerly on one end of the sofa and smiled at the two other people there. "Hi, Ms. Jamieson, Trevor. I appreciate your helping Sledge and me."

Sledge headed into the kitchen and busied himself in the refrigerator. There was bacon in the meat tender and a head of lettuce in the vegetable drawer. A carton of eggs rested beside a six-pack of his favorite microbrew. A package of cinnamon buns and a loaf of bread were shoved behind a bottle of French merlot, which his father said was Ellen's choice. A half-liter of the cream his father used in his coffee was slowly aging. Though it hadn't yet passed its best before date, it soon would.

Breakfast and blotto, he thought, as he pulled a can of beer from the plastic holder, except for the lettuce. Why it was there he wasn't sure. There was no salad dressing in the fridge and neither he, nor his father, were in the habit of adding lettuce to their bacon and egg sandwiches.

Still mulling over the lettuce issue, he brought a can of beer for Hammer and one for himself to the living room. He handed the can to Hammer and had to pretend he didn't notice the frown that leapt onto Ellen's face because he didn't also hand Hammer a chilled glass. Doing things in the proper way was important to Ellen and she expected everyone around her to act the same way. But Hammer didn't come from a family that favored formal manners and he'd be uncomfortable if he was expected to use them. Sledge was not about to put his friend on the spot, not when Hammer was not only grieving Vince's death, but was fearful that he might be charged with the man's murder.

"Did you get the e-mail?" Sledge asked, cracking his own can as he sat down beside Hammer.

Hammer nodded. His expression was morose. The e-mail from Vince's wife contained funeral details: viewing times, when and where for the service and then the private, family and close friends only, interment. Sledge and Hammer had both been invited to the private service two days from now.

Taking a swig of beer, Hammer said, "I hope to God I haven't been arrested when we put Vince in the ground."

Ellen winced. Trevor said, "That's why we're here today. What's that West Van cop—Szostalo, isn't it?" Hammer nodded. "What's he up to? Is he harassing you?"

"Yes. No." Hammer shrugged. "I don't know if he'd call it harassment, but I feel like it is when he asks me questions. He asks the same questions in different ways, over and over until *I'm* confused about what I did and where I was. He wants me to confess, but what do I have to confess? That Vince and I had an argument and said harsh words to each other before he died and now we'll never be able to make it right?"

"Not what he has in mind," Trevor said crisply. He pointed at Hammer. "The next time he tries to talk to you, tell him you need counsel present. If he tells you to come to the station, refuse. If he insists, say you want your lawyer with you. If he arrests you, say you won't talk to him until you have representation."

Hammer nodded gloomily. "I didn't kill Vince. I wouldn't. I couldn't. He could be a jackass and he'd fix on an idea, like the one that I dump Kyle because the cops were fingering him for the girl's murder. He could drive you nuts, but—" He shook his head before he lifted the can, then drank. When he lowered it again, he said, "He cared about the band, of course, but he also cared about us, Sledge and me, as people."

"And we cared about him," Sledge said quietly.

Hammer nodded. "I hate that Vince is dead."

Ellen, who was sitting on the small slipper chair with the yellow silk covering, reached out and laid her hand over Hammer's. "It will get easier once the funeral is over and you have a chance to grieve."

Hammer nodded. "That's what my dad says."

"We won't heal until we figure out who killed Vince. Szostalo isn't looking beyond Hammer, so we need to," Sledge said.

Hammer looked at him with raised brows. "You haven't solved the arena murder. What makes you think you can figure out who killed Vince?"

"We were all at the party," Ellen said. She folded her hands in her lap and looked at Sledge and Hammer with a cool haughty expression. "Sledge's house is in an exclusive development. There are no random passersby. It had to be someone who was at the party. That means you have a limited pool of suspects to choose from."

"That's why Szostalo is looking at you, Graham," Trevor said.

Sledge noted with amusement his father was using Hammer's proper name, probably in deference to Ellen's dislike of nicknames.

"He'd probably be after Rob too," Trevor continued, "but Rob was in the middle of things, with several people who can vouch for his whereabouts. He's fixed on you because you're easy. You went out of the building. You were alone, on your own, when the murder happened. You have motive and you had opportunity."

"I was halfway down the mountain when the murder happened!" Hammer said, outraged.

"So you say. Let's see if there is any hard evidence that will prove it," Trevor said.

Hammer's eyes flashed and for a moment Sledge wondered if he was going to surge to his feet, grab Trevor, then punch him out. He hoped not. If he did, Sledge would have to punch him right back, because no one, not even a best friend, hit his dad. Then there's be a brawl right here in Ellen's living room, which would probably turn all the antiques into broken junk to be disposed of. Ellen would be mad and he'd have to replace the busted furniture, which, come to think of it, might be a good thing, after all.

Hammer had a temper. Both Gowdy boys did. Most of the time he kept it under wraps. After a long moment of charged silence, Hammer asked, "What do you want to know?" There was an edge to his voice that said he was still annoyed, but he wasn't going to erupt right now.

"Take us through what you did, from the moment the argument ended. Don't hold back. It's the small details that are often the ones that are the most important."

Hammer drank more beer, then he said, "I was furious at Vince. I felt choked, like all the words I wanted to say to him were stuck in my throat. I had to get out of there. I didn't want to go back out onto the deck. Kyle was out there and if I saw him, I knew I'd only get madder. So I rushed up the stairs to the front door and went out. It was a nice night, a little cool, but there were no clouds and I could see the stars." He'd been staring at the beer can in his hands, but now he looked up and glanced from one to the other of his listeners. "As soon as I got outside I started to calm down. I knew I was going to have to sort things out with Vince and I figured that if I took a walk and thought things through, I'd be better able to make him understand me."

"So you left the property and headed down the street," Trevor said.

Hammer nodded.

"Did you see anyone who might know what time it was when you set off? Or who might notice where you went? Hear anything unusual?"

Hammer looked thoughtful. "I heard a rustling in the trees that surround Sledge's house. At first I thought it was the wind, but it couldn't have been." He grimaced. "In fact, I know it wasn't. It was that damned cat of yours, Ms. Jamieson. He was stalking the Siamese that lives near Sledge."

"You're sure of this?" Trevor asked.

Hammer nodded. He grinned, then glanced at Ellen and wiped the smile from his face. "I saw the cats near the end of the driveway. Together. They were, ah, mating." He cleared his throat. "I ignored them and turned onto the road."

"How long did you walk and how far?" Trevor asked.

Hammer considered that. "I was almost at the entrance to the development by the time I turned back."

"That's a five-minute walk," Sledge said. "The houses are on good sized lots. If you were there you couldn't have killed Vince and got back to my house when you did. Why is Szostalo hassling you?"

"Because unless he has proof Graham was where he said he was, it's only his word. Szostalo can ignore it." Trevor said.

"It might have been ten," Hammer said. "I wasn't walking fast and when I heard the cat howling, I had to run to get back to your place. Do you know how steep the grade is in your area?" he asked, aiming the question at Sledge. "I was panting by the time I got there."

"Why did you rush back when the cat howled?" Ellen asked.

Hammer frowned, then shrugged. "I'm not sure. I thought about the rustling sounds, then I wondered if there was a bear or a cougar in the area. I thought the cat might be in trouble. The old guy walking his dog might have been what caused me to wonder."

"An old guy walking his dog?" Ellen asked. Her eyes were open wide, her expression invited confidences.

Hammer nodded. "Yeah, Sledge knows him. He lives in the second house from the end of the street."

"You mean Mr. Hulbert? Has a black and white Sheltie?" Hammer nodded.

"You talked to him?" Sledge asked.

Hammer nodded again.

"Did Mr. Hulbert happen to notice the time, Graham?" Ellen asked. Her voice was even, soothing almost. There was no evidence of rush, though Sledge was certainly feeling it.

Hammer said, "He must have. He looked at his watch, then shook his head and said, 'Cougar's probably caught a cat. Stupid to let a pet out at five minutes past midnight around here.' I agreed, then I thought about your cat and the Siamese and I wondered if anyone in the house had heard them. I had this vague idea that I needed to help, so I ran back to your place, Sledge."

"Did you tell Szostalo this, Graham?" Trevor asked.

Hammer frowned, then shook his head. "I only thought of it now."

Trevor rubbed his chin thoughtfully. "Okay, don't." He looked at Sledge. "Can you phone this neighbor and see if he corroborates Hammer's story?"

"Sure." Relief washed over Sledge. He never believed Hammer had killed Vince, but he'd been afraid it would be impossible to prove his friend's innocence.

"Once we have a name, address, phone number and a willing witness, we'll hit the good detective Szostalo with our information and let him know he can start looking elsewhere for his murderer." Trevor's expression was smug, as if he was going to take great pleasure in making the detective's life more difficult.

Eliminating Hammer as a suspect would certainly shake up the cop, but how long would it take for him to find the real killer? If he did. Sledge hated the idea that someone had used his house and his party to take Vince's life. He needed to know who that was.

And he wouldn't rest easy until he did.

CHAPTER 22

The sky over the San Diego Zoo was a deep blue, dusted with the odd fluffy white cloud. The temperature on this March day was warm, but not hot, and the air was freshened by a light breeze. It was the perfect day to stroll along the many winding paths and enjoy the animal exhibits that were the best there were in providing a compromise between animal comfort and visitor viewing.

Christy, Quinn, and Noelle had entered the zoo about an hour after it opened. They'd wandered for a couple of hours then paused for lunch before they'd set out again to enjoy the exhibits they hadn't yet viewed. When they first arrived Noelle had skipped along the trail, full of energy and excitement. Now, several hours later, she was still in awe of the animals she was seeing, but her steps were dragging. Still, she didn't want to leave until she had viewed absolutely everything.

So they ambled lazily down the path, pausing to take pictures and point out animals that were difficult to see in their habitats, or watch others that were putting on a show. They could have been any of the hundreds of families wandering the grounds. A mom, a dad, and a daughter, happy and carefree on their day out.

But they weren't. Christy was still wrestling with the news that Roy had imparted to Quinn. Could it be possible that Frank was gone? That he had slipped away while she and his daughter were away? If she and Noelle hadn't come down here with Quinn, would Frank still be living in Stormy the Cat, irritating her with his comments and his apparent assumption that he remained her husband, even though he wasn't alive anymore?

Had Frank truly left Stormy's body? And was it her fault?

As if he sensed her dark thoughts, Quinn slipped his hand over hers and squeezed. She looked over at him and smiled. He'd been wonderful since Roy's phone call. He'd held her as her first blank shock had turned to grief and when tears started to trickle down her cheeks, he'd pulled her close and soothed her while she cried. Then he'd listened while she babbled about loss and endings and who knew what else. She'd fallen asleep in his arms, but he must have stayed awake, or perhaps merely dozed, because he woke her well before Noelle's usual time so that she could slip back into the bedroom she shared with her daughter.

He must be exhausted, but looking at him now she could see only the smallest hints of it in shadows below his eyes and the strain around his mouth. Instead he appeared alert, watchful, and ready for anything. She was so lucky to have him here with her, but was she expecting too much of Quinn by dumping her grief over her late husband on him?

He caught her look and smiled. In that moment she could believe that he didn't mind. That he was glad she felt comfortable enough in their relationship to lean on him. Their lovemaking had brought them closer. Perhaps Frank's passing would bring them closer still.

"We're coming up on another of the big cats," he said now.

Noelle, who was a little ahead, looked over her shoulder and asked, "What kind is it?"

"It's called a Clouded Leopard and it's only found in Southeast Asia."

Noelle still had enough energy to do a little skip while she processed this. "What's it look like?"

"You'll see," Christy said. She laughed at her daughter's scowl.

Quinn said, "We'll tell you all about it when we find it."

Noelle had to be satisfied with that. Christy could see that she was looking around with sharpened interest now that there was another of the big cats to view. They'd already passed the tiger exhibit, and the lions, leopards, and cheetahs. The white snow leopard had been a big hit as well. She'd thought they had already reached the end of the supply of felines and had been relieved. She had half expected Noelle to compare the cats to Stormy and she wasn't sure what exactly she'd say if her daughter brought up the family pet.

Last night, their second to last night in California, she and Quinn had talked about how and when to tell Noelle that her daddy would not be in Stormy when they got back to Vancouver. Christy wanted to choose a moment before they got back to Burnaby, but one that would not mar Noelle's pleasure in her holiday. They'd tentatively decided that she would do it once they deplaned in Vancouver. That way they'd be on home turf, and Noelle would already be transitioning from being on vacation back into everyday life.

The plan would work only if Noelle didn't mention her father. If she did, Christy couldn't lie outright. Or even lie by omission. She'd have to tell Noelle, then deal with the grief that would follow as best she could. This late in the day, Christy hoped that the clouded leopard, which was supposed to be rarely seen in the wild, would have decided that it had had enough of being on display and gone to ground for the night in some private part of its compound. Noelle would be disappointed, but the danger of a chance remark about her father would be over.

Christy was out of luck. When they reached the exhibit there was the clouded leopard, front and center in his enclosure, dozing in the late afternoon sun, clearly visible.

Noelle sucked in a deep breath. Her eyes widened and she said, "Is this the Clouded Leopard, Quinn?"

"Sure looks like it," Quinn said. He was staring at the clouded leopard with a fixed expression. Christy wondered if he was as horrified as she was.

As big cats went, the clouded leopard was one of the smaller ones. Its markings were not tiger stripes or leopard spots, but a combination of both. Big swirls, colored gold that tapered to greys and blacks, looked like clouds and had given the breed its name. They watched as the cat drew its paws under it, then stood and yawned. Its compact size and the unusual markings made it seem familiar.

"Stormy!" Noelle said, with delight. "Mom, look! Isn't he beautiful?"

Christy's heart sank. "Yes, he is, sweetheart."

Noelle moved closer until her face was jammed against the protective barrier and she was as close as she could get to the big cat. "Tell me about the Clouded Leopard, Quinn."

Quinn consulted the zoo's website on his phone, then said, "Clouded Leopards aren't really leopards. They are a separate breed of big cat. They live in Southeast Asia. Not much is known about them because they're shy in the wild and stay away from people."

Christy wished that this clouded leopard behaved like his wild relatives and hid from human eyes. Too bad the animal hadn't read the memo on proper species behavior.

"I'm glad he's not being shy," Noelle said, looking over her shoulder at Christy and Quinn. "He reminds me of Stormy so much! I bet Daddy would love this cat if he could see him."

In its compound, the clouded leopard did a full body stretch, yawned again, glanced their way, then padded to a treed area and disappeared into the shadows. They stood waiting for it to reappear, but after a few minutes, when it did not, Christy reached out for Noelle's hand and said, "Come on, kiddo. It's almost time for the zoo to close. We need to get moving."

Noelle sighed and said, "Okay, Mom," then let herself be guided away from the exhibit.

As they strolled along the pathway, Quinn dropped behind. He was leaving Christy with Noelle and giving her the space and privacy to explain Frank's silence and probable passing to her daughter. Christy wasn't sure how to begin. Or, indeed, what she could say to make the news easier on Noelle. She chewed her lip. Finally, she said, "Roy phoned the other night."

Noelle looked up at her. "Does he miss us?"

"He does, but that's not why he was calling. It was about Daddy."

At that, Noelle frowned. "Did something happen to Stormy?"

"No. Stormy's okay. It's Daddy. He's not talking anymore."

"Is he mad at Roy?"

"No. It's—" How to explain that Stormy witnessed a murder and the trauma may have convinced Frank it was time for him to move on? "Something bad happened and Daddy saw it. He hasn't spoken to anyone since. I think, honey, that he may have decided it was time to go to heaven."

Noelle's hand tightened in hers. "Without saying good-bye?"

Christy had wrestled with that too. "We knew Daddy couldn't stay in Stormy's body forever. It was just a matter of time..."

"No." Noelle said the word firmly. The expression on her face was determined to the point of stubbornness. "Daddy wouldn't leave without saying good-bye. He loves us, Mom. He wouldn't do that to us!"

"Sweetheart, sometimes we don't have the option of choosing our time."

They walked in silence for a minute. Noelle stared straight ahead, while Christy fought the urge to cry. When Noelle looked over at her again, there was both a plea and belief in her eyes. "Daddy wouldn't go without telling. I know he wouldn't. When we get home he'll talk to us again. I know it."

Christy bit her lip. She could press no further. Noelle might be right. Hadn't she thought the same thing? Maybe Frank still was there. Once she and Noelle were back he'd bitch about the decisions she made and start taking potshots at Ellen again, all in his usual way.

So she nodded to Noelle and said, "I hope you're right, kiddo."

Relief shone in Noelle's eyes. "I bet I am!" She tugged at Christy's hand. "You'll see."

Christy looked over her shoulder at Quinn as she allowed Noelle to pull her closer to the next exhibit. His smile said that she'd done all she could and that she'd let the subject drop at just the right moment. As they paused at the next exhibit, he caught up with them and slipped his arm around her waist. She leaned into him and thought, not for the first time, that she was a lucky woman.

Christy wrapped her hands around the coffee mug and said, for the third time, "I won't believe Frank's abandoned us."

The last night in California and their return flight home this morning had been quiet. Even Noelle's enthusiastic energy had been dimmed by worry over the change they could find at home. There had been hope, though, that Frank might not be gone.

Christy clung stubbornly to that hope now, even though Frank hadn't said a word since their return. "He wouldn't leave without saying good-bye. He wouldn't do that to Noelle."

Roy looked concerned and Quinn's expression was bleak. She knew that they both believed Frank had moved on to whatever came after death, and that she simply refused to accept what was, really, inevitable.

Part of her agreed with them. The sensible part, the practical woman who had a child to raise and a reputation to protect. But the part of her who had made excuses for

Frank almost from the moment they'd settled in Vancouver, the woman who accepted that it was possible for his essence to live in a cat's body, that part wouldn't let go. "Frank loved—loves—Noelle. He made a promise to her. He wouldn't break it."

"Seeing someone murdered…" Roy said, shaking his head. "It was tough enough looking at Vince's body. Watching it happen? I don't know if I could have handled it."

Christy pounced on that. "Exactly! It's post-traumatic stress."

Both men stared at her.

She felt herself coloring, but she continued resolutely, "He needs time and closure."

"Christy," Quinn said, but added nothing more, as if he thought her statement was so outrageous that there was nothing he could say.

Christy drank some coffee to hide the dogged resolution she was sure must show in her expression. She knew she sounded ridiculous refusing to accept what was clear to everyone else, but she couldn't let go. "We need to solve the murder, soon. Do you have any idea who could have done it?"

Quinn rubbed his forehead while Roy rattled off the list of suspects he, Trevor, Sledge, and Ellen had identified.

"I thought we'd eliminated Mitchel Crosier?" she asked.

"Of Chelsea Sawatzky's murder," Roy said. "But Vince's? Crosier was there that night and though he says he was wandering the house looking for Chef Rita around the time of the murder, no one saw him. He and Vince were in contract talks for the rights to the new SledgeHammer songs and Sledge says Vince wanted better royalties, more promotion and a lot of other benefits. I don't think giving up control would fit in with Crosier's world domination schemes."

"And you don't think the murders are linked," Christy said.

Roy shook his head. "I don't see how. There aren't a lot of similarities. I think the SledgeHammer involvement in Chelsea's death was just a timing accident."

If the murders weren't related, it didn't matter if someone had an alibi for Chelsea's. Christy drew a deep breath. "Okay, then we start fresh. Did you guys decide who was going to interview whom?"

Roy shook his head.

"I'll take Crosier," Quinn said. His expression was grim, his inflection flat. "I can tell him I want to do an interview. He'll be cagey, but I may be able to get him to open up. I can do the same thing for Brody Toupin, the backup guy with big dreams. He'll like the idea of some free promo now that he's looking for a new manager."

Christy put down her cup so she could slide her hand over Quinn's. He turned it under hers, so their fingers clasped. "Thank you," she said, trying to tell him how much his willingness to get involved meant to her. He squeezed her hand and his expression seemed to lighten.

"I'll talk to Hank Lofti," Roy said. He ignored the byplay between Christy and his son, though she was sure he'd noticed it.

"I take it Emily and Bernie Oshall weren't at the party?" Christy asked.

Roy shook his head.

"So they aren't suspects. What about the former band member, the one who ended up living on the streets? The guy with the creepy stare?"

"Sydney Haynes," Quinn said and Christy nodded.

"He was there, but he left early," Roy said.

"So he's not a suspect either. That leaves Hammer's brother, Kyle."

"He was out on the deck when the argument began and he stayed there when Vince and Hammer took it inside. Now that Hammer has a confirmed alibi, he'll probably be high on Szostalo's list of prime suspects."

Christy said, "Noelle and Mary Petrofsky are spending the day together tomorrow. I'll talk to Kyle in the morning, if he's free."

"I'll come with you," Quinn said.

Christy bit her lip. "It would be better if we split up." Truth be told, she planned on taking Stormy with her, in the hopes that Frank would emerge as she questioned the lead suspect in one murder who was also a potential suspect in another.

Quinn's expression closed and he slid his hand from hers. "Right then, I'd better get busy doing my research, since I've agreed to do two interviews." He shoved back his chair and stood up.

Christy stared up at him. She hadn't expected this reaction from him. "Quinn!" she said, but he ignored the plea in her voice as he walked out of the room, away from her. She jumped to her feet, ready to follow.

"Let him cool off," Roy said in a kindly way. "You lit a fire and it'll have to burn itself out before you two can talk any sense."

She sat down again. "I hurt him."

Roy studied her for a minute. "He'll get over it."

There was another silence in which Christy stressed over the choices she had made and was making.

Then Roy said, "I like Frank, at least the Frank who lived in Stormy. Part of me hopes he'll come back. I haven't had so much fun since I tied myself to a tree in Clayoquot Sound and dared the clear-cutters to take me down. That's the selfish part, though. The other part, the better half of me, my late wife Vivien would say, thinks it would be best if Frank was gone. A clean break." He paused again, then said, "It would be easier on all of you, but especially Quinn." His eyes twinkled. "It's hard competing with a dead guy, you know."

"I suppose it is," Christie said. She wrapped her hands around the coffee mug, feeling miserable.

Roy nodded once, then he said, "Something to think about."

Staring at the oily sheen gleaming on the top of the dark brew in her cup, Christy nodded. "A good reason to find the killer and sort this whole mess out. Then maybe we'll have some answers about Frank, as well as Vince."

CHAPTER 23

Kyle Gowdy lived in a modest bungalow in the East Vancouver area where he and his brother had grown up. Christy parked under a flowering cherry tree that cast its branches over the street to meet those of the cherry across the way. In February and as recently as a couple of weeks ago, the cherry trees were in bloom, but the season was over now. As she paused to study the house, she could see that some of the fallen pink petals lingered on the sidewalk.

The house was pretty much like every other house on the street. A pocket-sized lawn, bisected by a concrete walk, fronted the building. The foundation was concrete, as was the front porch and the steps leading up to it. Wood siding, freshly painted a mellow cream, covered the exterior. The front door and the trim were all a dark blue. A pleasing combination, she thought, as she headed up the walk. There were no flower beds in the minimalist yard, but there was a mature rhododendron bush almost ready to flower, and a cedar hedge separated this yard from the one next door.

Though the media had besieged Kyle's home when they'd first learned he was under suspicion for Chelsea Sawatzky's murder, interest had fallen off when no charges were laid. Now there were no media trucks parked in front of the house, or paparazzi lurking nearby waiting to snap the perfect picture, for which she was grateful.

Christy had called ahead to make an appointment, so she wasn't surprised when it was Kyle himself who answered the door. She was puzzled by the quiet in the house. She knew he had kids and since Spring Break wasn't over for another few days, she thought they would be home.

"Thank you for sparing me a few minutes," she said, smiling at Kyle.

He didn't smile back, but he opened the door wider to invite her in. He led her to a modest sized living room with a big plate glass window that looked out onto the rhodo bush and the lovely avenue of cherry trees. There was a television in one corner, a sofa, two chairs and a coffee table in between. A tower lamp was positioned between one of the chairs and the sofa. Apparently, this was where Kyle and his wife sat in the evening.

"Graham asked me to talk to you," he said, referring to his brother. "He says Rob told him that you are a hot-shot detective."

Christy stared at him. She couldn't think of a thing to say. *Hot-shot detective?* Her?

Kyle didn't notice her silence. "Between us, the Gowdy brothers have become suspects number one," he said.

"Trevor told me they found a witness who can prove Graham was well away from Sledge's house at the time of the murder." She smiled as Kyle indicated one of the chairs. Sitting down, she added, "Once the police take the witness's statement, your brother will no longer be a suspect."

Kyle's jaw flexed before he clenched it in a way that expressed his upset more effectively than his flat, unemotional tone or the words he chose. "I'll believe that when it happens. In the meantime, if you can help us, we'd appreciate it." He settled onto a corner of the sofa.

"I'll try." Christy sat and put her tote bag on the floor beside the chair. "I hope you don't mind, but I brought my cat with me. I thought your kids would be home and that they'd like to play with him." Stormy poked his head out of the tote and blinked at Kyle.

Kyle stared back. "My wife took them to the rec center. They've added extra family swim times for Spring Break and the kids love the pool." He looked up at Christy. "We're trying to keep them out of this as much as possible. They don't need to think their dad is some kind of monster."

That struck a chord with Christy. She wrinkled her nose and said, "I understand completely. When everybody thought my late husband Frank was an embezzler, my first priority was to shelter our daughter, Noelle."

Kyle nodded. He didn't say anything, but Christy wasn't fooled—the man was aching inside. Stormy emerged from the tote, stretched a lithe cat stretch and sauntered over to inspect Kyle. As the cat sniffed his leg, Kyle reached down to scratch behind his ears. Stormy began to purr.

Kyle smiled. It was only a little smile, the barest twitching of his lips, but it broke a bit more of the social ice.

Christy said, "I wasn't at the party when Vince was killed, so I'm trying to build a picture of what people were doing when everything happened. Where were you when the argument between Hammer—Graham—and Vince started?"

Stormy hopped up onto Kyle's lap, flopped down, and offered his belly for a rub. Kyle looked astounded, then he laughed and stroked the soft fur. Stormy's purr deepened. "I was on the deck," he said after a minute. "Graham was one of the hosts, so we hadn't spent much time together." He looked from the cat to Christy. "Kristine didn't want to get a sitter for the kids, so I went solo. I didn't want to go, but Graham thought I should. He said the cops would figure I really was guilty of that girl's murder if I didn't." He shrugged and his mouth twisted. "It was a mistake."

Christy frowned. "People wouldn't talk to you?"

Kyle shook his head. "No. That wasn't it." He hesitated, then shrugged again. "It was me. I wasn't in a partying mood. I hung around the edges and hoped no one would notice me."

He might be Hammer's brother, but SledgeHammer's world was foreign to him, Christy thought. She nodded and waited for him to continue. When he didn't she prodded gently. "So you were out on the deck…"

Kyle nodded. "Jahlina had wandered off somewhere and Graham had come out to schmooze with the people who were outside. When he noticed me hanging out in the shadows he told me I should mingle. I told him I didn't want to and that coming that night had been a mistake. That made Graham mad. He said I had to act like nothing was wrong or no one would believe I was innocent." A weary smile touched Kyle's mouth. "I told him to go to hell."

He sighed and patted the cat. Christy gave him a minute before she said, "What happened then?"

"Graham turned to go back inside. That's when he noticed Vince, who was between him and the doors that led to the great room. Vince must have heard what we were saying to each other because he told Graham he needed to stay away from me. He said any connection to me was poison for SledgeHammer. I heard Graham defend me, but I was furious. I was hurt too. What Vince said…It was so close to what I was thinking, but hearing someone say it aloud?" He sucked in a breath and pursed his lips as he shrugged. "I didn't want to be part of a scene. Hell, I didn't want to be there anyway, so I left them to it and slipped away. I took the steps that led off the deck and headed for the trees. I figured it was better to be alone until I could haul my temper under control."

"How long were you out in Sledge's yard?"

"A while."

"So you were outside when your brother stormed out of the house?"

Kyle nodded. "I'd been pacing and when I heard the door slam I was on the east side of the house and I could see the front from where I was. I saw Graham walk across the grass to the street. Even though I was outside, I'd heard the raised voices and I figured Graham was cooling off too, so I didn't say anything to him." His jaw flexed. "Now I wished I had. If we were together, neither of us would be under suspicion."

"Did you see or hear anything else while you were outside?"

Kyle's hand stilled and Stormy's purr quieted. He butted his head against Kyle's arm and Kyle resumed his petting. Stormy's purr echoed through the room again. "I didn't see anyone, but I heard rustling in the trees behind me and down toward the gate. It creeped me out, because from time to time Rob gets word that a cougar has been seen in the area. They're dangerous animals, silent and elusive until they're ready to pounce. I started to make my way back to the deck where there was noise and people."

"A sensible precaution," Christy said. She'd been told that cougars sometimes came down from the North Shore Mountains, swam across the Burrard Inlet, and made their home on Burnaby Mountain. She'd yet to see one, but Kyle was right. It wasn't likely she would, unless the cougar planned to strike.

Kyle laughed. "As it turned out, it was just a couple of cats." He tickled Stormy's belly. "This guy and a pretty little Siamese who were doing some kind of messing around."

"I heard about Stormy and the Siamese," Christy said, looking ruefully at the cat. "Sledge said his neighbor would be furious at him if kittens resulted."

Kyle laughed again. "Rob can handle it. She's a big SledgeHammer fan. All he's got to do is give her tickets to a concert and a signed album and she'll forgive him anything."

"Were you inside the house when Vince's body was discovered?"

"No. I was still outside." Kyle paused, looked out the window, then down at the cat in his lap. "I was feeling...raw, you know? Ashamed. Like it was my fault that I was suspected of that poor girl's death." He looked up at Christy and shook his head. "Stupid. I didn't do anything. To her or to Vince, but I still…" He looked away, to the calm view beyond his big window. He drew a deep breath, then looked back at Christy. "When I heard the cat howl I was on the deck. As I ran around the house I saw Graham coming up the road, toward the house."

"You didn't go from the deck through the house to the front door and out? Why?" Christy asked. "Wouldn't that be faster than running all the way around the outside?"

"I didn't know the cat was howling over a dead man." Kyle shrugged, then offered her a self-effacing, rueful smile. "All that popped into my head was a standoff between the house cats and a lurking cougar. I had this bright idea that if I charged around the house making a lot of noise I'd scare off the big cat and save the little ones."

Christy stared at him. "Kyle I…I don't know what to say except thank you on behalf of my daughter and myself. And Stormy of course." Stormy's purr rumbled blissfully, even though Kyle's fingers had stilled.

Kyle shrugged again. He was making light of his actions, but Christy knew that if there had been a cougar involved, he'd taken a big risk. Impulsively she leaned toward him and put her hand over his where it rested on Stormy's belly. "We'll find Vince's killer, and Chelsea's too, and exonerate you and Hammer."

"I hope so," Kyle said. "You're the Gowdy brothers' last hope."

CHAPTER 24

Quinn expected to interview Mitch Crosier in his office, but instead the record exec suggested he drop by the Crosier's Southlands estate after Vince's funeral was over. That gave Quinn a forty-five minute drive to wonder how Christy's interview with Kyle Gowdy had gone and whether she'd taken the cat with her. He pretty much figured she had, which meant she'd chosen Frank over him. Not a good sign. He was starting to think their affair was doomed to be the briefest one in the history of his life.

He found the address and turned into the drive, stopping at the gates to give his name. They opened slowly, but with silent, well-oiled precision, and Quinn drove through. The house was just as his father described it, he thought, as the gates closed behind him and he drove up the broad, curving drive. If the house, with its broad expanse of manicured grounds, was any indication, the record business was good and Mitchell Crosier was doing very well for himself.

He parked in front of the stairs leading up to the porch and double front doors, pausing to note down his impressions of the house and grounds on the pad he always carried with him. He planned to record the interview with Mitch, but sometimes people were intimidated by new technology and felt more comfortable with old-fashioned paper and pen method. Given the industry Mitch worked in, Quinn doubted he'd be one of those, but it was always best to be prepared.

As he wrote he wondered if Crosier had used the excuse of the funeral to stage the meeting here, in an expensive location designed to impress. If he had, too bad. Fancy trappings didn't have a lot of impact on Quinn's worldview. He finished his notes and thrust the pad into the pocket of the leather jacket he wore with a boat necked sweater and chinos. There was the possibility that Crosier wanted to include his wife in the interview. He thought this was less likely than a desire to impress. Crosier didn't strike him as the kind of man who invested emotion and part of himself into his relationship with his woman.

Kim was eye candy, he mused, as he got out of the car. She'd be sent packing once her youthful beauty surrendered to time. A cynical view, perhaps, but it went well with his sour mood. He climbed the steps to the double doors and rang the bell.

Kim Crosier opened the door, as she had for his father. She smiled at him with genuine warmth and said, "Mitch is in his office." She peeked around him as he moved past her into the house. "Did you bring that cute kitty with you?" She frowned, looking about as fierce as a beauty queen was able. "You didn't leave him in the car, did you? I'll be happy to watch him while you're talking to Mitch."

"I don't have the cat," Quinn said briefly. Christy had the cat. Christy was worried about the cat. Christy was obsessed with the cat.

Kim's frown dissolved into disappointment. "Oh, that's too bad. Well, come on through. Mitch is waiting for you."

She led him deep into the house to a quiet wing that seemed to be devoted to rooms with a purpose—a large screening room, an exercise room, a sewing room. That last one took Quinn aback. He doubted the sewing room was for Mitchell Crosier's use, but he couldn't quite see Kim, the pretty, rich man's prize, spending her days sewing...things.

He must have frowned as they passed the room, because Kim shot him an amused look and said, "Yes, I'm the one who uses it. I sew many of my own clothes." She indicated the dress she was wearing. It was sleeveless, with a mock turtle collar, cut to show off her shoulders. The sapphire blue knit material clung to her curves, but flared below her waist so it swirled around her thighs and showed off her long legs as she walked. "This is one of my creations."

Quinn was wrestling with that statement, and the superficial assumptions he shouldn't have made, when they reached Mitchell's office. The door was closed, so Kim knocked before she went inside. Still clothed in the white dress shirt he must have worn to the funeral, but minus a tie and jacket, Crosier was working at a glass topped, steel framed desk. His chair was leather and designed for comfort. He looked up from the computer monitor he was studying and smiled at his wife.

She sashayed into the office, the blue skirt swinging jauntily. "He's here, darling," she said, kissing her husband on the cheek. "Would you like me to bring coffee? Or something stronger?"

"Coffee," Mitch said. "Afternoon, Armstrong."

"Crosier," Quinn said by way of greeting. There was a chair—modern, rectangular, boxlike and leanly padded—in front of the desk. Quinn sat down and pulled his phone out as Kim slipped away to organize refreshments. "I hope you don't mind if I record our conversation."

Crosier considered the phone for a moment, then he shook his head. "I'm okay with that provided you give me a copy of the tape."

"Why?"

Crosier raised his brows. "My words," he said. "I like to make sure I'm being quoted correctly."

Quinn shrugged. Though he was here to find out if Mitchell Crosier could have murdered Vince Nunez, he also planned to write an article based on the interview. He wasn't concerned about misinterpreting Crosier's words, because he always checked his facts, so Crosier didn't need to worry about misrepresentation. "I don't intend to libel you."

A muscle flexed in Crosier's jaw. "I've had reporters do exactly that, promising just what you promised." He eyed Quinn, who eyed him back. "I'll level with you, Armstrong. The only reason you're here is because you're Sledge's friend and he trusts you. Vince's death has put my label under siege. The media loves the drama of it and while the publicity has been generating interest—"

"And sales?"

Mitch nodded. "And sales, right now at least. I can see it backfiring on us long-term. My company has a distribution agreement with one of the major labels. Right now they are willing to accept that I was only a bystander at Vince's death. If they think I'm involved?" He shrugged. "Not good news for us."

"I write balanced, investigative articles, not fluff pieces or smear attacks," Quinn said, keeping hold of his temper. "I want to know how Vince's death is going to affect those in the music business who worked with him. That includes SledgeHammer and your company. Most people only know the music business by what they listen to and the songs they purchase. I'd like to give my readers a wider picture, with more detail on how the industry works. Sledgehammer fans are worried. There's been a lot of ink shed about Vince's death being the end of the band the way Brian Epstein's death presaged the end of the Beatles."

Vince nodded gloomily. "Could happen."

"Or it might not."

"Bands break up all the time. Musicians are creative flakes and they can get wound up over the craziest things. SledgeHammer has had a long run." He shrugged. "Maybe it's their time."

"Sledge and Hammer don't think so," Quinn said, though truthfully he didn't know. He had Crosier talking now, even if it wasn't on tape, and he was getting impressions and ideas he'd be able to use.

Crosier grimaced. "They never do before they do it."

Quinn assumed he was speaking generically. *They* being musicians in general, not Rob McCullagh and Graham Gowdy specifically.

Kim Crosier chose that moment to arrive with two mugs, a coffee urn, a plate of sweet bread slices, and a stack of napkins, all balanced on a silver tray. A fragrant scent wafted from the bread. Quinn eyed it uneasily. He thought it might be banana bread; not one of his favorites.

She set the tray down and poured coffee into the mugs. "Do try the banana bread, Quinn," she said, confirming his suspicion. "It's just out of the oven."

"My favorite," Mitch said, eying it hungrily.

She laughed. "I know, darling. Today was difficult for both of us, but especially for you. I thought you needed a treat." She handed Quinn a mug. "If you like it, I'll give you the recipe for Christy." She smiled, then turned to provide the other mug to her husband.

Time to reassess, yet again, Quinn thought, as he watched Mitchell look at his wife fondly. Kim Crosier managed her husband with a deft dexterity that indicated a subtle understanding of the man. There was clearly more to her than appeared on the surface.

Mitch took a slice of banana bread, bit into it, and chewed. After he swallowed he winked at his wife and said, "Wonderful!" She winked back, then said, "I'll leave you to talk, then. Nice to see you again, Quinn."

She was gone before Quinn had time to sample her banana bread. Ordinarily, he wouldn't have bothered, but this time he didn't have the option with Mitchell Crosier watching him, waiting for his reaction with a possessiveness the baker herself didn't seem to share. With a mental shrug, he picked up a slice. He'd eaten worse when he had to. He broke off a chunk, then popped it into his mouth. And savored. "God, this is good," he mumbled. The texture was firm, but not heavy, the flavor sweet, but not over sweet. It was delicious.

"I know!" said Crosier, with enthusiasm. "That woman is a domestic goddess. She looks great, and she understands that sometimes I have to chat up the chicks. She is absolutely the best wife a man could want." He shook his head as he chewed another piece of banana bread. "I don't know how she puts up with me, but that's not why you're here."

Since Quinn had another mouthful of the bread, he couldn't reply. Mitch flicked his finger at Quinn's phone, which was still sitting on the desk. "Go ahead. Turn it on. Let's get started."

Quinn finished chewing, then wiped his fingers on a napkin, which was linen with cheerful red checks and a hand-sewn hem, ironed into crisp, perfectly even folds. He flicked on record and got started.

They talked for an hour about the music business and Crosier's position in it. That led to his plan for convergence marketing and inevitably, his hope that Roy would be involved. "Your father's agent turned me down flat," Mitch said, looking gloomy. "Too bad about that." He eyed Quinn thoughtfully. "If you talked to your father, do you think he'd override his agent?"

Quinn was prepared for this. He shook his head. "Wouldn't work. My dad always takes his agent's advice over mine."

"Pity," Mitch said. They went back to the music business and talked about SledgeHammer from their early days to the band's current world success. Quinn steered the conversation back to the night of Sledge's party and Vince's murder. "Give me your impression of the evening."

Mitch leaned back in his chair, cradling his second mug of coffee. All that was left of the banana bread was crumbs on the plate. "There was an edge, like everyone was waiting for something to happen." He took a sip while he reflected. "Not surprising, really, after that girl's death at the concert. There was a lot of looking over your shoulder, if you know what I mean."

"Explain it to me so I'm clear."

Mitchell leaned forward and put his elbows and the coffee mug on the table. Hands free he moved them in the air, using them to help him find the words for something he evidently hadn't tried to describe before. "I think there were several people in that house who wondered if Kyle Gowdy was guilty. They wondered and they watched. It struck me that no one was surprised when Vince told Hammer to keep away from his brother. It was as if everyone expected him to say that and an argument to follow."

"Where were you when the argument happened?"

Mitch hesitated.

Quinn raised his brows. "My dad told me Kim was in the great room talking to him. He didn't know where you were."

Mitch looked at the phone, looked at Quinn, then looked at the door before he said with a rush, "I was in the kitchen when the shouting started out on the deck. I was on my way to the music room when Hammer and Vince came into the great room."

"Why were you going to the music room?"

He hesitated again, before he said, "I was looking for the lady chef Sledge used to cater the party. One of the servers told me she had gone to the music room. I followed her."

Quinn blinked. Not the answer he expected. "Did you find her?"

"Not then. Later." Crosier had reddened.

Quinn wondered why. He imagined it was probably the usual one for powerful men, but he asked anyway. "Why were you looking for her?"

If anything, Crosier's face got redder. He stared at Quinn's phone, looking worried. "She made the most wonderful mini tourtiere pies. The crust was sensational and the filling..." He sighed. "Heavenly. Kim asked the chef for the recipe, but the bitch wouldn't give it to her. So I thought I'd see what I could do."

"You wanted a recipe," Quinn said carefully.

"Kim loves to cook. You tasted her banana bread. Imagine what she could do with a light as air pie crust and some ground meat."

From the expression on Crosier's face, Quinn figured he was doing enough imagining for them both. "Did you ever find her?"

"Later, after all the fuss happened," Mitch said looking annoyed. "Turned out she wasn't in the music room at all. She wouldn't give me the damn recipe either."

"Anybody see you between when Vince left the house and when Vince's body was found?"

"No." The annoyance was now in Mitch's voice.

So Mitch Crosier didn't have an alibi for the time of Vince's death. If his irritation was any indication, he realized he could be in a vulnerable position if the cops chose to take a closer look at him.

"How was your relationship with Vince? I understand he wanted a complete review of the contract terms between SledgeHammer and your company."

Mitch eyed him levelly. "He did and I respected him for it. Vince was a talent agent as well as the band's manager. His job was to get the best terms he could for his artists. He was good at it too, because he only represented quality musicians. I knew that whatever Vince and I agreed to, I'd still profit from the arrangement."

"And yet you played the game."

"Yeah, I played it. Why not? I wasn't going to just hand over the gilded plate to Vince. I was willing to make concessions, but he had to work for them."

"What happens now?"

Crosier shrugged. "SledgeHammer finds a new manager."

Quinn looked at him. "My research indicates that your label has interests in a company dedicated to managing artists. Sledge told me he'd already been approached by them."

"Yeah, so?"

"So it puts another spin on Vince's death."

"No, it does not," Crosier said shortly. "My company has an investment in the management company. I don't own it. Dig deeper into them. The artists they represent are recorded by a dozen different labels. If SledgeHammer decides to go with them, there's no guarantee they will keep the band with us."

No, there was no guarantee, but even if SledgeHammer signed with a new record label, Mitchell Crosier would still benefit.

The man had no alibi for the time of Vince's death and a lot gain from it. In Quinn's opinion, that put him right up near, or at the top, of the suspect list.

CHAPTER 25

The house was still when Christy woke up. Outside her window she could hear morning commuters on the way to work. Not as many cars passed as usual, but it was still Spring Break, so that wasn't surprising. She lay in the dim light that seeped through the curtains covering the windows and wondered why she'd woken so early when she didn't have to get up to make sure Noelle got to school on time. Then a cold damp nose pressed against her cheek and the sounds of loud purring echoed in her ear. Stormy was awake and wanted breakfast.

She kept her eyes closed and pretended she hadn't woken. Since their return Stormy had acted like a normal cat. A friendlier cat than he'd been when Frank was alive, but still just a cat. He snuggled. He sat on her paper if she was trying to write notes or a letter. He played with Noelle, chasing the ball she threw down the stairs, then made her retrieve it so she could have the privilege of throwing it for him again. He purred when he was stroked. He ate quantities of food.

But he didn't talk. To anyone.

Roy was upset. He worried that it had been his decision to take the cat to the SledgeHammer party that had caused Frank's silence. Roy figured that seeing the murder happen in front of him had brought back memories of his own murder and that he'd been traumatized. This had either convinced him to accept his passing and to flee Stormy's body, or it had left him so deeply unhappy that he had retreated from life and those still living. The result for both options was the same. Frank was no longer willing or able to communicate with the living the way he had before.

The purring in her ear grew louder and this time Stormy butted her cheek with enough force that Christy could no longer pretend to be asleep. She swatted at the cat and said, "Go away."

Still purring, Stormy positioned his paws on her shoulder, then began to knead. His purrs echoed through the room, in time with the slow rhythmic movement.

Christy groaned. His claws were in, thank God, or she'd be shrieking right now, but the loud purring and the kneading weren't going to let her go back to sleep. "It's too early to get up. I'll wake Noelle."

Stormy kneaded and purred, intent on his objective, paying no attention to her excuses.

"Oh, all right. I'll feed you, but then I'm coming back to bed." Fat chance that would happen, but she could hope. She wiggled out from under the kneading paws, then flung off her covers. Stormy bounded to the edge of the bed and leapt to the floor. He waited for her at the door as she yawned and put on her dressing gown.

They headed downstairs, Christy trying to be as quiet as possible so as not to wake the other occupants of the sleeping house, Stormy thundering down the stairs the way he did when he was intent on making his presence known. By the time she reached the kitchen, Christy knew that returning to bed to sleep was a forlorn hope, so she programmed the coffeemaker for a cup before she opened the pantry door to pull out a can of cat food for Stormy.

Stormy sat by his bowl and fixed an unblinking green gaze on her while she worked. She had deliberately fed him only canned cat food since she'd returned. She thought that if there were no treats—no tuna, no shrimp, no human food of any kind—that Frank would come out of his funk and complain. That he hadn't said a word was ever increasing proof that he was no longer living in Stormy's body.

She opened the cutlery drawer and picked up a spoon. "I have tuna in the fridge." She shoved the drawer closed. "If you want it, tell me now before I open the cat food."

Stormy stared at her, unmoving.

She went over to him, and stroked his head. "I don't know what happened that night, what you saw and what it made you think, but I want to help."

Stormy stared at her, then slowly blinked, but Frank didn't respond.

She sighed and picked up the bowl. She returned to the counter and put the bowl beside the can of cat food. The label said Tuna Dinner. Frank had always been scornful of the names given to the cat food she bought and said that all the flavors tasted the same. Stormy consumed the various varieties enthusiastically, though, much to Frank's disgust. But then, Stormy also happily ate grasshoppers, beetles, mice and birds, so he wasn't much of a gourmet.

She held up the can. "Last chance for real tuna."

Stormy abandoned the mat on which his food and water bowls sat and came over to wind around her legs. Then he stood on his hind legs and reached up toward the counter with his forepaws.

The message was clear. Feed me now.

The coffeemaker sputtered and completed its drip cycle. Despite the cat's silent demand, she took a moment to grab her cup and have a sip of fresh brewed coffee. "Oh, Frank," she said, staring at Stormy. "Why didn't you wait to say good-bye?"

Stormy was down on all fours again. His tail was now shivering with anxious anticipation.

Christy sighed again. There were moments when she wondered if Frank had chosen to leave because she'd gone away with Quinn. He probably guessed that she and Quinn had become lovers; that would have been hard for him to bear. Add the affront to his ego together with the trauma of witnessing a murder and you had a pretty good one-two emotional punch.

Unfortunately, the deed was done. There was nothing now that she could do about it. She took another swig of coffee, sighed again, and pushed guilt aside as she set about preparing Stormy's breakfast. She pulled the tab on the can and the seal broke with a hiss of air. She glanced down at the cat to see his reaction, but Stormy was simply being a cat. He paced to his mat then back again, impatient at her dithering, but nothing more.

She ripped off the lid. "Noelle is getting anxious. She refused to believe that you were gone, you know. She was so certain that you would say good-bye, that you wouldn't abandon her. Not a second time." She scooped Tuna Dinner into the bowl and chopped the paste into bite-sized morsels with the edge of the spoon.

Stormy paced from mat to counter and back once more, his tail straight up and shivering, muscles tense with excitement.

Christy picked up the bowl and took it over to the mat, then she crouched down as she placed it beside the water dish. Stormy made a great show of sniffing the contents before he dug in and began to eat with considerable enthusiasm. Christy stroked his back. "If you're in there, Frank, you need to come out and reassure your daughter. I don't care how traumatic seeing the murder was. You must put Noelle's needs ahead of your own, you know that."

Stormy paused to take a breath. He cast her one long unblinking look then he went back to vacuuming up his breakfast as quickly as possible.

Christy sighed and stood up.

"Were you talking to the cat? I smell coffee. Did you make a pot?"

Christy's heart skipped a beat and she jumped. "Ellen!" How much had she heard? Just the last bit where she'd talked about putting Noelle's needs in ahead of other ones? Or earlier where she'd used Frank's name? "Did I wake you when I came downstairs?"

"The cat woke me. Before I moved in with you I thought cats were stealthy and soundless. This beast can be noisier than a lawn mower on a Sunday morning."

Christy laughed. "At times. He can be quiet when he wants to be, too."

Ellen sat down at the kitchen table where she could watch the cat eating. Christy did the morning feeding, because she was always up early getting Noelle ready for school, but Ellen was the one who prepared Stormy's evening meal, while Christy made their dinner. Consequently, she had become more appreciative of the cat.

"I only made a single cup of coffee," Christy said, cautiously hopeful that Ellen hadn't heard anything amiss. "Would you like a cup, or are you going to try to go back to bed?"

"I'm up," Ellen said. "If I went back to sleep now, the day would be half over before I woke up."

"I'll make a pot, then. I doubt I'll be able to get back to sleep either."

"I don't think a cat can be traumatized by what people do, unless those people are hurting the cat," Ellen said, her gaze still on Stormy.

Christy's hand shook as she ladled coffee grounds into the paper filter. She swallowed hard and tried to act normally. "Roy told me Stormy was howling when you found him."

"He was." Ellen put her elbow on the table and her chin on her palm. "I've heard animals can sense a soul passing. The cat's behavior makes me think that might be true."

Christy focused on making the coffee and didn't comment.

"Has Stormy been ignoring Noelle or something? Is that why you were lecturing the poor beast?"

Christy's hand shook as she dumped the last scoop into the filter. "Something like that." She put the filter into the machine, added a pot of water, then set it to brew. "I think Stormy is mad at Noelle and me for going away. He's taking a while to warm back up."

"He certainly missed you. He spent most of his time outside or with Roy while you were gone. I hardly saw him until after the murder. Then he stayed inside and did a lot of cuddling."

Before and after, Christy thought. Before, when Frank was still in Stormy and resentful of his aunt. After, when he'd gone and the cat was once again just a cat. More evidence that Frank wasn't going to be talking in her head ever again, no matter how many lectures she aimed Stormy's way.

The cat finished his meal. He looked up, licking his lips. Then he sat down and took a minute to give his face and whiskers a good clean, before he strutted out of the kitchen, tail high and expression satisfied. He'd be off now to settle somewhere comfortable and have a snooze.

On an impulse, Christy reached down as he passed and scratched his belly. "Go up and cuddle with Noelle, but don't wake her. She can use a little more sleep, and she'll stay in bed if you're there to keep her settled."

The cat didn't pause, but Christy heard his footsteps as he galloped up the stairs.

CHAPTER 26

"What do you think?" Quinn threw a stack of paper-clipped printer paper onto the kitchen table beside Roy's laptop.

Roy emerged from the intricacies of plotting a mystery novel and blinked at his son. Quinn was looking particularly grim this afternoon. Roy thought he knew the reason why and sympathized, but there wasn't much he could do about it. This was a something Quinn had to work out on his own.

He picked up the paper and saw that this was an article on Mitch Crosier. "Thank you for showing me a printed copy. Gives these old eyes a rest," he said absently as he scanned the text.

Quinn grunted. The sound came from the vicinity of the coffeemaker. "When did you make this coffee, Dad?"

"Couple of hours ago. You've caught Crosier. But…Domestic goddess for Kim? I thought she was just a flaky bombshell."

"That's what Crosier calls her. It's over the top, but I think it says something about the man, so I included it." There was a whoosh as the stale coffee in the pot was dumped and then the sound of running water.

"Are you making enough for me, too?" Roy asked, without looking up. He pulled the paper clip so he could access the next page.

Quinn laughed. There was affection, but not amusement in the sound. Roy winced inwardly. Not a lot of lightness in Quinn's life right now.

"What do you think, Dad?" More gruff affection and the sound of pouring water.

"I think you wouldn't dare not to." This time when Quinn laughed, there was some amusement in the sound. Roy gave himself a pat on the back and read on.

He finished the article before the coffeemaker completed the drip cycle and looked up. "Excellent work. Well balanced and fair, but honest. Have you placed it yet?"

Quinn leaned against the counter. He was wearing jeans and a faded sweatshirt that he'd had for years. He hadn't shaved and the second day stubble added to the grimness in his expression. He should go over and see Christy, Roy thought. She was already attracted to him. The wounded warrior look would probably be enough to tip the scales so she'd slip back to him and forget about her difficult relationship with a dead man who might or might not be living in a cat.

"I pre-sold it to an online newsmagazine. Since Crosier is tied to Vince's death, they were all over it," Quinn said. The coffeemaker beeped. Quinn got himself a cup, and poured. He brought his mug over to the table and picked up Roy's to refill it.

"You only mentioned Vince's death obliquely," Roy said, as Quinn put his refilled cup on the table. He picked it up and sipped, enjoying the mellowness of fresh coffee on his tongue. "Do you think Mitch is involved?"

Quinn drank some coffee, then shook his head. "He claims he was looking for Chef Rita to see about acquiring a recipe for Kim." Roy laughed at that and Quinn smiled. "He didn't find her until after the murder, and he doesn't have anyone to give him an alibi for the actual time of death. That means he's still a suspect, but an unlikely one, I think."

"Because of the search for Chef Rita?"

Quinn nodded. "Yeah. He talked to a server in the kitchen, asking where Rita was. That can be checked. In fact, I've got a call into the woman now. If she confirms it, then we know where Mitch was when the argument took place. He says the server sent him to the music room to find Rita. If she confirms that, and tells me that she saw Mitch head off in that direction, it's likely he went to that part of the house. If he did, he wouldn't have time to get out the front door to confront Vince and murder him."

Roy sipped his coffee and nodded as he listened to this. "It's possible. But, unless the server watched him closely, he could have switched directions in time to get outside and do the deed."

"He could have," Quinn said, "though his motive is weak. With Vince dead, SledgeHammer will need to get new management. They might hire a company Crosier has a financial interest in, thereby bringing him in a new source of revenue from them. But managers are a key component in a band's career. With Vince dead, who knows what will happen to SledgeHammer. If the band breaks up Mitch stands to lose a lot more than he'll gain."

"So he's still on the list."

Quinn nodded. "I'd keep him there for the moment, though I wouldn't put him near the top."

Roy sighed. "I was hoping you'd put the finger on Crosier and say you'd solved this thing. Looks like I'm still on the hook."

"Haven't found Hank Lofti yet?"

Roy put his cup onto the table and grimaced. "Lofti is proving elusive. His address is a post box and he doesn't answer his cell, so I've been combing bars all week and have come up with zilch. I'm frustrated."

"Want some help?"

It was Friday night. Quinn should be doing something with Christy, not out prowling through seedy dives with his father. He shook his head. "I'm going to give the bar search one more attempt tonight." Quinn looked gloomy. Maybe he'd already tried to set something up for tonight and been rebuffed. "If I'm not successful I'll need someone to brainstorm other ways to find him. You in?"

"Sure." Quinn's smile was thin, his expression almost sad. He knew he'd been tossed a bone.

Roy said hastily, "Have you had a chance to talk to that Toupin guy? The backup guitarist who was on the tour?"

"Not yet. I arranged to meet him at his place on Monday morning."

"Not sooner?"

Quinn downed the last of his coffee. He pushed back his chair and stood. "I'm working on something for the weekend. I hope to be busy."

Good news at last! Roy grinned. "Good luck with that."

Quinn's mouth quirked up in a rueful smile. "Thanks." He scooped up his papers. "I'd better get this finished up. They want it before five this afternoon."

"I'm available to babysit, if you need it," Roy said to Quinn's departing back. He watched his son stiffen and his step hesitated.

Quinn didn't turn around. "Thanks. I'll let you know."

Roy sipped coffee and watched him as he left the room. He hoped Quinn would take him up on his offer, but he wasn't confident it would happen.

By eleven o'clock that night Roy had had enough. He stood in front of a bar was in the Downtown East Side, not far from Homeless Help. The area was a grim reminder of businesses gone elsewhere. Boarded up storefronts and old warehouses with broken windows outnumbered the places—like the bar—still in operation.

As with the previous nights, he had no success. He decided this would be his last stop tonight. Maybe his last attempt to find Lofti in a downtown bar. There had to be a more efficient way to locate the man. Lofti had been a jack-of-all-trades on the tour. Officially, he was part of the set up and take down crew, but he basically did what he was told by the foreman. If he wasn't working behind the scenes at rock concerts, what else might he do?

Construction? Possible. Loading and unloading trucks or trains or boats? Also possible. Both had unionized and non-unionized components. He doubted Lofti belonged to a union, so he'd be working or looking for work on non-union sites.

Roy was pondering how a person discovered active non-union construction sites in the greater Vancouver area as he pulled open the door to the seedy bar. Inside the lighting was dim, but he could see round tables spread throughout a large room with a worn wooden floor. The walls were painted a dull brown and in the poor light they merged with the long wooden bar. There were stools on one side of the bar and he could make out the tall handles of draft beer spouts rising from the other side. On the wall behind were shelves filled with dozens of varieties of hard liquor.

A single waitress worked a room half full of people clustered at the tables. The few who hung out on the bar stools were being served by the bartender. At one end of the room was a raised stage and on it was a band that clearly needed to spend more time rehearsing. Roy winced and decided he'd take a quick look around then get the hell out.

As his eyes adjusted to the muted lighting, he could make out faces. None of the people at the tables were Hank Lofti. Roy wasn't surprised; he knew this was a long shot. He moved deeper into the room, heading for the bar and the last few patrons he hadn't yet identified. No one paid him much attention. Those who weren't talking to a friend were deep into drink and listening to the band in a zoned out kind of way. Or maybe this was the kind of establishment where it paid to keep to yourself.

He wandered down the bar, pretending to look for a place to sit, but really scanning faces. As usual, no luck. Then, at the very end, he saw a man sitting with his back against the wall, his eyes on the band as he chugged beer from a long-necked bottle. Hank Lofti. Was it possible? Roy moved closer. Yes, it was.

He let his elation etch a smile on his face as he sat down on the stool next to Lofti's. "Hank," he said. "Is that you?"

Lofti lowered his bottle with the careful movements of a man who was a long way to being drunk, and peered at Roy. "Who's asking?"

"Roy Armstrong. We met at Sledge's party?"

Hank stared at him, clearly not remembering. He was intoxicated enough to blurt out, "No." Or maybe he was one of those people who didn't worry about the social niceties.

"Sure you do," Roy said. "I'm the guy with the cat."

Hank stared in an uncomprehending way. He put the beer bottle to his mouth and drank deep. "The cat that found Vince?"

"That's it," Roy said. "Shame about Vince."

Hank snorted and took another swig.

"I didn't know him well," Roy said, "but he seemed like a good guy."

The bottle crashed down onto the bar, drawing the attention of the bartender. He came over, cast an assessing glance at Hank, then looked at Roy. "What can I get you, mister?"

"A beer," Roy said. He cast a squinty-eyed glance at Hank's bottle, which was a well-known brand and one that was vastly overrated in Roy's opinion. "What do you have on tap?"

Turned out the bar stocked one of Roy's favorite microbrews. He ordered a pint then directed his attention back to Hank. "You worked for him, didn't you?"

"Who?" Hank asked. He stared at the bottle as he moved it back and forth over the bar surface.

"Vince."

"Bastard," said Hank and drank again.

The bartender brought Roy his draft and Hank held up his bottle. "Another."

"One more and you're cut off," said the bartender.

"Yeah, yeah," said Hank. "Like I'll believe that when it happens."

The bartender shot him an evil glance. Roy had a feeling that Hank's refill would be a long time coming. "Vince wasn't a good boss?" he said.

Hank pulled his gaze away from the actions of the bartender and refocused on Roy. "He screwed me big time."

Roy frowned. "How?"

Hank's face twisted. "He told me he wouldn't hire me again and he put the word out. Now I can't even get an interview, anywhere. I'm going to end up on the skids like his old pal, Syd Haynes."

Since the tour had ended only recently, Roy thought this was a bit extreme. "Why wouldn't he hire you again?"

"Said I was lazy, drunk, and not dependable."

Since he slurred the words together, indicating that he was already far gone toward intoxication, Roy thought that Vince might have had truth on his side.

"Told me I'd never work in the music business 'gain." Hank put the bottle to his mouth and chugged. Then he lowered it to peer owlishly down the neck, as if the bottle held a secret universe inside. Evidently it didn't, because his face twisted and he slammed bottle down onto the bar. "Hey, you there. Where's my refill?"

The bartender shot him a look and said, "Coming," then turned his back to Hank and his face to the other end of the bar.

"Stupid idiot," Hank muttered.

Roy sipped his beer. "That must have been upsetting," he said, watching Hank over the edge of his glass.

Hank snorted, apparently one of his favorite ways of expressing his displeasure. "Expected it. No surprise cuz he's done it before."

"Really? Who and how?"

Hank glowered at the still firmly turned back of the bartender. "He screwed Syd Haynes out of a fortune. Everyone knows that down here. Told lies about Syd, same way he told lies 'bout me. Once he was done, Syd didn't have a chance."

"Are you friends with Syd Haynes?" Roy asked. He was curious how well Hank knew the other man. The way he linked their names and fates indicated a relationship, but to Roy it didn't fit. Syd had come from a well-to-do family and had fallen on hard times before he reinvented himself. Hank, as far as he could see, was a man who had always scrambled on the edges and was now on his way down. Their trajectories didn't mesh.

Hank shook his head, confirming Roy's suspicions. "Syd's a legend around here. Everyone knows he founded SledgeHammer. If Vince hadn't forced him out, he'd be living in a fancy house up on the hill, like Sledge."

"Instead he's living down on the east side helping people find their way to better lives," Roy said.

Hank glared at his empty beer bottle and completely missed the approval in Roy's voice. "Bunch of no good losers," he muttered. "Syd deserves better." He picked up the empty bottle and tipped it to his mouth again, apparently hopeful it had somehow refilled since he'd last drunk. When nothing came out, he slammed the bottle down and shoved it away from him. Then he sat up, glared at Roy and said, "That bastard Vince had it coming to him."

Roy took another sip, then decided that was the last he'd drink of his draft, even though he had half a glass left. The brew had been fine, but Hank Lofti was curdling his stomach. He wanted to get his fact-finding mission over with and be gone. "Where were you before the cat started to howl?"

A crafty look slipped over Hank's features. "You mean when Vince was being offed?"

Not exactly, Roy thought, but close enough. He nodded.

The bartender came and slapped down a fresh brew in front of Hank. "Six-fifty," he said.

Hank stared at him myopically. Roy paid. The bartender went away.

Hank picked up the bottle and drank deep. "What were we talking about?"

"Vince's murder," Roy said, watching him.

"Right." Hank contemplated the bottle. "I was in the kitchen. Pretty fancy one it was, too."

"Why were you in the kitchen?" Roy was genuinely interested. Hank didn't seem like the kind of man who thought about cooking, especially high-end recipes. He seemed more the fast food type.

Hank's smile was close to a leer. "I was chatting up that pretty little chef Sledge hired."

"Chatting up. You mean talking to her in the kitchen?"

Hank began to laugh. "Been a while, has it, old man? No. I was putting the hit on her." The smile turned into what was definitely a leer. "I wasn't doing her in the kitchen, but close enough."

Roy thought about the chef, who was indeed an attractive young woman, and Hank Lofti striking sparks off each other. It was possible. Hank had a full head of thick dark hair and well defined pecs from the physical work that provided his income. It was also possible that Chef Rita might have flirted with him in the kitchen while she worked.

What Roy couldn't see as possible was a woman with a thriving catering business jeopardizing it by doing anything more than flirting at an event she was working. Since Chef Rita had come up in both Crosier and Lofti's statements, someone needed to talk to her. He'd suggest Ellen give it a try. She might not be great at interviewing, but he was sure she had lots of experience in dealing with caterers. She'd speak Chef Rita's language. That was for later, though. Right now, he needed to dig deeper into Hank's Lofti's story. He moved his glass back and forth, aware that Lofti's eyes followed it. "So you were in the kitchen when the cat started to howl? Making out with Chef Rita?"

"Yeah."

"That's strange. Mitch Crosier says there was a server in the kitchen about then and Chef Rita wasn't around."

Lofti's eyes darted upward. His hand tightened on the beer bottle. "Crosier lies."

"Really?"

"Look, old man, I said I was in the kitchen and I was." He shifted on his stool, away from Roy, and hunched protectively over his bottle. "I ain't got nothing more to say to you."

Hank Lofti was lying about where he was when Vince died, but that didn't mean he was the killer. He could have been with Chef Rita somewhere other than the kitchen. Did that mean they were both involved in Vince's murder, or that they were making out as Lofti claimed?

Roy couldn't see a motive for the pretty young chef, but he could see one for Hank. Bitter, angry, blaming Vince for his own failures, Hank had plenty of reasons for killing Vince.

But did he do it?

Roy added him to the growing list of suspects.

CHAPTER 27

Quinn ended the call from his editor and stretched. He glanced at the clock at the corner of his computer screen. Two in the afternoon. He rubbed his forehead and wondered if he should cancel the plans he'd made for this evening.

Yesterday, when he'd talked to his father, his afternoon stretched before him, full of opportunities. He wanted to give the article on Mitch Crosier another review and polish, but he didn't expect that to take more than fifteen minutes. Then he'd send it off and he could concentrate on arranging a romantic Saturday evening for Christy.

He finished the article, emailed it, then booked a table at Christy's favorite seafood restaurant and a room at one of the best hotels in town. She was stressing over Frank and his refusal to talk to her, or, more importantly in Christy's mind, to Noelle. He accepted that. He also guessed that living with the cat, waiting for it to speak, would be more than a little difficult. She needed time away where she didn't have to wonder, or worry.

He told himself that was why he was planning the evening, but he knew there more to it. They'd committed to each other in the middle of Spring Break, but now, mere days later, the school vacation was almost over and so was their relationship. He couldn't accept that; he had to do something.

He was about to go over to Christy's house to lay out his plan and invite her to join him when his phone rang. He considered not accepting the call, but it was from his editor at the publishing house that was putting out his book on Frank Jamieson's murder. It was late Friday afternoon. At this time of day, on the last day of the workweek, a telephone call would be to share some spectacularly good news, or to stave off imminent disaster. He decided he'd better take it.

Unfortunately, the editor wasn't calling to celebrate. Legal had issues with certain parts of the manuscript. The book was due to be sent to the printer on Wednesday and they needed those sections revised by Saturday afternoon so editorial could review the new text on Sunday, legal could okay it on Monday and production could make sure the changes were included in the final document on Tuesday. Quinn put his personal plans on hold and got to work.

The rest of the afternoon and all of his evening was a marathon of review, revision, and negotiation with his editor. He heard his father going out around seven. When Roy returned much later, he was deep in a confrontational call with his editor, arguing about changes the publisher wanted and which he didn't agree with. He crashed about two and was up again at six.

Now the changes were finally done, everyone was satisfied, and he had the rest of the weekend to himself. He could still take Christy out for that romantic dinner and night out. The arrangements were made; all he had to do was ask her.

When he made his plan for the evening, was he thinking of Christy's needs or his own? He wanted her to be focused on him, not on her dead husband. But was that what was best for her? He considered that moodily as he saved and closed files, methodically tidying up his on-screen workplace.

It was certainly best for him. By taking her out to dinner and then to a hotel he'd have her all to himself, which was exactly what he wanted. They could talk about each other, their feelings, the future they could have together. It would be like a recommitment to their relationship.

He brooded about that as he went up to his room to make himself presentable. It wasn't a good sign when a dating couple needed time and an artificially romantic environment to remember why they were dating in the first place.

Worrying, he thought, was a sign of fatigue, that was all. He shook himself out of the mood while he cleaned up. Once he had Christy's agreement and they'd organized timing, he'd have a quick nap. That would help his frame of mind.

He went down to his front door and then out and over to hers. As he rang the bell, he could hear shrieks of laughter echoing dimly from somewhere in the house. Those were followed by the thump of feet rushing up stairs moments before the door was wrenched open. Noelle, with Mary Petrofsky peering over her shoulder, grinned at him. "Mom! It's Quinn!" She opened the door wider to let him in.

He stepped into the small landing. He had the ominous feeling that his timing was off.

Noelle slammed the door shut and said, "Mom's upstairs."

Mary Petrofsky's less assertive voice said, "With my mom." She stopped, then added, "They're having tea."

"Using the Jamieson tea service," Noelle announced. "Aunt Ellen's there too."

He could just imagine the scene.

"They're having scones—"

"Yum," said Mary.

"And clotted cream!" Noelle said.

"And sandwiches. Little ones," Mary added, nodding.

"It's a proper tea!" Noelle's announcement was echoed by the sound of female laughter coming from the living room. Quinn didn't recognize the voice, so it wasn't Christy or Ellen. Must be Rebecca Petrofsky.

Not only was his timing off, but it was disastrously off. It was now two o'clock in the afternoon. He'd made the dinner reservation for seven, and thought they could check into the hotel about five. Those two hours would give them time to enjoy each other, then change before going out.

Part of the whole romantic evening plan was the way he would ask Christy to come out with him. He'd take her for a walk in the woods where they had spent so many intimate hours together. There he would invite her to go with him for the evening out.

No way she was going to go for a walk in the woods with him right now. In fact, it was unlikely he'd even have a chance to talk to her before five o'clock.

"Who is it, Noelle?" Christy asked, breaking into his thoughts as she appeared at the top of the stairs. She looked beautiful in a pair of dark slacks she'd topped with a sapphire blue sweater that did great things for her coloring and hugged her figure in all the right places. Her expression, though, was worried, but relieved at the same time. Quinn knew why. She was worried that Joan Shively, the social services worker who had made checking on Noelle's well-being her life cause, might take it into her head to do a random house visit. It was unlikely since it was Saturday and even Shively had a life, but Christy was always wary.

He hoped the relief was pleasure at seeing him. "Hi," he said.

She smiled and came down the stairs. "Hi, Quinn. What's up?"

Though she smiled at him, Quinn thought he saw some restraint there. He decided that it was best to ignore it. "It's a nice afternoon. I dropped by to see if you'd like to go for a walk."

Christy glanced up and over her shoulder. "Quinn, that's sweet…"

"My mom's here," Mary Petrofsky said.

"She is," Christy said. She came further down the stairs. "Noelle, why don't you and Mary go back to the playroom? I've got this."

Noelle looked from Mary to her mom to Quinn, then nodded. "Come on, Mary. I'll race you!" They dove back down the stairs to whatever game they were playing in the basement family room.

Christy paused on the stairs so she was eye-to-eye with him. "I'm sorry, Quinn. It was lovely of you to think of me, but…" She shrugged. "I can't."

"What about later?" he asked in a low voice.

"Mary is doing a sleep over and the Petrofskys are going out to a romantic dinner." Her lips twitched. "And having a romantic night as well, I expect."

He saw his own romantic evening slipping away while the Petrofskys had theirs. He wasn't going to let it go without a fight. Tonight might be out, but he could change reservations. "The Petrofskys obviously had the same I idea I did."

She looked confused.

"I came over to invite you to dinner."

Her face lit up. "That's sweet, Quinn." Her expression turned rueful. "But…"

"Yeah," he said. "Bad timing." He reached up to stroke a stray lock of hair away from her eyes, forcing her to look up into his. "What about tomorrow evening?"

Her gaze searched his for a moment, then she looked down and away. "Last day of Spring Break," she said. "I need to be here for Noelle." She lowered her voice. "Since Frank left, it's been hard. She's upset, but she's hiding it. I don't want to…" She hesitated. Her voice shook a little when she resumed, but her words were firm. "I can't go out tomorrow. It's a family thing. I need to be with her." She looked up at him, her eyes pleading. "You understand, don't you?"

Down in Pasadena they'd pretended they were a family: Christy, Quinn, and Noelle. Now they had returned to Burnaby they were back to the way they'd been before they went away together. Christy had a daughter and they were both Jamiesons. Whether Frank was still in Stormy didn't matter at this point. Christy had asked him if he understood, and he thought he did. She wasn't ready to commit to anything deeper than a sexual liaison.

So he had to decide—was that all he wanted from her? Was it enough?

He didn't know. He didn't think so.

Still, as he looked into her eyes he knew he couldn't end it this way, with Ellen and Rebecca in the living room, the kids downstairs and the cat somewhere in the house, probably spying on them.

"I understand," he said. He stepped away. "I'll let you get back to your tea party."

"Thanks," she said, but she made no move to climb up the stairs.

He nodded and let himself out, the image of her cool composed Jamieson princess expression burned in his mind's eye.

He was already canceling his reservations as he headed down her front walk.

"I'm going to tackle Brody Toupin today," Quinn said. He was eating breakfast with his father. The bacon and eggs Roy had fixed were congealing on his plate.

Roy set his own plate on the table and sat down. He looked pointedly at Quinn's uneaten food. "Something playing havoc with your appetite?"

Quinn cut a piece of bacon and ate it. "No." He looked at his plate, not his father.

Roy dipped toast into the soft yoke of his fried egg. "True love never runs smooth," he said, before crunching the bread.

"Oh, for God's sake!" Quinn said. He pushed back his chair and picked up his plate. "I'll be back later."

"See you," his father said affably.

Brody Toupin lived in Kitsilano, not far from Jericho Beach on the shore of English Bay. In the forty-five minutes it took Quinn to drive from Burnaby, he fumed about know-it-all fathers, women who couldn't move on, and idiots like him who put up with them. By the time he arrived at Toupin's address his mood was bleak and his outlook grim.

Brody Toupin's residence was a small mid-sixties infill house that had been sandwiched into a tiny lot between two much larger houses. The building took up most of the property. There was enough space left to provide a driveway and a pocket-sized lawn.

From the outside, the building didn't look like much, but in Vancouver's high octane housing market Quinn guessed it would sell for well over a million dollars. He knew from his research on Toupin that he was the owner of the property and he reflected sourly that the music business must be doing well by him.

Toupin answered the bell on his first ring, as if he had been hovering nearby waiting for Quinn to arrive. He said hello, then peered over Quinn's shoulder, frowning.

"Looking for something?" Quinn asked.

Toupin scanned Quinn up and down, then said, "You don't have a camera and you didn't bring a photographer."

Still standing on the front step, Quinn said, "No." He left it at that. He had a feeling he knew where Toupin was going with the question, but he wanted the man to say the words. Then he'd be able to act.

"You're not going to supply pictures to whatever rag you're selling the article to, are you? Will they accept it without images?"

Quinn was still standing at the front door. He reflected that Brody Toupin couldn't be all that bright. He expected Quinn to write a favorable article about him, but he'd begun the meeting with a confrontational statement and hadn't even bothered to invite him in. "The paper will supply a shot from their morgue," Quinn said. He sent Toupin a cool look and added, "I don't write the kind of fluff that requires more photos than content. People read my articles because they're interested in what I have to say and the opinions I offer, not because they want to ogle a pretty face or drool over a muscular body."

Since Brody Toupin possessed both of those qualities, he stiffened. "I'm not some pinup for teenyboppers."

"No, you're backup for one of the hottest bands on the planet." Quinn indicated the house with a nod of his head. "From your address and the value of property around here, I'd say you don't have a lot to complain about."

Toupin's brows snapped together and his expression hardened. "I was supposed to get headline status. Vince promised me that when he convinced me to participate in the SledgeHammer tour. Then the bastard screwed me, told me I wasn't good enough. That's bullshit."

"There are plenty of people who would envy you the success you've already got," Quinn said crisply. Brody Toupin was rubbing him the wrong way. Between the two of them and their equally negative moods, it was unlikely that he was going to get much of an interview from the man, even if Toupin agreed to one.

"I dumped the band I was with to go on that tour," Brody said. Anger reverberated in his tone. "We were doing okay. Not great, but we were making sales and getting airplay. In Canada, at least. Vince told me he'd push me into the stratosphere and I bought it." Now he sounded more disgusted at himself, than angry at Vince. "That band. The one I dumped? They had a US number one a month ago. They haven't made it yet, but they're on the way." Bitterness crept into his voice. "And I'm stuck here without a band. Without a label. Without even an opportunity to work back up on a big-time band because SledgeHammer is on hiatus."

"And you blame that on Vince?" Quinn said.

"Of course I blame it on Vince! Who else would I blame it on?"

Yourself, Quinn thought. *Your bad decisions. Your greed.* "I guess you were pretty mad at him."

Vince held up his hand. "Oh, no. I see where you're going. Don't try to pin Vince's death on me!"

Quinn shrugged. He was snarly enough to want to push this guy to the limit. Sure, he should be objective, but he was human and Brody Toupin struck him as the kind of guy who would never be satisfied. "Someone killed Vince. Why not you?"

Toupin allowed his mouth to gape open in astonishment. "Why would I?" At Quinn's raised brow, he said, "Look, Vince was my manager. Sure, I was pissed at the mess he'd made, but I couldn't afford to dump him until I found a new one. Now I don't have Vince behind me, I'm not going to get the kind of gigs I did when he represented me. Yeah, I was furious at him for lying to me, but killing him would be like cutting my own throat. I wouldn't do it."

"People do stuff for stupid reasons. Ever heard of revenge?"

Toupin's eyes narrowed. "I didn't kill Vince. Like I told the West Van cop, I was in the can when the cat started to howl. No way I could have gone outside, killed Vince and slipped back into the house without anyone seeing me. I'm in the clear." He stepped back from the door. "I think we're done here."

"Works for me," Quinn said. The door slammed behind him as he walked back to the street where his car was parked. Although Brody Toupin's defense sounded reasonable, his alibi for the time of the murder was thin. There was only his word that he'd been using the bathroom when Vince was killed. They would have to check his whereabouts with others before they wrote him off as a suspect.

Buoyed up by that thought, Quinn got into his car and headed back to Burnaby.

CHAPTER 28

"Why is that man here?" Charlotte Sawatzky asked. She was wearing a flowered spring dress, a little early for the season, but appropriate for the meeting this morning. Her eyes were narrowed ominously; she didn't look happy.

Ellen peered around the room. A utilitarian meeting room in the basement of the Library building on West Georgia, the room had been set boardroom style for the two dozen people invited to become the inaugural members of the East Side Beautification Committee. As they waited for the full contingent to arrive, people milled about, chatting, helping themselves to coffee and semi-stale pastries, and generally scoping out who they would be working with. "What man?" she asked.

As the genders were pretty much evenly represented, the question made sense. She recognized a few of the faces. The head of the city's Parks and Rec department, the owner of a well-known chain of garden stores, and the dean of English Bay University's downtown campus, to name only a few of the worthy citizens who had answered the call.

"That one. The agitator," Charlotte said, pointing. She didn't bother to be discreet.

"Oh," said Ellen, after a quick glance. "You mean Sydney Haynes."

"Yes!"

Ellen contemplated her friend, unsure why she would be so hostile toward the man. True, Sydney Haynes tended to be a single focus kind of person. He'd talk about nothing but his charity, droning on and on until his auditor wanted nothing more than to escape. Ellen thought he probably gained quite a few donations with that particular tactic. But to call him an agitator seemed a bit much. Still, Charlotte Sawatzky wasn't the type to make a fuss where none was needed. "I've only met him twice. Both times ended in unpleasant circumstances, but I don't think he caused the unpleasantness."

"I have not met him at all," Charlotte said, her tone dismissive. She sniffed and her chin tilted up. "I only know of his doings."

Ellen raised her brows and waited, but Charlotte didn't say anything further. She had apparently decided she should hold her tongue on the subject of Sydney Haynes.

After a moment, Ellen said, "How are your son and daughter-in-law coping?"

Charlotte seemed to deflate. "Badly," she said. "The police have botched the investigation completely. There are no new leads and not enough evidence to charge the brother of that dreadful musician."

Charlotte was talking about Hammer and Kyle Gowdy. Once, before she'd moved in with Christy and Noelle, Ellen knew she would have identified Graham Gowdy exactly as Charlotte just had. Now that she'd been to a SledgeHammer concert and partied with the band and the assorted characters who surrounded them, she had to squash irritation at Charlotte's comment. She realized, with some surprise, that she'd enjoyed the experience and liked the people. The thought threw her off stride and she missed what Charlotte said next. She became aware she'd been wool gathering when Jeff Darling, the city councilor who was representing the mayor, called the meeting to order.

They settled onto sturdy metal and fabric covered chairs around tables set up in a large square. Jeff talked enthusiastically about the changing requirements of the city and the need to create a plan to revitalize decaying areas on the East Side. Ellen listened attentively and made notes in a small leather bound book she drew from her purse. Charlotte, seated beside her, glared at Sydney Haynes.

Jeff identified the need for more green spaces, suggested flower boxes be erected at regular intervals along major streets, and then closed his opening remarks with the cheerful request for input from all present. "But first," he said, as he prepared to sit down, "let's introduce ourselves."

They went clockwise around the table. The EBU dean spoke first, in a self-depreciating way that did nothing to minimize the list of his accomplishments. He was followed by Portia Quance, a woman who owned a very high-end boutique hotel. Portia simply looked around the table with raised brows and said her name, expecting everyone present to know what it represented.

The next person was Sydney Haynes. He'd been sitting hunched over, as if he didn't feel he should be here. That was odd, Ellen thought. At the SledgeHammer concert he had kept to himself, but he had seemed confident and was open and friendly when spoken to. Then he didn't have the wary posture and almost furtive expression she was seeing today. She tried to remember how he had behaved at the party. He'd been there, she knew, because Sledge had announced that the party had raised a hundred thousand dollars for Homeless Help, and he'd presented it to Sydney not long before the fight between Hammer and Vince had begun. Sydney had left almost as soon as he'd received the donation, so no help there. But what about before?

Sydney's oddly penetrating stare flicked around the table, lingering on Charlotte before moving on. His behavior was strange, but Ellen couldn't identify what had triggered the change. She decided that anyone who dragged himself out of full-blown drug addiction to sobriety should be allowed the odd quirk.

After another quick glance at Charlotte, Sydney straightened and said, "I'm here to represent the downtrodden and ensure that the fat money cats don't throw them out with the garbage."

The statement was like a slap across the face. Ellen pulled away from the table in an instinctive reaction. The positive atmosphere created by Jeff Darling soured in an instant. All eyes were on Sydney, whose mouth was a grim line and eyes hard shards of calculated rage.

No one seemed to know what to do. Jeff said, "Ah…umm…no one said…I mean, that's not what…"

Sydney paid no attention. His lips curled into a sneer. "I know how it's done. People get together, whisper behind doors. Deals are made with no input from those who really matter." His voice rose, and he surged to his feet, his finger thrusting out aggressively. "Then before we know it buildings are being torn down to make way for some high-rise. Or the homes my people live in are being sold out from under them to be converted into condos that only the richest can afford."

"You're talking about the Regent Hotel conversion," Charlotte said.

Ellen shivered. Charlotte was furious, though her voice was even and her face was a mask of polite disdain.

"It's the most notorious example, but not the only one," Sydney said.

"The Regent Hotel was condemned," Charlotte said. "The building would have been torn down if Sawatzky Restoration hadn't rescued it."

"That redevelopment has been completed. Let's move on to the real reason we're all here," Jeff said, trying to regain control of his meeting.

Syd paid no attention. It was as if the councilor hadn't spoken. "All of the people living there—the poorest of the poor, the homeless—were evicted. People who had no access to other housing and who were forced to live on the street."

"Those people were squatters, putting themselves at risk by simply being in the building. There was no power. No water. No heat."

"I think we should talk about those flower boxes. What do you think?" Jeff asked, looking around the table and smiling hopefully.

"There was shelter!" Sydney roared. "A place to find warmth, to get in out of the rain. There may not have been the luxury accommodations that people like you expect, Mrs. Sawatzky, but it was home to many, many people."

"What nonsense," Charlotte said, contempt in her expression and voice.

"I'd expect nothing less from one of the privileged—"

"How did you know her name?" Ellen asked. She'd learned a bit from living along side the highly skeptical Armstrong men and Trevor McCullagh these past few months. Her question stopped Sydney mid roar, so she smiled as she looked around the table and said, "Ellen Jamieson here. I'm a director of Jamieson Ice Cream and I was born and raised in Vancouver." She turned back to Sydney. "We had hardly started the introductions, Mr. Hayes. I realize many of us at this table are known to each other, as for instance you and I are. I'm curious, though, how you know Charlotte? Would you care to enlighten us?"

The relief around the table at the interruption was almost a physical thing. It was short-lived.

Still standing, Sydney put one clenched fist on the tabletop and leaned toward Charlotte, pointing with his other hand. "This woman's son murdered the best man who ever lived!" He intoned the words as if this was a pronouncement from God. His thin, sharp features were twisted with grief and an inner agony that froze his audience in place.

"He did not!" Charlotte said. There were two spots of red in her cheeks, but otherwise she was pale.

"You're talking about the death of Reverend Wigle during the Regent Hotel riots," Ellen said.

"He was my mentor, my dearest friend," Sydney said. It was as if the air had been punched out of him. "If it hadn't been for the Reverend, I would still be a drug addict and one of those people you are all so anxious to drive into institutions or shove on to someone else's jurisdiction."

"No one said anything of the sort," Portia Quance said. She pushed back her chair as she glanced at her watch. "I have too much to do to waste my time with this." She was up and headed for the door before the city councilor could think of anything to say.

"Typical," Sydney said, sneering at her straight, elegant back.

At the doorway, she stopped and turned. "You know better than to behave this way, Sydney Haynes. Your father would be ashamed of you." She pulled open the door and strode out.

There had been a rumor years ago that Tate Haynes, Sydney's ultra respectable lawyer father, had had an affair with the glamorous hotel owner, but Ellen had always discounted it. Now, as Sydney flushed red, she wondered.

"The Reverend Wigle was my father! Tate Haynes may have bred me, but he made no attempt to raise me!" he shouted to the closing door. There was no evidence Portia had heard, but with the whiff of scandal, those who remained had become a willing audience. "I would do anything to keep Reverend Wigle's name and the causes he believed in alive."

"As Mrs. Quance said, I don't have time for this." Charlotte pushed back her chair and made to rise.

"Yeah, that's it. Run away," Sydney said, sneering again.

Ellen frowned. "She's not, you know."

Sydney scowled at her.

"Running, I mean. Really, Mr. Haynes, can't you see that this conversation is difficult for her? Family is important and she recently lost her granddaughter."

"Mine is a just cause," Sydney said. "What does the death of a girl matter to it?"

"Oh!" The word came out as a little gasp of anguish from Charlotte.

Jeff Darling suddenly found a spine and said, "You were invited to participate on this committee because we thought you would bring the viewpoint of the area to our discussions. I did not expect you to turn this table into a soapbox. I think you should go now, Mr. Haynes."

As other members of the committee nodded agreement, Sydney shot a poisonous look at the councilor before he stormed around the table. At the door he paused to say, "You can silence me in this room, but I will make my voice heard." The only reason the door didn't slam behind him was the hydraulic arm that controlled the speed with which it closed.

"Well," Jeff said into the silence that followed. "Shall we continue?"

CHAPTER 29

Christy kissed Noelle at the classroom door and gave her a hug. Noelle squirmed out of her grasp and danced away to visit with the other little girls in her class. It was the first day back after Spring Break and the kids were busy sharing vacation experiences. Christy didn't envy Mrs. Morton the task of bringing their attention back to their schoolwork.

She waited until the bell rang, then headed home using the path behind the school. She had a lot to think about and a quiet walk through the trees would give her the perfect venue to do it. Except it didn't. This was where she walked with Quinn. Where they shared their thoughts, where they kissed and learned each other's needs. She'd come this way so she could think objectively about her tangled relationship with Quinn and Frank. By the time she reached the townhouse development, she had decided objectivity was impossible, but she knew she couldn't move forward until she was certain Frank was gone.

The townhouse was quiet when she got home. Ellen was off at some committee meeting or other. Stormy was asleep on the couch. Christy was restless. They'd all agreed to get together around lunch time to pool their knowledge and brainstorm who the killer was, but there were too many hours between now and noon for her peace of mind. She wanted to do something to keep busy. But what?

She could ask Roy and Quinn if there was any research or interviews that still needed doing, but for the first time since she'd asked for Quinn's help to find Frank, she was shy about going over to the Armstrong house. She dithered about what to do, then finally decided that avoiding Quinn wasn't the answer.

As it happened, it was Sledge who answered the doorbell. He flashed her the smile that made millions of enraptured fans sigh with longing, and said, "Quinn's not here," before she'd even had a chance to speak.

Christy had never seen this side of Sledge. On their first meeting he had still been keyed up from the performance, then afterward he was preoccupied with the fallout from the murders. Looking at him now—the famous smile, the dirty blond hair perfectly cut so that it looked ragged and unkempt, gorgeous eyes, and the scruff of a beard emphasizing a lean jaw—she couldn't help but be a little starstruck. Well, maybe not a little. Maybe a lot. "Oh. I, ah…Is Roy around?"

Sledge nodded. The smile wasn't just on his lips; it warmed his eyes too. "Upstairs, with my dad." He turned to lead the way inside. He was wearing jeans and a T-shirt that hugged his form. Christy followed, enjoying the view.

In the living room the fragrant aroma of marijuana mixed with incense perfumed the air. Sledge settled onto the couch beside his father and took the joint Trevor passed him. Christy hovered at the top of the stairs. The joint explained Sledge's relaxed mood.

"Everything okay?" Roy asked, frowning.

"I just dropped Noelle off at school," Christy said. "I'm at loose ends. Is there anything I can do for the investigation?"

"Quinn's talking to the guitarist fellow," Roy said. He looked at Sledge. "What was his name?"

"Brody Toupin."

Roy nodded. "He's about the last of our suspects. We're going to pool our information later, once Quinn and Ellen are home, but you know that. There might be something to do after."

Christy nodded. Later didn't help. "Okay."

"What about that chef woman?" Trevor said, passing the joint to Roy. "She keeps coming up in people's alibis."

"Rita?" Sledge asked. His expression was mildly surprised. "Rita is a terrific cook and she's always prepared. I doubt she had anything to do with Vince's death."

"Someone should talk to her," Trevor said.

"I'll do it," Christy said. Talking to an unlikely-to-be-involved chef was exactly the kind of task she needed today. No pressure, but a small worthwhile achievement once she'd got it done.

Sledge offered to phone Rita to see if she was available. Thirty minutes later, Christy was in her car, headed to North Vancouver where Chef Rita Ranjitkar had her business.

She found Chef Rita's Catering Kitchen in a low-rise building off the Esplanade, North Vancouver's main east-west street. Traffic was heavy and the parking spots were few, but Christy managed to snag one a couple of blocks away. As she walked to the building it began to rain, and she shivered, reminded that it was still only March and temperatures in Vancouver could be unpredictable.

The door to Chef Rita's Catering Kitchen opened into a nicely appointed reception area. A middle-aged woman sat behind a beautiful antique desk, which had a telephone and a computer screen on the top and nothing else. No clutter. No evidence of work being done. "Can I help you?" she asked, smiling.

Christy gave her name and the woman nodded. "Please come this way. Chef is expecting you." She led Christy to an office that was as attractive as the reception area and looked as if it had been decorated by the same hand.

Chef Rita was not what Christy expected. She assumed she'd find an older woman dressed in chef whites. Instead, she found a gorgeous female who looked to be in her thirties, beautifully made up. She was seated behind a desk that appeared to be the twin of the one in reception, but she stood when Christy entered. The receptionist quietly left them together. The office door clicked shut behind her.

"Mrs. Jamieson," Rita said, holding out her hand. She was wearing a tunic style button front white blouse, belted at the waist and a pair of navy pants that emphasized her dark hair and slender shape. "I am delighted to meet you."

"And I you," Christy said. She felt underdressed in her jeans and sweater, but she had her Jamieson manners to draw on, so she smiled at the chef in a polite way and said, "I appreciate you taking the time to speak with me."

"Of course," Rita said. "Please sit down. What can I do for you?"

When they were both seated, Christy said, "I'm helping Rob McCullagh find out who killed his manager." She noticed Rita stiffen, but she continued. "He tells me that you catered the party that night."

"I did provide the catering, but—" Rita raised her brows. "Why would Sledge not leave the investigation to the police?"

Christy smiled thinly. "There are rumors flying around that could do serious damage to SledgeHammer's reputation. Sledge can't control them, but he wants them stopped."

"I suppose you mean the rumors that Hammer is the murderer," Rita said.

Christy nodded.

Rita drummed her fingers on the desktop for a few moments, then she seemed to come to a decision. "I understand, but I doubt I can help in any way. I spent most of the evening in the kitchen. I didn't see anything, not even the argument that I gather led to the killing."

"Several people are using you as part of their alibis…"

Rita's dark eyes flashed. "Who? That drunken lout Hank Lofti is one, I suppose."

"He is," Christy said cautiously.

"He came on to me earlier in the evening, when he was still relatively sober. I shooed him away, but he kept coming back. Finally, I told him to stay away from my kitchen."

"When was that?"

"About a half an hour before the argument."

"Someone else said that he tried to find you in the kitchen just after the argument ended, but couldn't," Christy said. "Were you in another part of the house checking on the buffet arrangements, perhaps?"

Rita stared at her, then she said, "I did go out to my catering van about that time. I was storing some of the dirty dishes. Getting a jump on the clean up, as it were."

This sounded promising. "Where was the van parked?"

"In the driveway, by the door that leads off the kitchen."

Christy thought back to the time they'd all gone to Sledge's place for the discussion on how to handle the first murder. "That door is at the side of the house, toward the back, isn't it?"

Rita nodded.

"Was anyone with you when you went outside?"

Rita shook her head. "I was alone, but when I returned to the house after I finished stowing my trays, I found Jahlina Vuong in the kitchen. She is employed at English Bay University as an event manager and we do a lot of work together. I featured a new appetizer at Sledge's party. Jahlina wanted to know if I could include it in an event she has coming up next week."

So Rita had an alibi for at least part of the time around the murder. "When you were out in the van, did you see or hear anything?"

"Two cats mating," Rita said, curling her upper lip distastefully. "And I heard some rustling in the trees. I thought it might be a predator of some kind. A bear, or a coyote, or maybe even a big cat. I stayed in the light and kept alert. Wild animals can be unpredictable."

"When you were outside did you see Hammer at all?"

"No. Nor anyone else." She hesitated, then said, "I couldn't see the front of the house from where I was, but I did hear something, though."

Christy perked up. She had begun to think her trip to North Van had been a waste of her morning. "What was that?"

"Someone speaking angrily. A man. He said, 'Leave it! We've been over this before.' Then another voice spoke, but I couldn't make out what was said."

"Could you tell if the second person was a man or a woman?"

"No." Again Rita shook her head. "I went back inside just about then. I didn't want to eavesdrop, and besides I was done stowing my trays."

"And that's when you met Jahlina?"

Rita nodded.

There was something about the woman's expression that fanned Christy's curiosity. "Did you tell the police what you'd heard?"

A wary look crept into Rita's eyes. "I don't know who the voices belonged to and the snip-it of conversation I heard didn't mean anything."

"It might have meant a great deal," Christy said, shooting Rita an austere look.

"Look, Mrs. Jamieson, I mind my own business when I am at a client's house. I don't listen in on conversations or flirt with the guests. I depend on word of mouth referrals and I won't get them if I'm involved in a murder investigation. I think I've said enough." She stood up and offered her hand.

The meeting was over. As Christy shook Chef Rita's hand, she decided she'd discovered a lot more than she'd expected.

Perhaps the morning hadn't been a total waste of time.

CHAPTER 30

◆

"I had the most dreadful morning," Ellen said. She put the large white carton she was carrying onto the Armstrong's countertop. Roy cut the string that held it closed and opened the lid. Inside a cardboard tray covered in golden foil was mounded high with an assortment of crustless quarter cut sandwiches. "Am I the first to arrive?" she asked.

"No." Roy carefully drew the tray from the box. "Quinn's downstairs with Sledge and Trevor. Christy called a half an hour ago and said she was leaving North Van. She should be here any time."

"Why was she in North Van?"

"She was talking to the woman who catered the party. Chef Rita."

"I hope she brings back something fabulous," Ellen said. "That woman's food was wonderful."

Roy grunted agreement. He pulled plates out of the cupboard and handed them to Ellen.

Once she would have stared at the dishes in amazement and not had a clue what to do with them. Now she was simply impressed how quickly she could set the table for six. It would be a squeeze, but the Armstrongs and Jamiesons did their best work crowded together around a simple kitchen table. Today they planned to discuss Vince's murder and pool their information.

"What made your morning so crappy?" Roy asked, as he put the platter of sandwiches onto the table. "Or do you want to wait until we're all here before you tell the story?"

"It has nothing to Mr. Nunez's murder," Ellen said. "Although that odd man Sydney Haynes was involved. Since he was also at Sledge's party, I suppose I should wait."

Roy nodded. He had just set coffee mugs on the counter by the coffee brewer when the doorbell rang. He cocked his head. "That will be Christy."

There was the sound of footsteps and voices. Sledge and Quinn appeared in the kitchen doorway. Sledge was dressed in his usual jeans and T-shirt. He flashed her his friendly, regular guy grin as he passed, rather than the sexy rock star smirk. Quinn merely nodded. His eyes were shadowed, and his expression unusually gloomy. He was dressed in a sweater and slacks, but he looked…rumpled. Ellen frowned, adding Quinn's appearance to the absence of Christy. Over the months she had lived in Burnaby, she had seen them moving closer and closer to each other. What was going on here?

Perhaps Roy was wrong and the person who rang the bell wasn't Christy, but someone else. Someone…random. How unlikely was that? Very, she decided, as Christy, followed by Trevor and Stormy the Cat, entered the kitchen. "Hi everyone. Sorry I'm late."

She was carrying a white box as well, and like Ellen she put it down on the countertop. Hers was taped closed so Roy had to slit it open. When he did, Ellen saw that it was filled with luscious looking deserts.

"Not late," Roy said as he closed the box, clearly planning to leave it until they'd eaten the main course. "We're in no rush."

Trevor deposited a shopping bag beside the box of pastries and began to pull out giant sized bags of chips. Roy handed him several large bowls and there was the sound of crinkling plastic as Trevor filled them up. He left two bowls on the counter, within easy reach, and put the other two on the table beside the sandwich tray.

Roy looked around. "Okay, everyone, we're all here. Grab a plate and a chair. Coffee is ready and I've got ice tea in the fridge."

They settled around the table with their beverages and plates and tucked into the food. Ellen noticed that Christy sat at one end of the table, with Sledge between her and Quinn. Her expression was carefully blank, while Quinn's was a dark storm cloud. As the cat hopped up onto Christy's lap, Ellen saw Quinn look away. What, she wondered, was going on?

"Let's start with your morning, Ellen," Roy said. "You mentioned you had a run in with Sydney Haynes, I think?"

"Nothing quite so dramatic," Ellen said. She chose a curried chicken sandwich and added sour cream chips to her plate. "I was at the inaugural meeting of the East Side Beautification Committee with a few others, including Charlotte Sawatzky. Mr. Haynes made rather a spectacle of himself, I'm afraid."

Sledge frowned. "What did he do? Syd has always been about Syd, but he used to be able to turn on the charm when he wanted."

"If so, he didn't want to this morning," Ellen said. She didn't sniff in disapproval, but she did raise her brows critically. "He became quite agitated and verbally attacked Charlotte. He bears a grudge, I believe, over the conversion of the Regent Hotel and the death of Reverend Wigle."

Trevor picked up a sandwich without paying much attention to the filling. "Tate Haynes tried to get him to go into therapy when he was sixteen, but Syd wouldn't do it. He had started to say Tate wasn't his father and that Tate had abandoned him." Trevor bit into the sandwich and his eyes widened. As he chewed he peered at the contents. "I think I just ate an eggplant."

"Roasted red pepper and eggplant," Ellen said. "I don't know what the spices are, but I love this combination."

"Right," Trevor said, frowning. He stared at the sandwich quarter as if trying to decide if he could abandon it or if he had to finish his portion. "When Syd got into the music scene, Tate thought it was a good thing, then the drugs happened."

"Syd's been doing pretty well since he cleaned up and started working with Homeless Help," Sledge said. His hand hovered over a sandwich with a filing that looked like the eggplant and red pepper one, then moved away. He finally zeroed in on salmon. "He was at the party, but he'd gone by the time Vince and Hammer started arguing."

"So he's out of the picture," Quinn said. He drank coffee, but left his plate bare. "The guy I talked to this morning, Brody Toupin, is probably in the clear too. He thought Vince was going to make him a star—"

"Brody? Really?" said Sledge, surprise in his voice.

Quinn nodded.

"Brody is a great guitarist, but he has zero stage presence," Sledge said.

"Apparently, Vince felt the same way. Anyway, that gives Toupin motive, but he claims that with Vince's death he now has no manager and no future. He's feeling pretty sorry for himself."

"Where was he when Vince was killed?" Christy asked quietly from her end of the table.

Quinn shot her a quick look, then inspected his coffee cup. "He says he was in the bathroom. Can't be corroborated. I also talked to Mitchell Crosier. He claims he was searching for Chef Rita so he could ask her for a recipe."

"A recipe? What kind of recipe?" Trevor asked. He sounded incredulous.

For a moment humor lit Quinn's eyes. "The kind that your domestic goddess of a wife can have fun with."

"Blew me away when you told me Kim Crosier is a domestic goddess," Roy said. "I thought she was just a flake." He chose the eggplant and red pepper sandwich Sledge had avoided and bit into it with gusto.

"Apparently she's both. Mitchell didn't find the chef until later, so he has no alibi. Like Brody he claims that Vince dead causes more problems for him than Vince being alive, though he does have a motive, I think. His label has a management subsidiary he claims is independent." Quinn looked over at Sledge. "I understand you're in negotiation to have them represent you."

Sledge nodded. "It's early days yet, but yeah, they're on the short list."

"So," Trevor said, "he kills Vince and not only does he eliminate a hard negotiator, but he also gains a new revenue source." He drank some iced tea. "Could be."

Christy toyed with the shrimp sandwich on her plate, then Ellen saw her pick out a shrimp and feed it to Stormy, who was still crouching on her lap. She also saw Quinn staring at Christy, a brooding expression on his face.

Roy waved a chip. "I had the unfortunate task of tracking down Hank Lofti. Not," he said, selecting another sandwich quarter, "a pleasant experience. Lofti is a drunk and lazy with it. He considers himself one of Vince's victims. I think he's got a lot of potential, motive wise, but to get himself organized to kill?" He shook his head. "I can't see it."

"Who are Vince's other victims?" Ellen asked.

"Syd Haynes," Roy said. "He figures Vince deliberately pushed Syd out of SledgeHammer when Syd was the one who originated the band."

Sledge straightened. "He didn't! Hammer and I started SledgeHammer. Syd was just along for the ride. He wasn't a bad musician, but he was unreliable. Vince tried to get him into rehab, but he wouldn't go."

"Chef Rita said Hank was drunk the night of the party and that he came on to her. She turned him down," Christy said. She snuck another shrimp to the cat.

"No surprise there," Quinn muttered.

Christy shot him a frowning look, then she shook herself and said, "Rita was out loading her van just before the murder. She claimed she heard a rustling sound in the woods around the time the cats were mating. Kyle Gowdy mentioned it too. Anyone else say anything about that?"

"Hammer did," Ellen said. "He heard something as he left the house and started on his walk. He thought it was Stormy, because he saw the cat shortly afterward."

"Hammer isn't guilty," Sledge said. "I checked with the neighbor he met."

"The one walking the dog," Ellen said.

Sledge nodded. "He confirmed the meeting and Hammer's timing. There is no way Hammer could have killed Vince and be where he was when the cat started to howl."

"I contacted the West Van cop, Szostalo, with that information," Trevor said briskly. "He was not pleased. He believed Hammer was the perpetrator and he apparently does not have any back up suspects." He looked at Christy. "Did Chef Rita mention that she'd heard something in the woods to Szostalo?"

Christy grimaced. "No, and she won't. She says it's bad for business." She picked up a chip, but only toyed with it. "Both Kyle Gowdy and Chef Rita thought the rustling sound was made by a wild predator. A coyote, or a bear, or maybe a cougar. Sledge, does this seem likely to you?"

"Sure. Animals come down the mountain regularly. Bears are usually in the summer, though. I think they'd still be hibernating now. We hear coyotes at night, so I know they're around, but I can't say I've seen any recently. Cougars are rare, but not unheard of."

Christy patted the cat. "Rita also said that she heard Vince say 'Leave it! We've been over this before,' and someone else reply, but she couldn't hear what the second person said and she didn't recognize the voice. So the rustling sound, which happened before Vince's death, could have been an animal. Or…" She looked around, still stroking Stormy and apparently not noticing. "It could have been Vince's killer."

"Christy."

She stiffened at the sound of Quinn's voice behind her as she was about to follow Ellen down the Armstrongs' porch stairs. In front of her Ellen paused and looked over her shoulder, making Christy pause too, when all she wanted to do was run away from the crisis she knew was brewing.

Ellen said, "I'll see you at home."

"I have to pick up Noelle," Christy said, to Ellen and to Quinn, even though she wasn't looking at him.

Ellen nodded. "Later, then," she said, leaving Christy to deal with the crisis Ellen probably didn't even know was looming.

As Ellen trotted down the steps carrying her elegant leather binder, Christy slowly turned to look at Quinn. He'd taken the short time she'd paused to talk to Ellen to grab his leather jacket and shrug it on.

He closed the door. As their gazes made contact, he said, "I'll walk with you."

She wanted to say no. She wanted to put off this conversation as long as possible. She was certain it would be painful. Worse, it would lead to a set of questions she didn't know how to answer and a decision she wasn't ready to make.

"Sure." She turned away from him and started down the front walk. Two houses away she heard her own front door close as Ellen returned to the house. She wished she was with her.

This situation was all her fault. When Quinn suggested they go to Disneyland for Spring Break, she thought she was ready. She and Frank had fallen into old habits, bickering and sniping, sometimes laughing together, but more often finding fault with each other. It didn't help that he remained critical of Ellen most of the time, but often took his aunt's side against Christy if there was a parenting issue over Noelle. It really was her old life, except there was no Frank in the flesh, only his voice in her mind and his essence in Stormy's body.

In this limbo her relationship with Quinn had been a quiet, stolen pleasure. The walks in the woods, evenings out for dinner, or perhaps dinner and a movie. They weren't a couple, not officially. The excuse she used for herself and everyone else, but mostly herself, she thought now, was Joan Shively. The woman continued her regular home visits, though as January drifted into February the time between visits lengthened. Christy was careful to make sure Shively had no excuse to find fault with her parenting. She was terrified that if Shively used her clout within Child Services and decided Noelle had to be removed from her home, that even the legal help of Trevor McCullagh wouldn't be enough to keep Noelle with Christy.

But as February drifted into March and Shively became much less intrusive, Christy started to believe she was safe, that her child was safe. She let herself look forward to a time when she could focus on her own life. Her own needs.

Quinn's suggestion they travel down to Disneyland during Spring Break caught her on this high note and gave her a boost of optimism she couldn't resist. She said yes and they started to make plans, clearing the holiday through Shively first. Planning which southern California attractions to see and how long to spend at each. Booking the hotel and plane tickets.

Noelle had been ecstatic at the thought of going to Disneyland. Christy had monitored her reaction to the suggestion carefully. If Noelle had had any reluctance to going with Quinn she would have put a stop to the adventure immediately. But Noelle had been as delighted that Quinn was coming as she was with the idea of visiting Disneyland itself.

Christy knew Frank didn't want her to go. He was resentful that it was Quinn who would be there with Noelle, not him. Before the trip Christy didn't have much sympathy. In life, Frank had lots of opportunity to take Noelle on a theme park holiday before he died. He didn't. His loss. She'd left Vancouver, buoyed up on a high, ready to move her life forward into one that included a much deeper relationship with Quinn.

And she'd done it. Those days and nights with Quinn? Probably the best ones of her life. He was so good with Noelle and she had so much fun with him. At the same time, he showed Christy in big ways and small that he cared for her. She wasn't used to a man in her life who made her a priority. It had been wonderful.

Then came Vince's murder, Frank's retreat, and a crushing burden of guilt she couldn't ignore. She hadn't been there when Frank's voice was silenced. Had he truly left Stormy? Had he deserted her and Noelle because they deserted him?

In California, Noelle refused to believe that her daddy was gone. Even though he hadn't said anything since their return, she still believed he'd come back, that he'd talk to them again, because he had promised her he wouldn't leave her without saying good-bye. It had been days, almost a week, since they returned, and Frank still hadn't spoken. Even Noelle, with her trust and optimism, was beginning to believe her daddy hadn't stayed to say good-bye.

It crushed Christy to see the doubt in Noelle's eyes when she patted Stormy. The small frowns when she thought Christy wouldn't notice. The hunch to her shoulders. The sleepover with Mary Petrofsky had been a desperate attempt to redirect her attention, the return to school, a relief.

She knew Quinn wanted clarity, to define what they were together and where their relationship was going. But how did she make him understand her tangle of emotions without hurting him? Now the moment was upon her she couldn't see a way.

He came up beside her, matching his strides with hers. "I have a little time. I was going to go the back way," she said. Her voice was husky with emotion tightly bottled.

"Works for me," he said.

There was a grimness to his tone that clawed at Christy. Her throat worked and she fought for control. They walked up the street in silence. She kept her head down, studying the black asphalt surface of the road as if each tiny flaw, each lump on the surface could trip her up and cause her to fall flat on her face.

The silence stretched, tightened. Quinn made no attempt to talk about the murder, about the fruitless discussion that followed Christy's suggestion that Vince's murderer had been lying in wait for him. He didn't want to talk about the murder. Neither of them did.

They reached the top of the street and turned onto the path. The trees closed around them, bright new leaves bursting out on the cottonwoods and maples, shoots of vivid, almost neon, green beginning to open on the pines and cedars. The woods were coming alive after their winter sleep and she should be celebrating the joy of a season of rebirth. Instead all she could feel was the bleak despair of crumbling decay.

"I thought we had something together," Quinn said. He was staring ahead, not looking at her. His voice was low, a rumble of sound filled with all the hopelessness she was feeling. She opened her mouth to reply. He continued.

"Down in California, I thought…" He paused. She saw his jaw tighten, the muscles flex as he fought for control. "I thought we could be a family."

A vise tightened around her heart. She had thought they could be a family too. Instead, they returned to despair and crushing guilt she couldn't get out from under. "Quinn, I…" The words wouldn't come. How did she ask a living man to wait while she dealt with the emotions she felt for a man who was already dead?

They were near the place where the path forked, one arm leading down to the school, one going forward. He stopped and she did too, standing so that they were facing each other. Close, but not intimately so.

He looked down at her, his expression serious. His finger traced the shape of her face, a slow sensual touch that evoked other, intimate, memories. "I get it, you know. I understand where you're at. Noelle comes first, always."

"Yes." Her choked voice was thick with unshed tears. She had a sense where this conversation was leading and it terrified her. "Quinn…"

He put his finger over her lips, asking for silence. She stared up into his eyes and saw sadness there. "This isn't the right time for us, is it?"

She wanted to break her silence, shout that the timing was perfect, that he was perfect, but she couldn't. His touch, light, almost a caress on her lips, demanded honesty. She couldn't give him the reassurance he needed, so she said nothing. But her eyes searched his face, begging him not to push this conversation to its inevitable conclusion.

"I've been telling myself to be patient. That you care for me…"

"I do!" The words burst from her. His finger left her lips, and he stroked her cheek and dug his hand into her hair.

"But not enough." His mouth quirked up into a rueful smile. "My problem is, I care too much. I want more, Christy. More than I think you can give."

Christy had no answer to that, because he was right. "Quinn." His name was agreement, and they both knew it.

"It's time for me to move on."

"No." The word came out as an exhaled breath. Her throat closed. She couldn't say anything more.

"We live so close," he said. "Noelle has fun with my dad and he loves her. I'll try to keep this civilized so neither of them notice."

But Roy would, even if Noelle didn't, and they both knew it. Quinn didn't ask for her help in the deception, though, and that spoke volumes.

They were done.

He tugged her closer with the hand tangled in her hair, then lowered his mouth to hers. The kiss was tender, a mere brushing of his lips on hers. Tantalizing, expressing all that was lost. When he lifted his head, his smile was wistful. He pulled his hand from her hair, trailing his fingers along her cheek before he let it drop. Then he turned and strode away, leaving her staring after him until a turn in the path hid him from view. Only then did she move, trudging down the fork that led to the school, where she went to collect her daughter.

CHAPTER 31

Christy's suggestion that the rustling sound Kyle and Chef Rita had heard was not made by a cougar, but by the killer, had sparked considerable discussion yesterday afternoon, but they'd been unable to come to any conclusions. If it was a person, then who?

There were far too many suspects, Ellen thought now, as she carefully laid out her working materials on the kitchen table: the leather binder in which she kept all her notes; a stack of lovely, vellum writing paper, delicately tinted a mottled blue and engraved with her name at the top; her collection of fountain pens, each filled with a different color. She set everything precisely, then stood back to admire the effect. She could almost pretend she was about to sit down at the pretty little secretary in the small room she used as her office in her condo to make notes about the meeting she'd attended yesterday morning.

She suffered a pang at that thought, both because she missed her condo, with its prime location and wonderful views, and because the meeting had been…disturbing, to say the least. She straightened the leather binder a fraction of an inch for no other reason than to comfort herself, and sighed.

The cat, who had been snooping around its food dish, jumped onto the table and sniffed at the binder.

"No," Ellen said. "Off." She reached for him and Stormy lifted his nose in the haughty way of annoyed cats and glared at her. As she picked the beast up, she said, "Christy may have no concerns with you leaping onto the table where we eat, but I do." She put him on the floor, where he sat on his haunches, shot up a leg, and inspected his nether regions. Ellen pointedly looked in another direction as she moved around the counter to the coffee machine to make herself a cup.

By the time the machine had finished its hissing and gurgling, Stormy was sitting at his food dish, back straight, front legs neatly placed in front of him, tail wrapped around his feet. He stared at her pointedly as she passed, on her way back to the table and her carefully laid out work materials.

"You have food," she said.

He didn't move. His stare was unwavering.

When she left this morning, Christy had muttered something about grocery shopping after dropping Noelle. She'd looked dreadful, so Ellen had suggested that she should come home and go back to bed once Noelle was in class, but she'd shaken her head and said that the cat needed food.

After Christy and Noelle went off, Ellen had checked their supplies. The cat had plenty of food. That made her wonder if something was bothering Christy, but as she looked at the beast, sitting there refusing to eat because whatever had been dished out to him wasn't up to his high standards, she accepted Christy's explanation at face value. The cat had food, all right, just not the *right* food.

Well, the creature might con Christy into wasting her money on treats to stimulate his picky taste buds, but Ellen wasn't participating. He had food. He wouldn't starve. Not her issue.

She placed her coffee cup opposite the binder, by her right hand, and sat down. Her purpose this morning while all was quiet, was to make another list. This one would lay out the suspects for Vince's murder using the clues they'd identified during their discussion yesterday.

Ellen was a great believer that writing down details focused the mind and cleared away confusion. Her little list might not move the investigation forward—it hadn't been effective in finding poor Chelsea Sawatzky's killer—but it might provide a path for them to investigate, one that they'd missed when discussing the problem verbally.

She picked up a pen, a lovely handmade creation with a quartzite barrel and a beautiful German made nib. The barrel was a sea blue and the ink inside matched. She pulled forward a sheet of the vellum and started to write.

"Graham 'Hammer' Gowdy. Had an argument with Vince that caused him to storm out the front door," she said, itemizing the details as she wrote. "Vince followed him out of the house, but they did not talk. Hammer proceeded to walk to the end of the development where he met a neighbor walking a dog. He was talking to this man when Stormy started to howl."

Hearing his name, the cat abandoned his post by his dish and came over to the table. He stared up, sizing up the distance to the top of the table for a jump. Ellen glared at him. Stormy glanced away, then back at the table, but when he leapt, it was onto the chair beside Ellen's.

She gave him a pat. "Good cat," then she went back to her work. Stormy sat in his tidy way and watched her.

"Hammer," she said, writing his name, then tapping the vellum with her finger, "is no longer a suspect."

She went on to Kyle and Chef Rita, noting that they both had opportunity and Kyle certainly had motive, but they had separately mentioned a rustling in the trees prior to the murder. Would they have brought this up if they themselves were guilty? Unlikely. Of course, it could have been that the rustling *had* been a cougar, but Ellen was inclined to believe Christy's suggestion that the sound had been made by the killer. She looked at the cat. "Christy told us Chef Rita spoke with Hammer's girlfriend, Jahlina, just after she returned to the kitchen, so that pretty much rules her out. Kyle Gowdy doesn't have a witness who saw him return to the deck, so I'll leave him in for the moment. Who else should I consider?"

The drunk and whiny Hank Lofti, who had motive and no true alibi; the self-absorbed Brody Taupin who had motive, but reasons that explained it away; and Mitch Crosier, whose motive was business related. Would a man kill because of a difficult contract negotiation? "Hank Lofti and Mitch Crosier both said they were looking for Chef Rita. She, of course, was out at her van, loading it with dirty pots and pans, so they couldn't find her." She made notes on her sheet, then tapped the lovely pen against her lips.

She looked over at the cat. "Sledge's house is huge. Rita stayed in the public areas—the kitchen, the great room, some of the side rooms on the ground floor—but a man like Lofti, who has his mind in his pants…"

The cat's eyes seemed to widen and Ellen found herself blushing for some reason. She pressed on. "A man like that, and intoxicated as well, might think he'd find her flat on her back in one of Sledge's bedrooms."

Stormy licked his forepaw and didn't look at her.

"Mitch Crosier said he wanted a recipe. He claims he eventually did find Chef Rita and asked her for it, but she refused. He might have had time to both look for Rita and kill Vince. But would he?" She looked at the cat, who stared back, unblinking.

"Then there is Brody Taupin. He says he was in the washroom and saw no one." She sniffed. "A thin excuse, one that I've heard used before." She thought about Chelsea's murder, the one that had been superseded by the more immediate and intimate death of Vince Nunez. "Bernie Oshall and Kyle Gowdy both said they were in the washroom when Chelsea was killed." She sighed. "I believed them. I suppose I should believe Brody Taupin as well. Though," she added reflectively, "I did like him as the perpetrator of the crime. He is so self absorbed. He could well be the one who was talking to Vince when Chef Rita heard two men arguing outside."

Stormy sat in his familiar, alert pose and she thought with some amusement that she had his full attention now. "'Leave it! We've been over this before.' Who would Vince say those words to? Brody, certainly. Hammer, but he's been cleared. Would he say it to Kyle Gowdy? I don't think so."

She picked up a new pen. The barrel on this one had a milky white base, with a pattern in cinnamon red swirls. The ink was a vivid crimson. It stood out well on the fresh sheet of beautiful vellum as she made her notes. "Kyle doesn't fit in any way. I'm going to rule him out."

The cat butted her elbow and she put her pen down to give him a pat. "Hank Lofti needs to remain on the list. Vince's words are just the sort of ones he'd say to a man he had no intention of employing again." She tickled Stormy under the chin. "I like this fellow, Lofti, for the crime. What do you think?"

She wrote down her thoughts, then looked at the first page she'd written. "I must not forget Mitchell Crosier, but the tone of Vince's words doesn't fit with his relationship to Mitchell. Now if it had been Mitchell talking and Vince the voice Rita couldn't make out, that would be different."

She tapped the pen against her chin as she thought about this. Stormy yawned. "You don't appear to be impressed by this argument," she said, then shook her head, amazed at herself for attributing rational thought processes to a cat. "Chef Rita didn't know the voices because she didn't know the people, so it could have been Mitch, not Vince, talking. Oh!" she said, throwing her pretty pen down on the table. A spot of crimson ink marred the surface of the elegant paper. "Damn!" She dabbed at it with a tissue she found in the pocket of her trousers. "Look at the mess I've made."

Stormy put his paws on the tabletop and stretched his body full length so he was standing, staring at the paper. Ellen pointed sternly to the chair and he subsided back into his tidy sitting position.

"This murder is as complicated and unlikely to be solved as poor Chelsea's is," she said. She heard the frustration in her voice and sighed. If she didn't watch herself, she'd sound as whiny as Brody Taupin or that dreadful man Syd Haynes. She shuddered as she thought about the meeting yesterday morning. Haynes had attacked Charlotte Sawatzky. There was no other way to describe the vicious accusations he'd made against her son and his company.

The Regent Hotel riots and the Reverend Wigle's death had been a dreadful slur on Vancouver's reputation. She could understand Haynes grieving the loss of a man he admired and may even have loved, but he had no right to accuse Charlotte's family of purposefully causing the man's death.

"Or did he?" she muttered, pulling out a fresh, undamaged, sheet of vellum. "Syd Haynes," she said as she chose another pen. This one was clear acrylic, tinted a lovely hunter green. "Green for envy," she said, writing. The ink, of course, was green as well, a bright emerald that lay garishly on her pale blue paper. "Syd Haynes hated Vince because Vince fired him from SledgeHammer." The impatience in Vince's words was perfect for a discussion over a decision made long ago and impossible to change. "Syd Haynes left the party before the argument between Vince and Hammer happened. Could he have been the creature hovering in the woods that Rita and Kyle heard?"

Writing furiously, she didn't even notice when the cat put his paws up on the table again and angled his body to watch her work.

"No one has considered him as a possible suspect because he left before anything untoward happened. Because he wasn't part of the argument in the great room, and we all thought the argument was the trigger. Even the policeman thought that." She looked up, noticed the cat, and didn't chastise him for having his paws on the table. Instead she stared vaguely at him and took a moment to tickle behind his ears. Stormy began to purr.

"Haynes was at the concert too. After it was over, he left the box and didn't go backstage. He could have left the arena with the rest of the audience. Or he could have found a place to hide out, stayed behind, then killed Chelsea."

She made a note. Stormy butted her elbow again and she smiled a little smile. "You want more patting, don't you?" She rubbed his fur, the rumble of his purr putting wings to her thoughts. "If he approached Chelsea after we were all gone, she would remember him. She'd be willing to speak to him. She wouldn't feel threatened or wary." Stormy licked her hand. She looked into the cat's eyes. "But would he have been capable of such a horrendous act? He didn't simply murder her. He raped her as well."

As she thought about the girl's end, tears sprang into her eyes. Stormy hopped up onto the table and butted his nose against her cheek, then he licked her with his rough sandpaper tongue, capturing the tear that trickled from her eye. Ellen sniffed, patted his head, and said, "Silly cat." Stormy licked again, his rough tongue scratchy against her skin. Ellen sighed. His cat caress soothed her, surprising her.

She straightened and the cat sat, curling his tail around himself. He stared at her watchfully. "There is absolutely no evidence that Sydney Haynes is our killer," she said. "No one thought to ask him his movements after the party because he had already left. The police probably asked him about after the concert, but with tens of thousands of people emptying out of the arena, it would be difficult to contradict his statement if he said he simply went home." Detective Patterson was thorough, though. If she thought there was a possibility that Syd Haynes had perpetrated the crime, she'd dig until she found her evidence. She had to identify him as a viable suspect first, and up till now no one was even considering him.

Ellen capped her pen, placed it with the others, then gathered her papers into a neat pile. She looked at Stormy. "She'll look if she has evidence. I can produce motive. I can connect one murder to the other using that motive, but I can't provide the evidence because no one has thought to ask the questions needed." She shoved her sheets into the leather binder, then put her beautiful pens on top. "Sydney Haynes may have a shady past, but he is now considered a benefit to the community. I can't simply accuse him. I'd be laughed out of the detective's office. Worse," she said, waving a finger at Stormy, "I'd be indulged. A silly rich woman filled with prejudice against a man of the people."

She placed her hand on top of the pens and binder. "I need to have proof before I make any accusations."

Stormy meowed and put his paw over hers.

Ellen looked at the cat and smiled. "Sweet kitty. You shouldn't be on the table." She glanced at her watch before she picked him up. "The morning is still young," she said, with some surprise as she put Stormy on the floor. "He's bound to be in his office at this hour."

She tapped her chin with her forefinger. "Time, I think for a visit."

CHAPTER 32

Christy couldn't bear to go back to the townhouse after she'd dropped Noelle off at school on Tuesday morning. She'd spent the night brooding about Quinn and her relationship with him and where she'd gone wrong. Ellen had poked at her a bit, posing leading questions, making remarks about the Armstrong men. She was looking for answers that Christy didn't want to—couldn't!—give. So she took her purse with her when she walked Noelle to school, then got into the car when she got back to the townhouse, instead of going inside.

Her excuse was grocery shopping. It worked as well as anything as a way of sectioning off time that belonged to her alone. In the grocery store she could wander the aisles, speak to no one, and let her thoughts drift at the same time as she did something useful for the household. Grocery shopping was a task she'd done with her mother when she was a kid, but she hadn't had the opportunity when she lived in the mansion. The cook did the shopping, or one of his helpers did. Doing the weekly grocery shopping had been an unexpected bonus to moving into the townhouse.

The supermarket was the anchor store for a sprawling strip mall that also boasted a hairdresser, a liquor store, a pizza delivery outlet and a very nice bakery and coffee shop. Wanting to spin out her time away, Christy went to the bakery first. There she ordered a Viennese coffee and a chocolate croissant, and found a place to sit in a corner, alone.

She took a sip of the sweet coffee and reflected that the beverage and the croissant probably contained half the calories she usually consumed in a full day. There was nothing redeeming about either. They were simply sugar bombs that would lift her mood for a short time, then dump her down into the emotional dumpster. Since she was in that dumpster right now she figured she couldn't get much lower. And it would be nice to have a boost, even if it was only short-term.

She bit into the croissant, felt the pastry flake, then melt on her tongue as the chocolate shot sweet comfort to her brain. The bakery was a little place, nothing much to look at, but the people who ran it certainly knew how to create delicious confections. She took another small bite and savored, letting her thoughts drift.

She'd screwed up big time with Quinn. She could see it now, or at least thought she could see where she'd gone wrong. She'd taken him for granted, and he'd walked.

Picking up the coffee mug, she held it in her hands and inhaled the fragrant scent of chocolate and coffee combined. How would she get him back? She sipped the coffee. *Could* she get him back? Or was it over for good? That thought put her mood into a nosedive, so she took another bite of the croissant.

They'd been teasing each other for months, building a sexual fire that simmered and gained heat until it came to a boil in a California hotel. When Quinn suggested they take Noelle to Disneyland for Spring Break, she'd known that she was going to go to bed with him while they were there. She'd wanted it. She looked forward to it. And when it came to the actual event he'd made her feel…well, cherished.

Then what did she do? She came back to Burnaby and froze him out.

She didn't want to split with Quinn. She wanted him to be in her life, but not as a pleasant, civilized neighbor. How did she get him to come back to her?

She ate more croissant, but the melt-in-your-mouth pastry and the rich, perfect chocolate weren't doing their job. Her mood wasn't being elevated at all. In fact, it was sinking lower than before.

The key to the problem was Frank. Well, not Frank, but her relationship with him. Instead of accepting that he was finally gone, she'd worried that he had. Christy sat up a little straighter. Duh! That behavior had sent a clear message—her heart still belonged to Frank Jamieson.

Did it?

She picked up the coffee mug again and sipped as she pondered this. For a very long time, even before Frank's death, she told herself she no longer loved him, but was she being truthful with herself? Did she need Frank in her life? If he was still in Stormy, but not talking for some reason, how would she feel if he started talking again? Glad? Happy? Relieved? Annoyed? All of the above?

Would her heart be filled with tenderness and a wish that somehow she and Frank could go back into their past and recreate their perfect life? Except their life together wasn't perfect and never had been. What had linked them at the end and linked them now was Noelle. She looked gloomily down at the croissant before she popped the last section into her mouth. It was like Frank had divorced her and she'd never gotten over his decision to leave her.

For some reason that thought buoyed her up. Divorced women got over their exes. They co-parented, but moved on to other mates. She could do that too. With Quinn. Somehow. She finished up her sinfully sweet coffee, collected her shopping bags, then headed over to the grocery store.

Her cart was filled with milk, eggs, chicken and a dozen tins of cat food when she joined the checkout line. Stormy would have turned up his nose at the brand when Frank had been living in him, but he now ate it without complaint. Her cell rang.

It was Ellen. "Will you be home soon, Christy?"

"Probably." She put the phone between her chin and shoulder so she could dump items onto the conveyer belt. "I'm at the checkout now."

"How long do you think you'll be?"

"I should be home in about fifteen minutes. Why?" The woman ahead of her plugged her debit card into the chip reader while the cashier bagged up her items.

"I'm going out. I'm trying to decide if I should take the car or call a cab."

Getting a taxi to Burnaby Mountain could be a slow process. "I'll probably be home before the cab gets there."

"Yes. It's not like finding a taxi downtown."

No it wasn't. "They're checking me out now, Ellen. I've got to go."

"All right. I'll wait for you, then take the car." Ellen rang off and Christy paid for her groceries, then she hauled the bags out to parking lot and stowed them in the van.

She used back roads to return to the townhouse, so there was no traffic. She was there in less than the fifteen minutes she'd expected. She opened the hatch and picked up a bag, then reached for another.

The cat hopped into the car. She ruffled the fur behind his ears. "Hey, Stormy. I got you new food."

Something better than what you've been feeding him, I hope.

She stared at the cat, who stared back. "Frank?"

Of course it was Frank. It wasn't Stormy who was talking in her head.

Chris, you need to stop Ellen.

But Christy wasn't listening. "You're silent for a week— a week!—when we're all worried about you and the first thing you do is complain about food?" Furious, Christy hauled the bags out of the back of the car and stomped up her walk to the porch. She dropped the bags, then went back for another load.

The cat was still sitting there, beside her groceries. Waiting for her.

Chris, she's putting herself in danger.

Christy picked up the remaining bags. "How could you not talk to Noelle? She has faith in you. She refused to believe you'd go without telling her. She assumed you'd talk to her once we came back. But you didn't! How could you do this to her? She loves you!"

I...

Christy turned her back on the van and headed for the porch.

The cat hopped down and followed. *I saw the murder. I couldn't stop it. I tried. The weaselly little bastard hit him with a rock and there was nothing I could do. I saw him die, Chris.*

She put her bags with the others and turned to face him. "You've seen death before. You were murdered!"

That was cold.

She put her hands on her hips. "There's nothing cold about the anger I feel right now!"

They glared at each other. The cat didn't blink. It was Christy who looked away. She dug into her purse looking for her house key.

The murder made me think it was time to move on, to whatever comes next.

Christy froze in place, her hand in her purse, her back stiff and straight.

But I couldn't go. I thought it was because I needed to wait until you and Noelle were back, so I could say good-bye, but...I'm still here.

She turned back to him. "Why couldn't you go on?"

The green eyes stared into hers. *I don't know.*

Probably the most honest answer she'd had from Frank in years. "Maybe you need to work on it? Talk to Noelle. Reassure her, then give it another try."

His answer was lost in the sound of the door opening. "Oh, good. You're back," said Ellen. She held out her hand for the car keys. "I shouldn't be long."

NO! Stop her, Chris!

Christy frowned at the cat. "What are you talking about?"

"I need information," Ellen said. "I was working on my notes, but they were incomplete. I think I've had a breakthrough, but I need to confirm it."

Christy handed her the car keys. "Okay. I'll see you later then. I'll close the hatch for you."

"Thanks, Christy." Ellen headed over to the van and opened the driver's door.

Don't do this! Stormy bolted for the car and dove in just before Christy slammed down the hatch.

"What are you doing?" Christy shouted.

Saving Aunt Ellen!

The van started to move as Ellen eased away from the curb.

"From what?" Christy demanded, as Ellen stepped on the gas.

The murderer. She's visiting the murderer. Call the cops, Chris!

CHAPTER 33

A private vehicle was one of the finest benefits of living in the suburbs, Ellen thought as she guided Christy's van out of the development and onto Woodland Drive, the area's main street. It would eventually lead her across Lougheed to the access ramp for Highway 1, part of the Trans Canada highway system. Though the Trans Canada skirted the city of Vancouver, bypassing it to cross the Second Narrows Bridge into North Vancouver, Highway 1 was the fastest way to connect to the main roads into central Vancouver. It was also the most fun to drive, with a hundred klick speed limit and a generous peppering of speeders.

Woodland Drive wound down Burnaby Mountain in hairpin turns that were tight enough to satisfy the road rally enthusiasts who had once used it for their events before the area was developed into residential housing. Ellen swooped down the mountain, taking the first turn more quickly than she should. The wheels squealed and elation filled her. A second hairpin came up, this one leading to a stop sign where she would turn left to head for the highway. She took it fast again and skidded to a stop at the white line.

Stormy the Cat tumbled into the passenger seat with a hiss and a growl.

"What on earth!" said Ellen. She stared at the cat, who glared at her for a minute before he carefully began to groom his chest and shoulder. "What are you doing here?"

There was no answer, of course. She shook her head. Living with Christy was giving her bad habits, like talking to cats as if you expected them to talk back. "Stupid cat. You must have jumped in when Christy was unloading her groceries."

She drummed her fingers on the steering wheel. She should go back and return the cat to Christy. But she'd have to drive quite a distance out of her way. She'd be adding a half an hour at least to her commute.

Behind her a car honked. She glanced in her rearview mirror. There was a small lineup of vehicles all waiting to access the connector street. The honk made up her mind. She turned right and aimed the car for the highway access ramp.

The car gained speed and the cat hissed. He crouched down in the seat. Ellen reached the access ramp and gunned it.

There was a surprising amount of traffic for late morning. Some passenger cars and a lot of trucks, from pick-ups to panel trucks to mammoth tractor-trailers. Ellen's blood began to pump hard as she judged the speed of the vehicles whizzing by and prepared to merge with the on-going vehicles.

The cat began to howl.

Ellen jerked the wheel and almost rammed a black 4-by-4. She straightened and managed to join the flow of vehicles without further mishap, but she was shaken by the near miss.

"Be quiet, you bad mannered beast!" Stormy fell silent and she drew a deep breath. She should have taken the cat back to Christy, but she was committed now, and the cat appeared to have calmed down. She breathed deeply, relaxed a little. The cat went everywhere with Christy and Roy. He was used to cars. Why shouldn't he come with her and behave?

They whipped past an exit ramp, the next was the one she planned to use. The cat growled. She looked over at him. He was crouched on the seat, his green eyes fixed on her. His tail lashed from side to side and his lips were curled back in a frightful display of temper. "I get it," she said. "You're trying to intimidate me. Well, it won't work. I am not going back. You have come with me to Homeless Help. Then you'll have to wait in the car, because you are being rude."

The growling stopped. She glanced over at him again and saw that the snarl was gone, although the tail still lashed. Feeling quite pleased with herself for having bested the beast, Ellen saw the sign for her exit coming up and switched into the inside lane.

Her exit led her onto Hastings Street and necessitated a much slower speed, but Hastings was almost as much fun to drive as the highway, since street parking was allowed. Every block there was a car pulling out or one attempting to parallel park, which meant that you had to nip into one lane or another to avoid being stuck. It took concentration, though, for someone with the limited experience Ellen had of driving herself. She was completely focused on avoiding a delivery van pulling out of a spot in front of a butcher shop, when the cat meowed and put his paw on her leg.

She screamed and jumped. Her foot pressed heavily on the gas and she lurched into the left-hand lane, cutting off the car behind her and earning an annoyed honk. Her heart pounding, she said, "Don't do that!"

The cat meowed again, a plaintive sound that made her feel like a horrible person. She drew a deep breath to help herself reestablish her equilibrium. She did not scream at people. Or cats, for that matter. She didn't scream at all. She might want to, but she didn't. She showed a calm, controlled face to the world, no matter what the situation. That's what a Jamieson did. Hadn't she lectured Christy on that very subject time and again while she was married to Frank?

The cat meowed again, but she ignored it. She breathed in through her nose and then let the air out in a whoosh through her mouth. Her heartbeat slowed. That was good. She was herself again, which was important because she had almost reached her destination.

It occurred to her that finding a spot to park in this busy and congested part of town would not be easy. She began to watch for openings along the street, or a lot where she'd probably pay a fortune, but which might be easier than parallel parking.

As she drove, the area around her changed. What had been a prosperous street filled with pedestrians moving in and out of small shops, became one where few people milled and the storefronts were either vacant, or rundown. She saw the sign for Homeless Help, and there, right in front, was a parking spot.

"Perfect!" she announced and put on her indicator to let the impressive line of cars behind her know that she was about to become the one who was the cause of the traffic congestion.

The cat stood on his hind legs and put his front paws on the dash. His tail lashed and he howled just as Ellen cranked the wheel as she began to back in.

Rattled, she snapped, "You. No more nonsense, or you'll go into the back." The cat dropped down from his upright position onto the seat, to hunch there as she guided the car smoothly into the space. She killed the engine then half turned in her seat to stare at the cat. The cat stared back, defiant. "I have no idea why Christy puts up with you."

Because she's married to me.

Ellen blinked as shock rolled over her. "What did you say?"

Because she's married to me.

The first time the words had sounded in her head there was an annoyed and impatient tone. Now there was smugness, as if the speaker knew how much he had shaken her and was pleased about it.

That rallied Ellen as nothing else could. "Nonsense," she said, and opened the car door.

Her intention was to get herself out quickly enough to leave the cat locked in the van. A passing car made a swift exit impossible. Stormy was out the door and under the vehicle before she'd managed to turn back to the van.

Annoyed, she slammed the door shut. She looked over the roof, hoping the cat had made it onto the sidewalk, and saw that a young woman was coming out of Homeless Help. Her hair was a rainbow of neon colors and was cut in a short, ragged style that could have been done by an expert or by someone who simply hacked off her locks with scissors. There was a ring in one eyebrow and another through her nose. She was wearing jeans and a cloth jacket that had both seen better days.

As she paused to change the *open* sign to one that said *closed until 1 pm*, Stormy slipped past her ankles and into the building. The girl looked down and saw the cat. She waved her hands ineffectively as she said, "Shoo!"

Ellen dove around the back of the van to the sidewalk. It had never occurred to her that Homeless Help would close for lunch. Or that Sydney Haynes wouldn't be in the building all day. Yet beyond this young person, the storefront was empty, which fit with her putting up the closed sign.

For the first time, Stormy was proving useful. "Excuse me," Ellen said, hailing the young woman.

She looked up, her expression blank. "Yes?"

"The cat that just rushed into your building. It's mine."

The girl blinked. "So you'll get it out?"

"He. The cat is a he," Ellen said, surprising herself. She wouldn't have expected to champion a cat in a million years.

The girl's expression didn't change. "Who cares?"

"He does." Ellen almost shook her head at herself in exasperation. This was not necessary!

The girl shrugged. "Hurry up, then. I want my..." She shot Ellen a sideways glance, as if she was considering something. Then she smiled, tightlipped. "Fix."

Ellen stiffened and the girl's smile widened. Ellen narrowed her eyes and looked down her nose at the girl. She said coolly, "I have come to see Sydney Haynes. Is he in the building?"

The girl glowered at her. "Who's asking?"

Ellen raised an eyebrow and didn't reply. The girl shrugged and pointed inside. "He's got a private office in the back. He's there now."

"Thank you," Ellen said. The girl didn't reply. Ellen went into the storefront. The girl hunched her shoulders and headed off to wherever it was that she would acquire her fix. Ellen took stock of her surroundings.

The interior of Homeless Help was simple and utilitarian. Beside the door where she stood was a plate glass window, which had two metal folding chairs in front of it. The walls were a faded cream, dingy with years of dirt. On one was a calendar with pictures of monster trucks advertising a garage that serviced them. On the wall facing the door a large round clock showed that it was now five minutes after twelve noon. A wooden counter stretched the width of the room, bisecting it. Behind it were shelves full of goods.

At first, Ellen could see no way for her to get to the back office the girl had spoken of. Then she noticed there was a door on the far side of the back wall and in front of it the counter was hinged so that it could be folded back to allow access to the area behind the counter and to the door itself.

She lifted the countertop.

Don't do this, Aunt Ellen! Syd Haynes is dangerous.

She passed through and made her way to the door, ignoring the voice in her head. The cat tangled around her feet, making her stumble, as if he didn't want her to go into Sydney Haynes' back office. How absurd. She pressed forward.

The cat leapt up, snagging his claws in her pant legs, reminding her of the day he'd punished the odious social services woman for searching through Christy's private things. "Stop that!" she hissed, not wanting to have her trousers ripped. Or to be treated in the same way as Joan Shively.

Stormy meowed. *There's still time to stop! Turn around. Walk out the door.*

The damned voice was unnerving her. "I'm here now. I can't turn around."

Yes, you can. The voice became more urgent. *Aunt Ellen. Listen to me! Go. Now!*

She lifted her hand to knock, but hesitated. Perhaps the voice was right. Perhaps she should leave without talking to Sydney Haynes. She lowered her hand, took a step back.

The door opened. "Sadie? What the hell is going on out here? I thought you were going to lunch?"

Ellen pasted a confident smile on her face, even though panic assailed her at the fierce glower on Sydney Haynes' face. In that instant he looked mean and dangerous. But then maybe she was seeing something that wasn't there because of those negative comments the voice in her head was making. "Hello, Mr. Haynes." She shoved out her hand. "I'm Ellen Jamieson."

He narrowed his eyes and frowned at her hand, but didn't take it.

"I hope you remember me. We've met a few times. I've come to ask you some questions."

His eyes searched her face and Ellen held her breath. At her feet the cat growled.

Sydney Haynes scrutinized her a minute longer, then he smiled, a friendly smile that reassured her and told her that the voice in her head was nothing but nerves talking. "Of course I remember you. Come in, Ms. Jamieson."

He held the door wide and Ellen passed through into the private area behind. The cat scrambled between their feet, determined not to be left behind.

Frowning, Christy watched Ellen drive away with Stormy in the van. Saving Ellen from the murderer. As if. That was Frank all over, dramatic, expecting her to react to his pronouncements as if she had nothing else to do. As if he hadn't been silent for the last week, upsetting everybody. Making them grieve. Filling his daughter's eyes with sadness whenever she looked at her beloved cat.

She turned back to the house and walked to the porch where she opened the door before she picked up a couple of bags of groceries to cart inside. Ellen wasn't the kind of person who faced down murderers. What had she said? That she'd been making notes and needed more information? Frank had it wrong. He was overreacting.

She reached the kitchen. As she put the grocery bags on the counter she noticed Ellen's leather binder and her pens on the table. She went back to the porch to get the final bags. She'd check Ellen's notes when she was finished putting away the groceries.

As she shoved the door closed with her hip, having retrieved the bags, a frightening realization shivered through her.

Frank knew who the murderer was.

Christy dropped the grocery bags on the landing and sprinted for the kitchen.

A few minutes later she'd read over Ellen's notes and realized who she was zeroing in on. Christy put her hand to her throat in an unconscious gesture of dismay. If Ellen was right, the man she was about to interview was a rapist as well as a cold-blooded murderer.

She surged to her feet. What was Ellen thinking? What was Frank thinking? There was no way Stormy was protection enough if Ellen got into trouble. She had to do something, but what?

Call the cops. If Ellen was right, Sydney Haynes had murdered Chelsea Sawatzky, so that case was Patterson's. Patterson might not believe Haynes was guilty, or feel that they had amassed enough evidence to prove he was the killer, but she would at least intervene between Haynes and Ellen.

Christy's hand shook as she dialed the detective's number—and got voicemail.

Who knew how long it would take Patterson to call her back. The detective might be on an active case, at a crime scene, interviewing a suspect. It could be hours. She disconnected, then started to call 9-1-1. And stopped.

What could she say? That Sydney Haynes, the guardian angel of the Downtown East Side, was a murderer and her aunt was in danger because she'd gone to talk to him? No one would believe her. She dropped the handset back into the cradle.

What to do?

She needed to save Frank and Ellen. She needed help to do it. She picked up Ellen's notes, then grabbed her keys from the counter where she'd dropped them and raced out of the house.

She went to Quinn.

At the Armstrongs' she was relieved to see that their car was still in the carport. She rang the bell, then pounded on the door, as impatient as Noelle when she had a new toy to show off.

It was Quinn who opened the door. He was frowning, as well he might when someone was hammering on his door like a mad person. Or maybe it was because she was the one who was doing the pounding and it wasn't civilized or polite. "I need you," she said, before he'd even opened his mouth. "I need your help."

His frown deepened, but he opened the door wider. "What's up?"

She stepped inside. "Ellen identified the killer. She doesn't know it though. She thinks his actions are suspicious, but she's not sure it's really him. But he's the one and she's on her way to interview him. She's taken the car, and Patterson isn't answering."

The words poured out of her in a stream that had her breathless by the time she finished. Quinn put his hands on her shoulders and said, "Calm down. Come upstairs. Dad's in the kitchen writing, but I think he should hear this."

Christy nodded. She headed up the stairs while Quinn shut the door and followed. She could hear the clatter of laptop keys as she headed for the kitchen. It didn't stop as she entered the room. Nor did Roy look up from his screen.

"Dad," Quinn said. His tone was sharp. "Crisis."

Roy went from focused on his imaginary world to immediately aware of his real surroundings. He looked from Christy to Quinn, then said hopefully, "Are you back together?"

Christy froze and she saw Quinn stiffen. So much for not noticing.

A muscle leapt in Quinn's jaw. "Christy says Ellen has gone off to confront the killer. She needs our help."

Roy looked from his son to Christy. "Who did it?"

Quinn frowned at that and turned to Christy, his brows raised.

"Sydney Haynes," she said.

Roy rubbed his bristly chin. "Really? I can't see it. Haynes left the party long before the argument."

"He didn't just kill Vince. He also killed Chelsea." Christy went over to the table. She spread Ellen's notes out beside Roy. Quinn followed behind her and looked over her shoulder as she pointed to the conclusions Ellen had made and the questions they'd raised.

"If I've worked it out correctly, she was sorting through the information we've gathered for both murders and she found a link. That link was Syd Haynes."

Roy and Quinn scanned the information. Roy said, "There are questions about Haynes here, and depending on the answers he gives, she might be right. But there's nothing that indicates he'd murdered anyone, let alone two people."

She's visiting the murder. Call the cops, Chris!

"Haynes is the killer," Christy said. She couldn't look at Quinn.

"How do you know?" he asked. His voice was quiet, but there was something in his tone that told Christy that he knew exactly how she knew.

"Frank's back," she said.

CHAPTER 34

Christy's statement created a sensation.

Roy slapped the table and said, "I knew he couldn't be gone," even though he'd been one of those who had been saying they all just had to accept it.

Quinn swore. If Frank said the murderer was Sydney Haynes, he would know. What was it about these Jamieson women that they assumed they could take on the most violent of criminals? "You called Patterson, but couldn't connect," he said instead, staring at Christy.

She nodded. "I was going to call 9-1-1, but I wasn't sure how to spin this so it is an emergency."

"Instead, you came to us," Roy said. He sounded happy. He should sound worried. What was with his dad?

"I thought…" She glanced from Roy to him then down to stare at Ellen's notes. "I thought Quinn could take me to Homeless Help." She shot him a sideways glance. "With his gun."

"The gun's gone. Patterson confiscated it."

"She…she didn't give it back?"

Quinn shook his head. Christy wanted him to rescue Ellen and somehow he'd do it, but not with the gun, not even if Patterson had returned it to him. He directed a look at Christy. "How long ago did Ellen leave?"

"Not more than ten minutes," Christy said.

"It will take her at least twenty minutes, if not half an hour to get to Hastings. I'll head down there now. With luck, she's stuck in traffic and I'll beat her there. If not, I'll have to intervene. Dad," he said.

Roy nodded, eyes bright, alert and prepared for anything.

"Call Patterson again, and keep calling. If she doesn't answer, try 9-1-1 and see if you can convince them to send a car to Homeless Help."

"Roy, if we're not back by the end of school, can you pick up Noelle?"

"You're not coming with me," Quinn said. No way was he risking Christy with a murderer. Again.

"Yes, I am."

"No, you're not." He didn't want an argument, so he headed out of the kitchen.

Christy didn't bother to argue; she simply scurried after him.

In the carport they stood on either side of the car, and glared over the roof at each other. He told her going after Haynes was dangerous. She retorted she knew that and two was better than one in a crisis.

Roy followed them down and positioned himself at the back of the car. He broke the standoff. "You're wasting time, both of you. Stop bickering and rescue Ellen."

"And Frank," Christy said. "Frank's gone with her to protect her. That's why he broke his silence. For Ellen." She climbed into the passenger seat.

Quinn settled in behind the wheel and started the car. Roy got out of the way and waved as Quinn headed up the hill, as if he was seeing them off on a shopping trip to the mall.

"Tell me exactly what Ellen said when she left," Quinn said, as he guided the car onto the highway and gunned it. Christy told him as he drove, so by the time they reached the area where Homeless Help was located he was feeling more hopeful. "This may turn out to be a non-event," he said as he looked for a place to park. "Ellen can't hear

Frank, so she doesn't know Haynes is the murderer, at least not for sure. He's not going to come out and tell her, so they can both dance around the question, without either of them coming to blows."

"I hope so," Christy said. "Look! There's my van."

Ellen might have scored a prime spot right outside Homeless Help, but there was nothing else available in the block. Quinn came to an intersection and turned, hoping to find something on a side street. Eventually, he did, but wasted several minutes looking. As he parked, he said, "Stay in the car."

She got out.

So did he. "Christy."

"Quinn."

They stared at each other over the hood for a moment, then she turned away and loped toward Hastings and Homeless Help. He had to hustle to keep up. They paused in front of the storefront. A sign on the door said the operation was closed for lunch, and the room inside was dark. "Before we go in, try Patterson one more time. If she doesn't answer, leave a message."

Christy nodded. Quinn pulled out his own phone and called his father. Roy answered on the first ring. "Did you get hold of Patterson?"

"No luck," Roy said. "I just finished talking to 9-1-1. They told me my problem wasn't urgent and that I should call the station house. What's happening at your end?"

"We're in front of Homeless Help. There's no one inside, but Haynes may be in his office at the back. Christy's car is parked out front."

"You're going in," Roy said.

"Yeah."

"With Christy?"

"Yeah."

There was a moment of quiet, then Roy said, "Take care. I'll keep trying Patterson."

"I will. Thanks, Dad." He disconnected at the same time Christy did.

He raised his brows in query. She shook her head. "No answer. I left her a detailed message, but who knows when she'll pick it up."

"Then we go in." He tested the door. It was unlocked. That was strange, but it could simply mean someone had forgotten to lock up when he or she left. Quinn caught Christy's arm and turned her to face him. "Let me do the talking. We want to defuse this situation, not escalate it."

Her eyes widened. "Too late! Frank is broadcasting and he's furious."

Quinn shoved her behind him and pulled the door. It opened soundlessly. He entered cautiously, remembering the way the troops he'd been embedded with in Afghanistan had entered buildings in villages they were trying to clear. They'd hoped for no problems, but expected them anyway, and looked everywhere for clues that might keep them safe. Senses alert, edgy, he scanned the room.

Satisfied there was nothing in the shadowed interior that was a danger to them, he walked softly toward the door behind the counter that led to Syd Haynes office in the warehouse area. Christy followed close. He sensed her behind him, so when he reached the door he turned so that he could see her. He put his finger to his lips asking for her silence and motioned her away from the door. She nodded and slipped to one side.

He cracked open the door.

The back area was dimly lit. Floor to ceiling shelves covered the walls and were stacked high with goods rescued from dumpsters around the city. To the untrained eye it looked like junk. For all Quinn knew, it was junk. Syd's office was a partitioned area, carved out of the warehouse space and located to the right of the entry from the storefront. Even as Quinn eased quietly into the big space he could hear the raised voices coming from the office.

"Put that down!"

Ellen's voice, authoritative, haughty.

"Shut the fuck up!" Haynes, edgy and stressed.

"I'll thank you not to speak to me that way!" Ellen again.

Quinn looked back at Christy, who rolled her eyes. He motioned her back into the storefront, then followed her. Once there, he closed the door to the warehouse. "I think Haynes is holding a gun on Ellen."

Christy nodded. Then she grimaced. "She seemed to be holding up well."

"Maybe too well. Haynes sounded pretty strung out." He looked around the room. "We need a diversion. Something that will bring the cops and distract Haynes at the same time."

Christy prowled through the area behind the counter, poking through the items on the shelves built in under the countertop. Suddenly she pounced. When she stood she was holding a pair of hand weights. "What if I used these to break the window? Think it's alarmed?"

Quinn grinned at her. "Even if it's not, you could call 9-1-1 and report a break-in in progress. That should bring a squad car on the run."

"While I'm destroying property, what will you do?"

He came over and took one of the weights from her. "I'm going to create a diversion of my own."

She stared up into his eyes and he could swear he saw caring and concern in hers. It made his heart do a little flip and his mind wonder if there wasn't hope for them after all.

"Be careful, Quinn," she said. Her voice was calm. Her eyes begged.

He nodded. "I will." Which was a complete lie. How could anyone about to rush a guy with a gun be careful? But he wasn't going to say that to Christy. He didn't have to. She knew.

She slipped past him, around the end of the counter. There she paused. "Frank's here and he wants to protect Aunt Ellen. Once I break the window, I'll yell my head off. He'll hear me and know we're here. He'll help you take down Haynes."

The way the cat had helped her when Frank's killer had broken into Christy's house in Burnaby. Quinn nodded. He didn't like working with the cat, but if they both had the same goal he could deal with it.

He crept over to the outer door, while Christy headed for the window. He saw her raise the hand weight high, then swing. He was half through the warehouse door when the front door opened.

"What the hell are you doing?" a female voice shouted.

He looked over his shoulder, even as he kept moving. A woman with rainbow colored hair, tattered street clothes, and a myriad of piercings, was staring at Christy as she swung.

"Stop!" the woman cried.

Christy screamed. The round head of the weight hit the glass with a solid whack. A crack appeared and raced up the length of the window. Christy raised the weight again and the girl dove for her. She screamed again. The weight flew out of her hands and bounced against the window. Another crack appeared and almost as if in slow motion the glass began to crumble. The rainbow-haired woman screamed too as she grabbed Christy and the two of them wrestled. Their momentum pushed them away from the window toward the counter as window glass flew everywhere.

"Go!" Christy shouted. "I'm okay!"

In the back Quinn heard Haynes say, "What the hell was that?" And Ellen's coolly critical reply, "It sounds like a break-in. I expect the police will be here momentarily. I would advise you to put down that gun. They will treat you more leniently if you are unarmed." Quinn envied her *sangfroid*, but he didn't think Sydney Haynes would feel the same way. He eased toward the office door.

In the storefront he could hear the sounds of a scuffle still in progress. He sincerely hoped the windows were alarmed, because Christy wasn't going to have a chance to call the cops any time soon. "Cat," he said in a low voice he hoped only the animal's more acute hearing would catch. "I'm coming in. Be ready."

The cat didn't answer, of course, but he thought he heard a low growl from behind the partition. He reached the opening and risked looking inside.

The room was small and the desk Haynes used was large, so instead of bisecting the room, it was pushed against the far wall. In front of it was the big executive desk chair Haynes was so proud of. He was using it now, lounging in its deep cushion, swinging it from side-to-side while he held a gun on Ellen. She was just beyond the door, standing near the back wall of the room. Two cube-shaped packing boxes were stacked one on top of the other to her left, the door side. On her right was a standing lamp and beside it the reading chair with the ruined upholstery and escaping stuffing. Together they filled up most of the opposite wall. While Quinn watched, he saw the cat creep silently around the lamp and behind the chair, positioning himself so that he was within striking distance of Sydney Haynes.

"The cops won't come," Haynes said. "They don't care about this place. Or this area. They let us police ourselves."

Ellen looked remarkably bored for someone facing down a gunman. "I doubt that is true. You are respected in this community. Of course the police will come to deal with a break-in."

Haynes snorted his disbelief.

Ellen raised her eyebrows. "They will be quite surprised when I tell them they've also nabbed a murderer."

He laughed. "They won't believe you. You said it yourself. I'm respected in the community. I help the helpless live better lives. I have value. Who cares if I offed a leach like Vince Nunez?"

"What about that young girl? Why did you kill her?" Ellen asked. Her voice had softened. She sounded sad, almost disappointed.

Haynes bristled and his casual grip on the handgun tightened. Out in the front the sounds of the fight faded away. "An eye for an eye," Haynes snarled. "Her father took the Reverend Wigle away from me, so I took his daughter away from him."

"But you didn't just kill her. You raped her as well!" Now there was anguish in Ellen's voice.

"Sawatzky needed to suffer the way I have suffered."

"But she was so young. So pretty and sweet. How could you?"

"She was a tool, nothing more."

Quinn shivered. The man's voice was empty. There was no remorse, no pity for a life cut short. The indifferent words almost sounded like a shrug acknowledging something unimportant.

He wondered if Sydney Haynes was using again, or if his mind had gone. Either way he was unpredictable and dangerous with it. He didn't think they had the luxury of waiting for the police to come to their rescue. He looked over at the easy chair and thought he saw the cat crouching behind it. "Be ready," he said, in a normal voice.

Haynes frowned and looked toward the door.

Quinn shouted, "Now!" and charged Syd, the hand weight raised. At the same time, with a blood-curdling howl, the cat leapt. Ellen dove for the floor and the gun went off, the roar adding to the chaos as Haynes screamed under the assault.

The melee went on only a few minutes. When it was over, Sydney Haynes had cat scratches on his face and a large bruise forming on his shoulder where Quinn had whacked him with the weight. Quinn had him on the floor, his hands behind his back, and he was tying them together with a connector cord Ellen had detached from Haynes' computer and printer as he knelt on Hayne's back. The bullet had flown harmlessly over Ellen's head and lodged itself in the back wall. Ellen was now standing by the door, holding the standing lamp like a baseball bat, ready to take on all who tried to enter unauthorized.

"Christy's okay," she said as Quinn tightened the knot around Haynes' wrists.

Quinn glanced over at her. Ellen looked...mischievous. He frowned. How would she know? She hadn't been out of the room.

But the cat had.

"Not you, too?"

"Yes! Imagine. He talked to me the whole time I was here." She looked down at Haynes. "It was tremendously empowering. Mr. Haynes had no idea he was dealing with two people, not one."

Haynes arched, trying to dislodge Quinn's weight. "She's mad," Haynes said breathlessly, as Quinn rode him down.

"You're probably right," Quinn said. "Anyone who decides it's a good idea to face down a murderer is most likely crazy." He looked over as the cat slipped back into the room and took up a position by Hayne's face. He met the cat's eyes and allowed his mouth to quirk up in a wry smile. "Or a Jamieson."

CHAPTER 35

The police arrived not long after. They relieved Ellen of her lamp, replaced Quinn's printer cord with handcuffs, and confiscated the hand weights and the gun. Then they hauled everybody down to the local police station, including the rainbow-haired girl.

The station was in a modern building that was simple in design, with clean lines to the point of being stark. The walls were an institutional white, the floor a hard-wearing gray linoleum, and the lighting was provided by brilliant white fluorescents. The place was crowded with people, all of them busy and surprisingly noisy. There was an odor of strong cleaning products and sweat. It was not a smell Christy was enjoying.

The cops herded the rainbow-haired girl in one direction—she was evidently a run-away, no surprise there!—Syd Haynes in another and sat Ellen, Christy and Quinn down on hard chairs lined up in a row against a wall in front of the duty sergeant's desk and told them to wait. Stormy had tagged along in the cruiser, despite the protests of one allergic officer, and at the station he settled himself on Ellen's lap. When the sergeant admonished them to keep the cat under control, Quinn snorted and said, "Good luck with that," which didn't go down well.

While they waited for someone to take their statements, Quinn phoned Roy to brief him on what had happened and where they were. Christy could hear Quinn's part of the conversation, but not Roy's reaction. After he hung up, Quinn sighed and put his head back against the wall.

"Problem?" Christy said.

"Just Dad being Dad." Quinn turned his head to look at her. He smiled faintly. "He's afraid the system will swallow us up and we'll never see the light of day again, so he's calling Trevor to come down to look after us."

Sensible.

"Oh," Christy said. Her lips twitched. She actually wanted to laugh, but she was afraid that if she started she wouldn't be able to stop. Instead she said, "Possibly a bit extreme, but kindly meant."

"Trevor will make a production of it, just you watch," Quinn said.

"I am glad Trevor will be coming here," Ellen said. "I agree with Roy. It is a very sensible of him. I do not trust that these people understand *we* are not the criminals."

Ellen wasn't exactly speaking quietly. The desk sergeant looked up and frowned and they subsided into silence. Stormy curled into a ball on Ellen's lap and went to sleep. Quinn closed his eyes and apparently did the same thing. Christy watched the comings and goings of the busy station house, while Ellen stroked the sleeping cat.

Trevor, when he arrived, did indeed make a splash, as Quinn predicted, but it wasn't exactly Trevor who caused it. It was Sledge. Trevor strode into the station, a man on a mission. He marched up to the desk sergeant's desk and said forcefully, "I'm Trevor McCullagh. I am here to see my clients. Where have you put them?"

The desk sergeant didn't look impressed or intimidated. "Who are your clients?"

Sledge, who had wandered in behind his father, saw Quinn, Christy, and Ellen sitting against the wall and came over. A young woman passing by, carrying a load of files, dropped them as she raised her hands to her face and cried, "Oh my God! It's Sledge!"

Behind her someone said, "What? Sledge? Here?"

Someone else said, "Why? Couldn't be."

A crowd gathered. Sledge signed autographs, flashed his famous grin and catered to his fans. Quinn turned to Christy and said, "See?"

She laughed. "Technically it wasn't Trevor."

"Trevor brought Sledge. I rest my case."

Trevor spied them and came over while Sledge was working the crowd. "Has anyone been taken into interrogation yet?"

Someone in authority bustled over and ordered everyone to get back to work. As the crowd dissipated, Detective Patterson appeared. She looked at Sledge signing a final autograph, Christy, Quinn and Ellen sitting along the wall on the hard chairs, and Trevor hovering beside, a guardian angel. She shook her head. "Mrs. Jamieson. Why am I not surprised you and your friends are involved?"

"Detective Patterson, I did try to contact you," Christy said, her tone polite, she hoped.

"Yeah," said Patterson, "you did. Okay. I'd like to begin with Ellen Jamieson, since I gather she was the first of you to arrive at Homeless Help."

Ellen said, "Very well. I will state right now that I wish my attorney to be present."

Christy thought she heard Patterson sigh, but all she said was, "I take it that is Mr. McCullagh?"

Ellen nodded. Patterson indicated Trevor with a nod. "Come along then, both of you."

Ellen put Stormy on the floor, then rose. She waited for Trevor, then they both followed Patterson down the hall. Stormy trotted along behind.

"I wonder how long it will take for Patterson to evict the cat?" Quinn asked.

Christy shook her head. "If he's stealthy enough she won't even notice."

"I can't believe Syd murdered Vince and that girl," Sledge said. With the last of his fans gone, he settled on the chair beside Quinn. "How did you figure it out?"

"Ellen did," Christy said. "Quinn found out that Reverend Wigle was not just Syd's mentor, but that he cared deeply for him. Syd was shattered when Wigle was killed in the Regent Hotel riots and he blamed the company planning to redevelop the hotel for the Reverend's death. Ellen discovered that Syd not only blamed the company, but the man who owned the company."

"It was personal for him," Sledge said.

"He wanted revenge," Quinn said. "He lost a mentor and a man who was almost a father to him. He wanted to inflict the same kind of pain on the man who had done it."

"So he killed a young woman who had done nothing to him," Sledge said. He shook his head. "Nasty."

"Ellen was going over the information we'd gathered for both murders and she realized that Syd's alibis weren't very strong because he had no one to corroborate them. He could have committed both murders, but no one was looking at him for either," Christy said. "He's done a lot for the Downtown East Side, so the cops were taking his word for where he was. Once she realized how obsessed and how angry he was, she thought his word wasn't enough and decided to accost him."

"Which was not a good idea," Quinn said.

Sledge laughed.

A uniformed policewoman appeared and asked Christy to come with her. She nodded and stood. Quinn caught her hand and squeezed it. He flashed her a smile when she looked down and her heart twisted. She smiled back, then turned to follow the policewoman.

As it was, she didn't have to worry. Trevor stayed in the room while Patterson asked her questions, which were simple and straightforward. She was amused to realize that Stormy remained underneath the table, since Frank made comments throughout the process. When Patterson let her go, she passed Quinn whose turn was next. She managed a brief smile and touched his hand as she passed.

It wasn't long before Quinn's interview was over and he returned to the line of chairs. He brought Trevor with him. Stormy trotted along behind.

"What now?" Sledge asked.

"They have to decide if they're going to press charges," Trevor said.

"Charges!" said Ellen. "Why would they want to charge us with anything? We captured the killer the police were too incompetent to even suspect."

You tell 'em, Aunt Ellen. Stormy hopped up onto her lap then put his head under her chin and nudged her to give him a pat.

"She can hear him too?" Sledge said.

Quinn closed his eyes and put his head against the wall.

"Assault and battery," Trevor said. "Property damage."

"Assault and battery to whom? Sydney Haynes?" Ellen asked. "A confessed murderer?"

The desk sergeant looked up at Ellen's imperious voice and frowned again.

"I'd be the one charged," Christy said. She'd spent much of their time in the station thinking about the consequences of their desperate acts that day and she'd come to some conclusions even before her interview with Patterson. "I broke the storefront window and I wrestled with the rainbow-haired girl when she came in unexpectedly. I don't think you and Quinn need to worry, though, Ellen. Haynes had a gun and was threatening you."

She was aware of Quinn beside her, sitting up straight, and she could feel his narrow-eyed gaze on her. She guessed that he hadn't thought about charges when they made their plan.

"Shively," he said.

She turned to look at him, and managed a smile. "Yeah. Could be a problem."

He reached for her. "Christy, I should have…"

She understood what he meant without his saying it and shook her head. "You had to be the one to confront Haynes. We both did what we needed to." He didn't look convinced. "I refuse to worry until I must," she said, with a smile that she hoped would reassure.

"I can make a good case to justify your actions," Trevor said. "You won't serve time."

That wasn't the point, and both Quinn and Christy knew it. Shively would pounce if she caught even a whiff of improper behavior on Christy's part.

Fortunately, Patterson chose that moment to arrive. They all looked at her expectantly and Christy discovered that she was holding her breath.

"You are free to go," Patterson said, speaking to Quinn, Christy, and Ellen. "No charges are being laid, although you may find that the landlord of the building that houses Homeless Help will demand that you replace the window."

"They will not have to contact us," Ellen said. "I will see that the window is repaired immediately. I will also make a substantial donation to the organization itself to compensate for the time they were forced to close."

Patterson raised her brows. "You may want to hold off on that, Ms. Jamieson. Homeless Help is under investigation for financial irregularities."

Sledge said, "Syd was stealing from his own charity?"

Patterson said carefully, "The Reverend Wigle set up the organization and let Mr. Haynes run it. Since Wigle's death, some of the directors have brought suspicions to the police and requested an investigation. There hasn't been enough evidence to charge Mr. Haynes, but now that he is under arrest for the murder of two people his affairs will be scrutinized closely. There is no telling what we'll find." She nodded, then strode away.

Now that they were free to leave, Trevor offered to drop Ellen, Christy, Quinn and the cat back at Homeless Help where their cars were parked. On the way there he and Sledge agreed to go to Burnaby for an impromptu celebration suggested by Ellen.

At Homeless Help the storefront looked as forlorn as Christy was feeling. The window had already been boarded up and the closed sign was on the door. Christy looked at Quinn. "I guess I should ride with Ellen."

He looked at her for a long minute, then he said, "Why? You came with me."

"It's true, I did. But…I thought you might prefer…"

His gaze was intense. "Come home with me, Christy. Please."

She searched his expression, then she smiled. "Thank you, Quinn. I'd love to."

THE
9 LIVES COZY MYSTERY
SERIES

The Cat Came Back
The Cat's Paw
Cat Got Your Tongue
Let Sleeping Cats Lie
(More to follow)

Turn the page for an
excerpt from

LET
SLEEPING CATS
LIE

The 9 Lives Cozy Mystery Series
Book Four

Louise Clark

"I expect to see a substantial portion of the funds returned to the Jamieson Trust by the end of summer."

Christy stared at the broad, beaming face of Harry Endicott. To say she was blindsided by his announcement was putting it mildly. When he'd asked her to come to his office for a meeting, she thought he planned to tell her the Jamieson fortune was gone forever.

She drew a deep breath, reminded herself this was good news, and summoned her Jamieson princess persona to steady herself. No matter what the situation, show no weakness. Smile, raise a brow, display interest, but not too much. Give praise for work well done to those in your employ. "This is welcome news, Harry. How did you discover the location of the funds?"

Her question allowed Endicott to launch into an enthusiastic, and very detailed, explanation of his process. Beside her, Christy sensed Detective Billie Patterson was listening carefully. The information was of particular interest to her, as it would tie into the cases she was building against two of the former Jamieson Trust trustees.

As Endicott talked, Christy searched her mind for questions, but she was still reeling from the shock of his news. Questions would come, she knew, but not until she had time to think and plan. When the meeting was over, she smiled at the accountant and said, "Thank you, Mr. Endicott. I'll be in touch."

Endicott nodded and stood. He stretched out his hand. "It has been a pleasure, Mrs. Jamieson. As always."

Christy shook his hand. As she left the office, Patterson said, "Mrs. Jamieson, if I might have a word."

Christy paused and half turned, her brows raised.

Patterson said, "You've heard about the murder of Fredrick Jarvis?"

Christy nodded. "It was the topic of a discussion at a recent social gathering I was at." A fancy way to describe one of the Armstrongs' back yard barbecues, but she was still in her Jamieson princess persona. Fancy was the norm not the exception.

"Fredrick Jarvis was a national political figure. His death is being considered in the context of his status as a member of provincial government and his campaign for national leadership. I'm part of a taskforce drawn from national and local police forces. We're looking at his political life, at the people who have protested his policies, his competitors in the current leadership campaign, anyone with international connections."

Christy stared at Patterson. She thought of the barbecue and heard again Roy's voice reminiscing about the protests he'd participated in while Jarvis was minister of the environment and his still firm view that the man was dead wrong in his policies. She thought about Tamara Ahern, held captive by radicals, and so newly returned to Canada.

And Quinn, Tamara's former, and possibly current, lover. A journalist who had spent years in war zones, interviewing friends—and when he could arrange it—foes as well.

The cold of stark fear washed over her. "Everyone?"

Patterson nodded. "The taskforce will put anyone they are investigating under a spotlight. The glare will be intense. Every flaw revealed. Every weakness exposed."

Christy studied Patterson's expression. If she read the woman right, Patterson was telling her that Roy and Quinn were in danger.

Patterson returned her gaze with a steady one of her own. "However, I don't believe Mr. Jarvis was killed by an international terrorist or a political enemy. I think he was killed for one of the usual reasons—money, revenge, jealousy, fear. There were at least a half a dozen people in his private life who have a motive to kill him."

"If you believe Jarvis was killed for personal reasons, why don't you investigate that angle?" And leave Roy and Quinn out of it.

"I'm a lone voice. I don't have the time or manpower. As I said, the focus of the taskforce is on his political life and I am part of it. Everyone involved is working flat out to sift through a mound of data. I had to get special permission to come to the meeting this afternoon."

Christy frowned. Harry Endicott kept meticulous records, which he would turn over to the police once he was done. He'd also write a detailed report for their use. It wasn't necessary for Patterson attend this meeting. There had to be another reason she had made a point to be here today. "Did you come to warn me Quinn might be under investigation?"

Patterson didn't immediately reply. Christy had the sense that she was wrestling with herself. Finally she said, "Mr. Jarvis moved in the kind of social circles the Jamiesons play in. I'm sure you, or your aunt, know his wife and children. You might even be on a first name basis with them."

"His daughter was on one of the committees I belonged to before Frank died, but—" Realization dawned. "You want me to investigate Fred Jarvis' family?"

"Ears, eyes and feet, Mrs. Jamieson. You can go where I cannot."

"Detective, I don't think this is a good idea."

Patterson's gaze was steady on hers, but she didn't respond. She stayed silent and let Christy stew about spotlights, and consequences and danger to those she loved.

"All right," Christy said at last. "I'll do it. Give me the names on your suspect list."

———◆———

LET SLEEPING CATS LIE

available in print and ebook

Louise Clark is the author of cozy mysteries and contemporary and historical romance novels. She holds a BA in History from Queen's University.

For more information, please visit her at www.louiseclarkauthor.com or on Facebook at www.facebook.com/LouiseClarkAuthor.